WHAT HAPPENED TO RUTHY RAMIREZ

WHAT HAPPENED TO RUTHY RAMIREZ

CLAIRE JIMÉNEZ

GRAND
CENTRAL

New York Boston

Grand Central Publishing
Hachette Book Group
1290 Avenue of the Americas, New York, NY 10104
grandcentralpublishing.com
twitter.com/grandcentralpub

First Edition: March 2023

Grand Central Publishing is a division of Hachette Book Group, Inc. The Grand Central Publishing name and logo is a trademark of Hachette Book Group, Inc.

The publisher is not responsible for websites (or their content) that are not owned by the publisher.

The Hachette Speakers Bureau provides a wide range of authors for speaking events. To find out more, go to www.hachettespeakersbureau.com or call (866) 376-6591.

Unless otherwise noted Scripture quotations are taken from Holy Bible, New International Version®, NIV®. Copyright © 1973, 1978, 1984, 2011 by Biblica, Inc.™ Used by permission of Zondervan. All rights reserved worldwide. www.zondervan.com. The "NIV" and "New International Version" are trademarks registered in the United States Patent and Trademark Office by Biblica, Inc.™

Print book interior design by Marie Mundaca.

Library of Congress Cataloging-in-Publication Data

Names: Jimenez, Claire, author.
Title: What happened to Ruthy Ramirez / Claire Jiménez.
Description: First Edition. | New York, NY : Grand Central Publishing, 2023. | Summary: "The Ramirez women of Staten Island orbit around absence. When thirteen year old middle child Ruthy disappeared after track practice without a trace, it left the family scarred and scrambling. One night, twelve years later, oldest sister Jessica spots a woman on her TV screen in Catfight, a raunchy reality show. She rushes to tell her younger sister, Nina: This woman's hair is dyed red, and she calls herself Ruby, but the beauty mark under her left eye is instantly recognizable. Could it be Ruthy, after all this time? The years since Ruthy's disappearance haven't been easy on the Ramirez family. It's 2008, and their mother, Dolores, still struggles with the loss, Jessica juggles a newborn baby with her hospital job, and Nina, after four successful years at college, has returned home to medical school rejections and is forced to work in the mall folding tiny bedazzled thongs at the lingerie store. After seeing maybe Ruthy on their screen, Jessica and Nina hatch a plan to drive to where the show is filmed in search of their long lost sister. When Dolores catches wind of their scheme, she insists on joining, along with her pot-stirring holy roller best friend, Irene. What follows is a family road trip and reckoning that will force the Ramirez women to finally face the past and look toward a future-with or without Ruthy in it. What Happened to Ruthy Ramirez is a vivid family portrait, in all its shattered reality, exploring the familial bonds between women and cycles of generational violence, colonialism, race, and silence, replete with snark, resentment, tenderness, and, of course, love"-- Provided by publisher.
Identifiers: LCCN 2022047942 | ISBN 9781538725962 (hardcover) | ISBN 9781538725986 (ebook)
Classification: LCC PS3610.I474 W53 2023 | DDC 813/.6--dc23
LC record available at https://lccn.loc.gov/2022047942

ISBNs: 978-1-5387-2596-2 (hardcover), 978-1-5387-2598-6 (ebook)

Printed in the United States of America

LSC-C

Printing 1, 2022

For my sisters

¿Cómo habré de llamarme cuando sólo me quede
recordarme, en la roca de una isla desierta?
                    —*Julia de Burgos, "Poema para mi muerte"*

What shall I be called when all remains of me
is a memory, upon a rock of a deserted isle?
                    —*Julia de Burgos, "Poem for my death"*
                    (Trans. Vanessa Pérez-Rosario)

If you drew a map of our family history, you might start it off with my dad, young, fat, and handsome, eighteen-year-old Eddie Ramirez, plotting to get with my moms, who was dark-skinned, small and freckled, long black curly hair. Freshly turned seventeen. Her name is Dolores. And you can probably start it off in Brooklyn. Canarsie. Draw a bump underneath my mother's wedding dress—that's Jessica. Then shortly after, in 1981, you can make Jessica a separate person, angry and red, pale-skinned like my dad, screaming in my mother's arms. Two years later draw Ruthy in pencil, lightly, because you're going to need to erase her in a couple of minutes. Now, draw the Verrazano, the water, the Island, the dump. Draw my proud family, Puerto Rican and loud, driving over the bridge and a little pink town house in West Brighton. I'm the one born in 1986, in Staten Island. They named me Nina. Make me look cute. The five of us seem normal for a while, up until Ruthy turns thirteen and disappears. Now you can rub her body away from the page. Draw my mother sixty-two pounds later. Give her diabetes. Kill my dad. Cut a hole in the middle of the timeline. Eliminate the canvas. Destroy any type of logic. There is no such thing now as a map.

Call that black hole, its negative space, the incredible disappearance of Ruthy Ramirez.

CHAPTER 1

Nina

Afterwards, sometimes, as a teenager, I would stand at the bus stop where my sister went missing, concentrating on the deli down the block, the way the sign on its front door would blink the word *Open*. I tell you, I would stand there squinting for so long that sometimes a bus would stop and mistake me for somebody waiting. I tried to picture it, 1996: thirteen-year-old Ruthy standing there outside after track practice, five o'clock, alone, book bag graffitied by Sharpies, her red hair knotted and wrapped into a bun. In my head, I'd play out all the different scenarios—our family, shakily divided across a three-way split-screen mounted on the wall in my brain.

While Ruthy was shivering at the bus stop waiting for the S48, as she always did after track practice, me, Jess, and Ma would have already been at home, the handouts for my fourth-grade homework scattered on top of the table, Ma flicking the last pieces of wet onion clinging to her fingers into a hot pan. That night Jess had taken the phone from the kitchen into the small downstairs bathroom so she could whisper into the receiver in private—some sophomore-year secret that nobody even really cared about anyway; still, she lowered her voice. On the other side of the Island, by the mall, my father, who managed a hardware store, would be in the middle of a shift, helping the receiving crew unload a truck of refrigerators, jamming a finger between the twenty-foot shelving and a hand cart, cursing out the motherfucker who sideswiped him with a shopping cart, "Puñeta."

The alarm did not sound until seven o'clock, when Ma stood on her toes to pull a stack of dishes out of the cabinet and plate the pollo guisado.

Ruthy should've been home by six.

Six fifteen at the latest.

Suddenly aware of the time, Ma wiped her hands on the back of her tight jeans and blinked, then tilted her head to the side and stared past me, as if she were having some otherworldly vision.

"Nina, where is your sister?" she asked me from the stove.

As if I could answer.

I was still trying to remember how to add two fractions with different denominators. A series of multiplication signs were floating on my handout. The paper was disintegrating where I tried too hard to erase away my mistakes.

I wasn't worried about Ruthy. During Christmas she had single-handedly beat up a boy-cousin thirty pounds heavier for calling her butt-ugly: "Oh, you going to cry? Look who's fucking ugly now," she'd said, while he blubbered on the basement floor and tried to hide his face.

In my fourth-grade mind, Ruthy was invincible. Thirteen-year-old Queen of the Quick Comeback, hoop earrings and Vaseline, Patron Saint of the Fist and the Late-Night Call Home from the Principal. Who in the world could touch her, my sister?

No one.

My mother, now more agitated, stepped quickly to the bathroom and shouted through the door. "Jessica, get off the fucking phone already, God."

Once Ma got her hands on the receiver, she dialed the school, but nobody was picking up. Then she called my father at work and started flipping out in Spanish. It was now approaching seven thirty, and Ruthy wasn't home. No phone call. No nothing. (Though Jess had tied up the line for God knows how long.) "And I'm telling you right now, Eddie. I'm not playing games. If I find her sitting outside, chilling with her little friends..."

But the edge in my mother's voice softened and trailed off, betraying the unmistakable fear that sometimes surfaced at the cash register after her credit card was declined and she'd send me back to return whatever brand-name box of cereal I'd begged her to put in the cart. Ruthy was never late coming home from track practice. Not once that I could remember. After she ran, Ruthy always arrived on time, six p.m. for dinner, hungry and eager to replace whatever energy she'd lost.

It was twenty-eight degrees outside that night.

Ma made me and Jess put on a coat and loaded us into the car to drive out to IS 61. Then she told us to roll down the windows and call out for Ruthy, "Loud, girls, so she can hear you." But our voices only echoed across the street against the brick walls of the empty school building.

"For how long?" I asked, the fourteenth time around the middle school.

"Until I tell you not to," Ma said.

When Ma got tired of circling Castleton, she took Forest Avenue and turned left on Victory Boulevard, drove down that long hill towards the water, where we could see the city's skyline twinkling ahead, the buses gliding past us away from the ferry. The long gray lines of electricity suspended between a stretch of wooden crosses erected along Victory Boulevard like the pictures I'd seen of the Calvary in our Sunday school textbook.

3

Sometimes it feels like the three of us are still stuck in that car. Shouting out Ruthy's name into the unanswering dark.

For a straight month the cops rolled up and down the block asking everybody the same questions, whether or not Ruthy had a boy-friend? "Or maybe one of youse saw her after school walking back that night to the house? A skinny-looking girl?"

Five foot one. Long red hair. A beauty mark beneath her left eye.

Look, a picture of Ruthy cheesing on a bus on a seventh-grade trip to Six Flags, probably getting ready to argue about something she said somebody was spitting behind her back. Probably about to roll up her FUBU sweatshirt to show you the place in her belly where she'd pierced herself with a safety pin. Our Ruthy'd been a special kind of pain in the ass. She took more liberties than any of us did; once she even snuck out at night and came home at two in the morning, inspired by a dare and unafraid of the epic ass whupping she would receive from my mother, who sat there in the living room on the couch, waiting in the dark for her return. Even though she was only thirteen, she'd been practicing disappearing since she was twelve.

But people didn't talk about that. Not at the praise and worship service at Our Lady of Hope, where they lit candles afterwards and the pastor chanted, "That Ruthy Ramirez will return to us safely." And certainly not in the Ramirez house, where we'd taped her eighth-grade class photo to the wall above Mom's dresser and surrounded the picture with candles and rosary beads as if she were a small deity.

But I knew.

For years I argued with Jessica about whether Ruthy'd run away or whether somebody had taken her. For me it was clear that Ruthy had simply left. The morning she disappeared, Ma had yelled at her for the fifteenth time for not bothering to properly clean the bottom of the caldero when it was her turn to do the dishes, and Ruthy had shaken her head and muttered underneath her breath, "I can't wait to get out of here."

"Look, even her favorite shirt is missing," I would say. To which Jessica would whisper, "Don't be saying that shit in front of Mom, Nina. You hear me? Because I will kick your ass."

There were no clues in the diary Ruthy left.

Just her bubbly shaped script describing kicking it with her best friend Yesenia, several page-long takedowns of the teachers she hated, and then a couple of moments of infighting with the crew of girls she hung out with at school. A poem. A few raps that sounded suspiciously like Left Eye's part in "Waterfalls." One brief breakup with Yesenia, in which Ruthy called her "a fake corny bitch," and then numerous passages in which she made fun of me and Jessica. "Poor Nina, she's got no rhythm. It's like the girl, she was adopted." Or: "Jessica needs to stop plucking her eyebrows so thin. It makes her forehead look extra big." There were descriptions of our childhood fights, sometimes lists of rules: if you fall off the bed while wrestling and don't get up, you lose; if you blink in a staring contest (even if it was because you had to sneeze), you lose; if you cry while getting roasted by one of your sisters, then, oh Lord, were you finished! Crying was a mortal sin in the Ramirez house. The ultimate sign of weakness.

In Ruthy's journal, there were no suspicious boyfriends or predatory grown-up men. No kindly male mentors with hidden agendas. Just pages of her logging in how fast she ran that day during track practice or descriptions of the pale green hamburger she forced herself to eat during lunch.

Our father waited at the precinct after work every day for a month, with his puffy leather coat folded in his hands over his lap, not for good news (my father was a pessimist) but to make sure the cops did not forget us.

"They got to know that we're watching. And that people care about her," he'd say, his head bent to the plate as he shoveled rice into his mouth late at night, long after all of us had already eaten.

The cops had suspected him at first. Dad knew they looked at him like he was a piece of shit, until they called his boss who confirmed that he'd been working overtime, a late shift, the night that Ruthy disappeared.

Still, it broke my father's heart.

That somebody could think that about him, and those types of rumors, they don't ever go away.

Our mother, shocked, spent large amounts of time stuck at the kitchen table. And if outside people or one of the extended family became restless or moved around the house to clean or to cook, or if people wanted to take her out to dinner or to a movie to cheer her up, my moms would tell whatever people, "Why don't you sit the fuck still?"

"Pues, stay still, then!" people started to say, the church folks especially—who'd always looked down on her for being thirty-two with three daughters, for having the first kid when she was just seventeen—they left my mother alone. Even after the gossip and the heartbreak finally killed my father five years later, these people, they kept on whispering. "Besides, you can only sympathize so long for somebody else's loss before you run out of encouraging things to say." So my mother stood still.

For many years. By herself.

So that she blew up like a balloon, eleven different sizes.

And what did I do?

That little fourth grader sitting at the kitchen table with minimal math skills and no rhythm, surrounded by her scattered handouts, squinting through Coke-bottle glasses?

Well! The first fully funded chance I got for Promising Minority Students (first-generation or otherwise), I ran away from home, too. Spent most of college making excuses not to come back for Christmas. Not because I did not love my family or was ashamed, but because it hurt too much to see up close what had happened to us over the years. And sometimes, during those rare holiday visits, the gravity of our situation was so strong it felt like being pulled into a black hole. Summers, I avoided seeing Mom by staying on campus upstate to work as a research assistant for one of my biology professors. And sometimes when Jess called, I didn't pick up, because I worried that if I did, she would provide some urgent reason for me to find the next bus ticket home. I didn't go back to New York, not even when Jess had the baby.

Mostly, this strategy worked.

Until I graduated, and Jessica put her foot down. "Cut the shit out, Nina. It's your turn to take care of Ma now."

Jessica had done it for years.

Driven Ma to appointments.

Made sure she was taking whatever necessary meds.

Four times a week she went to Ma's house for dinner, helped her clean the dishes afterwards, and then drove back to her boyfriend's to sleep...but now she had little baby Julie and a full-time job at the hospital and only five hours to close her eyes at night. "And that's if I'm lucky," she said. "I need your help."

Which was something Jess rarely ever admitted.

"All right, I got you."

After graduation, I flew back to New York, and at the airport, when the three of us met at baggage claim, for a split second we didn't recognize each other. I hadn't seen Jessica or Mom in almost two years. Jessica's cheeks had grown chipmunkish. Her arms and shoulders had rounded so that she looked like a football player, and dark wrinkles had formed around her neck like a noose. Still, she was prettier than me. Even after a kid. Her eyeliner and mascara crumbled around the lids, reminding me of the teenage Jessica who a

7

decade of boys had worshipped and loved, year after year. An arc of rhinestones dotted her collar, and I could tell that she'd dressed up to meet me at the airport, because her long black hair was still wet.

Mom had changed, too. She'd lost weight since I last saw her, sophomore year, and the flesh on her arms had deflated. And you could tell she was in good spirits because of her makeup; it had that sharp Rocío Jurado eyeliner and dark lid, circa 1972.

"She was sleeping a lot last month, but she's doing better now. She doesn't do Catholic church anymore because she says they're a bunch of fucking phonies. But she's got a new job at the Pentecostal church teaching parenting classes," Jessica had told me over the phone as I packed up my dorm room, throwing out old folders and notes. "When you get here, you gotta get her out of that bed. Keep her moving around."

At the airport Ma was full of energy, though. "Mamita, look how beautiful you are," she said. She kept on hugging me, then pulling away to smile and hold my chin up for inspection, then hugging me again.

But in the bathroom mirror at LaGuardia I'd already seen how my thick black curls had frizzed and shrunk in the airless compartment of the plane, how the brown skin on my face had yellowed and turned greenish underneath the eyes: too much caffeine, too much staying up all night, finishing finals, giving birth to ugly research papers, the shape of whose declining arguments reflected that night's consumption of seventy-five-cent vending machine candy and cigarettes.

Here in the terminal, I felt too aware of the body I had forgotten about while studying late at night. My arms and thighs had grown awkwardly over the last few years from being hunched in front of a computer. And when Jess came in for a hug, I wondered if she could feel the soft slope I'd developed between my shoulders from bending over my textbooks at all hours.

"Looking good, sis," she said extra loud as she pulled me in.

There in her arms, I realized, to my surprise, that I felt shy. In front of my own sister. My mother.

The baggage carousel beeped and the conveyor belt lurched forward and sighed as it rotated the luggage. "Mamita, which one of these is yours?" my mom asked, looking urgently at the bags tumbling onto the carousel.

"Let me get that, Ma," Jess said.

But Mom insisted, not only on pulling the bag off the conveyor belt but also on rolling it through the bright terminal all the way to the parking lot, where she had one last surprise hidden in the car. "Just a little something!"

She pulled out a bouquet of sunflowers from the front seat.

Nestled in between the blooms was a stuffed bear with a miniature graduation cap, complete with a tiny yellow tassel.

"And we got you a cake at home, too," Jess said.

"From Valencia," my mother whispered, before pinching my cheek.

The bear was holding a little card with my name on it.

"Go ahead," Ma said. "Open it."

In the envelope, folded, were three crisp twenty-dollar bills, and I thought to myself, Dear Lord, I am so sorry.

Nowhere in the world could there have been a bigger asshole than me.

In the car I tried to redeem myself. I sat in the front seat with the directions Jessica had copied off Mapquest on a napkin in crayon, while at the same time folding and unfolding a map of Queens, all this while Jessica kept taking a series of wronger turns. Later, over the water, on our way back to the Island, Jessica told stories about the baby's growing teeth. And I told stories about college, aping my professors' gestures and verbal tics.

Our mother, she sat quietly in the back.

CHAPTER 2

Nina

That July, two months after I landed in New York, I got a job selling lingerie at the Staten Island Mall—Jessica's idea. She was the one who dragged me to the interview at Mariposa's, because one of her girlfriends worked nights there and said they needed a salesgirl bad; it was swimsuit season. And Mariposa's had just put out a whole line of bathing suits. "Make sure you call them, Nina," Jess demanded. "First thing tomorrow."

I tried to get out of it, but there were not many other options. Despite my best efforts, I hadn't gotten into med school. And though newly graduated from a top university, I was broke and blessed with the brilliant luck of the 2008 recession; all the newspapers that year were saying the economy hadn't been this screwed up since 1929. Plus, nobody would hire me because they said none of my skills was actually marketable. And if you've got some kid who's worked five years at Dunkin' Donuts, and he already knows how to work the register, and you can pay him eight dollars an hour, and he's not going anywhere, and he's not going to complain because he never had a degree to begin with, who needs a bio major anyway?

"Plus, we'd have to train you," they said. "I mean, what have you actually *done*?"

A few weeks into the summer, one bad interview after another, I gave in. "Fine. Okay, I'll apply to Mariposa's," I said.

And Jessica was like, "Don't act like you're doing *me* a favor. I *got* a job." Because Jessica loved to point out that she worked at St. Lucy's Hospital, even though she was only a nurses' aide.

On the application, I put down a pile of irrelevant stuff I'd done in college, even my GPA—though it was mediocre. I added that I'd worked in the alumni office during the phone-a-thons where we had to call former students to get them to donate money. ("Frankly, I think you should be refunding me tuition," this one guy said, because he'd been unemployed for the past eight months.)

At Mariposa's, the manager raised one drawn-in eyebrow, its fakeness barely perceptible. The brow kit she used must have been expensive. "You have like zero sales experience, sweetheart."

On her pink-and-gold name tag it said *Savarino*.

"This is true." I adjusted my glasses. "But I think you'll find me to be an excellent addition to the sales team. First of all, let me tell you that I'm enthusiastic." I stuck out a thumb.

"And I'm hardworking," I said. "I'm detail-oriented, a team player."

I mean, how many more repulsive things could I say?

"I don't know." Savarino looked down at the résumé. Shook her head. And you could tell she was sizing me up, probably thinking that I wasn't cute enough, wondering if customers would buy bras from a dopey-looking girl like that.

Savarino was probably like fifty, but she'd preserved herself so she looked closer to thirty-five. Dark red pin-straight hair that she'd probably been burning with a flat iron for the past seventeen years. And she was a vain woman—the type of woman, you could tell, who'd looked down at those less attractive than she was her whole life. Picture the evil queen in *Snow White*, except with the illest old-school Brooklyn accent.

The one thing that comforted me was that she was a smoker. And I could smell it, the burnt enamel of her teeth. When she spoke, she wheezed a little bit. And even when she stopped speaking, her breath would creak like a piece of air blowing through an open window. Whenever I felt anxious, I looked at the thin noisy crack between her teeth.

She shrugged and reshuffled a stack of résumés. "I'd really like to do something for you, but…"

Bitch stopped.

And I was thinking, Okay, fine, that's it. I give up. Nobody will ever hire me. I'm done. Let me crawl my broke ass back to Ma's place and babysit Jessica's kid forever. Then just like that, an idea seemed to eclipse the doubt on Savarino's face. The air conditioner in her office coughed and came back to life. "You speak Spanish?"

Shit. "Of course," I lied. Then I looked at her and smiled.

"Your English is pretty good, too, huh? That accent's not even that bad."

Which made me think: *Wait, who's the one with the accent?* I tried not to look too surprised, though.

After all, there was an opportunity here.

"You know," I said to Savarino. "I learned English at a very young age."

Because I was new to Mariposa's, the more experienced salesgirls (who were sixteen years old and still skipping high school) made me work the shittiest hours. Six to eleven p.m. every weekend. During closing, I'd spend twenty-five minutes untangling drawers of string thongs that became stuck on each other's rhinestones and security tags. If I was lucky, sometimes my teenage bosses put me in the fitting room, where it was possible to sit down in secret without Savarino aggressively whispering into the headset to stand the fuck up. Literally: "Stand the fuck up, Ramirez. What do you think this is?"

The downside of working the fitting room was that sometimes you got stuck measuring the customers for new bras. Watching these strangers unclothe, I'd struggle for the right way to look at their bodies: a stomach, an armpit, a mole. Once this woman came in, casually threw her sweatshirt on the floor and stood there, arms lifted. I could tell she was a mom by the way she gave zero fucks about her body while taking off her clothes. There were stretch marks along the sides of her breasts that extended from her nipples like stars. And the skin around her stomach was puckered where somebody had cut her open to take something out.

She must have seen my glance in the mirror as I wrapped the measuring tape around the bottoms of her breasts because she said, "If you don't want to look like this, sweetheart, stay away from the booze. Don't smoke. Don't have kids. Drink water."

Then she looked at me and laughed.

With that $7.50-an-hour check from Mariposa's, I helped my mother pay the rent. I took care of half the groceries and at least one utilities bill. Before I'd returned to Staten Island, she'd survived on SSI checks and crochet work that she'd accumulated from the ladies at church: toilet seat covers, baby blankets, intricate borders and tassels for other women's towels and rugs. Sometimes I'd even babysit Julie for Jessica, but what I'd really wanted to do was to get into med school, and when I hadn't gotten in, the rejection made me feel as if all of my insides had been lacerated and thrown into a blender. At least three times a week after work, I purchased a six-pack of Coors Light and some Newports at the bodega across from my mom's apartment building, and every time I had to tell the same old dude at the register who hit on me that yes, I had a boyfriend.

Even though I didn't.

Then I'd walk up the block to where I lived and smoke most of the cigarettes by myself in my room. I had not been able to write the professors who'd recommended me to tell them I wasn't accepted into school, and for several months I refused to update my Facebook status, until Matt, one of my friends from college, noticed my absence online and suggested I go to therapy.

Immediately, I defriended him.

Mostly because I was proud of my depression. I'd read somewhere on the internet that it was a sign of extreme intelligence, and I'd started to consider depression as some type of X-ray vision, with which I could see the world clearly in ways that others could not— that is, not only the skin but also the skeleton.

It was like that for a while. Things stood the same for me, even when the stock market crashed, and Lehman Brothers went bankrupt. Nothing much changed. The Ramirez family was broke before Wall Street failed and remained broke afterwards. "As it was in the beginning," me and Jess would laugh, "is now, and ever shall be, world without end. *Amen.*"

Then one night, early November, Jessica called me saying, "Hurry, Nina, channel six."

In the background, over the phone, I could hear the baby crying for attention. It was midnight, and probably Jessica was camped out in front of the television, squishing her nipple into the baby's angry mouth.

"Come on," I said, irritated, because she had disturbed an important dream of mine. In it I was getting paid more than $7.50 an hour.

"Just turn on the fucking TV, okay?"

"Fine," I said.

But, it was just one late-night news show after another; all of the hosts were talking about how Obama kicked John McCain's ass in the polls—the First Black President. A sign of hope. But in Staten

Island, they reported that three boys from Rosebank had attacked a Black teenager with bats in response to Obama winning. "Fucking losers," I said.

"Are you doing it?" Jess asked.

"Yeah."

I kept flipping through the channels until *bam*: there was this woman who looked exactly like Ruthy, except ten years older, with the same brown beauty mark beneath her left eye.

"No way." The blood underneath my skin started to itch, and for a second I thought I might vomit.

"You see it?"

I put the volume all the way up and stared at this new Ruthy, who was not so much Ruthy as she was a parody of Ruthy. It was a late-night reality show, and the television version of our sister looked like she'd dyed her hair red with Kool-Aid. She wore the type of hoops from the nineties with the name suspended in the middle, except these earrings spelled out *Ruby* in that bubble font we used to use in sixth-grade love letters. Ruthy or Ruby or whoever she was had drawn in her eyebrows past the corners of the lids, and her lipstick was purple.

"That's not Ruthy," I said. "That girl looks like a fucking Muppet."

"No, Nina. That's her."

The TV show flickered to a beat like the sound of Tetris blocks landing on one another before increasing in speed. Different shots of Boston flashed across the screen. The Prudential Center. Copley Square. Then there was Ruthy again, smiling and dragging her bags up the stairs into a two-floor condo while the name of the show pulsed above her head in bright red letters: *Catfight.*

"What is this?" I asked.

"That's that mierda where all those girls are always beefing and showing their asses," Jessica said.

On TV, Ruthy/Ruby came out again in a bikini, slipping a finger in her mouth and pulling down her lip. Then she slowly slid one bright blue nail along the top of her cleavage.

"Jesus," I said.

The TV screen flashed with multiple faces: a white blond sorority chick from Jersey, a Black girl from the Bronx, and an Indonesian punk girl from Florida.

An invisible dude spoke: "There are rules," as the camera refocused on Ruthy/Ruby's distorted face. She leaned back, elbows upon bed, then spoke into the camera: "Always come looking correct."

Now there was a new shot of the punk girl, small and boyish, half of her head shaved, straight black hair swept over one side of her face. "You must be the last bitch standing."

More music. A scene fast-forwarding to a fight later on in the season with two of the girls trying to drown each other in a pool while an emptied wine bottle bobs between their fists. More music. A shot of the sorority chick nodding in mock agreeability. Then: "Never apologize," she said, her blond hair parted straight down the middle of her head.

"Listen, Nina," Jessica said. "Are you listening?"

"Yeah, I'm here," I told her, though the inside of my head was buzzing.

"You cannot tell Mom."

I turned off the TV. I thought, It is very likely that the Ruby on television is not our Ruthy from real life. True, there was a likeness and the beauty mark on her face, but there were plenty of loud redheaded and freckled Puerto Rican girls, a ton of them in West Brighton alone.

Most likely our Ruthy was dead.

After all, how many years had we spent looking for her?

I went into the living room to find my mom, who'd fallen asleep on the couch with the window open. A breeze snuck through the black iron safety bars, lifting curtain away from sill. In the dark, I almost bumped into the chinero. My mother was snoring and gasped when I woke her as if she were coming up for air after swimming too long.

"I fell asleep," she said.

"You did."

As I walked her to the bedroom, a fire truck drove by, rotating light and noise around us, and each time the light captured a new and grimmer angle of my mother's face: the bottom of her soft, disappearing chin. The blue skin beneath her eyes.

The next day, after work, I took the bus straight over to Jessica's house. If this was really our sister, we were going to find her, Jess said. We were going to bring her back home.

When I rang the doorbell, Jess answered with little Julie's fat legs clutched around her waist. The kid was possessively holding Jessica's right boob.

"Hello, baby girl," I said, my face exaggerated with surprise. I reached out to pinch her cheek.

She smashed one side of her face into Jessica's chest and gave me side eye with her little one-year-old head.

"That baby's got an attitude problem, you know that?" I said.

"Oh, yeah, she's the one with the attitude."

And when Jess turned around to walk into the house, I swear Julie glared at me over her shoulder. In the kitchen, Jessica flipped open her laptop, and we waited four minutes for its dusty ass to buzz, beep, rattle, and blink on.

"That shit sounds like it's going to catch fire," I said.

Jessica rolled her eyes. "Oh well, dale. Buy me a new one, then."

We tried to find Ruthy on the internet by googling her suspected alias. Maybe an email address? A phone number? But there was no Ruthy Ramirez on Facebook, and there wasn't a Ruby, either, who even in the slightest way resembled our sister.

"I think the heffa changed her last name," Jessica said.

She scrolled down the *Catfight* website searching for the most current season, then kept X-ing herself out of the window by accident, because when it came to technology, Jessica kind of sucked. She still did things like send whole emails unnecessarily in caps.

"Just let me do it," I said, trying to muscle the laptop away.

But she grabbed the computer back and made sure to point out that we were in her house, and we were in her kitchen, and this was her laptop.

"Relax," I said. "Damn. It's not that serious." I stepped back and hoisted myself onto the counter.

For a while, we didn't say anything to each other, and I surveyed the kitchen that Jessica had crafted—its blue flowered wallpaper, the GOD BLESS OUR HOME plaque she'd nailed above the sliding patio door—until she slammed a hand on the table. "Found it."

On the screen was Ruthy/Ruby's face. A metal heart dotted her upper lip like a mole. It was a head shot. And below the picture her bio read in pink bubble letters:

My personal motto: Don't start none, won't be none. Otherwise, I dare you. I'm five feet of sexy fun.

Then in more official font:

Interested in writing Ruby? Leave a comment below. (Inappropriate sexual comments will be deleted by the webmaster.)

"*None. Fun,*" I said. "Such wordplay. Our sister's become a poet."

The light from the screen flashed on Jessica's face as she scrolled down. "What are you thinking? Should we leave a comment?" She reached absentmindedly for my pack of Newports.

"And say what?" I asked, snatching the pack away.

Not because I cared, but because she was always getting on me about smoking. *Do you know what your lungs probably look like right now, Nina? Huh? I'll tell you what they look like, girl—they look like one of Tío Ralphy's burnt-up hamburgers on Fourth of July. You want to die with a tube in your neck at forty-five? Half your teeth missing? Huh, Nina? Trust me, we see it all the time at the hospital. All the time.*

Jessica was always telling us about what she saw at the hospital *all the time*.

"I thought you don't smoke no more?" I said, before passing her one. Very generously, I'll add.

"I'm having a very stressful time right now, Nina. Besides, I don't even smoke as much as you," she said.

"Whatever, I just don't want you to have hamburger lungs, that's all."

Jess waved a hand in the air and ignored me, then started reading the message she was drafting aloud. "Dear Ruthy, This is Jessica, your sister. Please contact us at..." She'd put on her official business voice as she read. Like she was a midwestern newscaster on CNN.

"Don't be putting your personal shit down there. That shit is public. Everybody is going to see what you wrote," I told her.

She exhaled and blew the smoke in my direction, mostly, I think on purpose. "How is she going to write us back, then?"

"I don't know, but you're going to have a whole bunch of fucking creeps emailing you if you put your contact info down. Don't be stupid."

She started again. "Dear Ruthy, this is Jessica." Her voice had reached new inflections of whiteness.

"And Nina," I said.

"Jesus Christ." She pounded the backspace button several times with one finger, ashing on the keyboard. "This is Jessica and Nina... Please contact us—" Now Jessica screwed her face up into a question, then nodded as if she'd found the answer: *Nina is on Facebook.*

"Don't give her my shit *neither*. What is wrong with you?"

My sister... good-looking girl. But not too smart.

I pulled the keyboard away and pretended to type. "Dear Ruthy, this is Nina and Jessica. After all these years, we have found you, long-lost sister, who left us on purpose."

"Oh, stop!"

"Do you think it is that easy to escape, my dear disappeared one? I myself have been trying to escape this family for many years!"

"Stop," Jessica said. "Be serious."

"I am being serious."

Jessica pulled the keyboard back towards her, then typed:

Dear Ruthy. This is Jessica and Nina. (Your sisters.) Who love and miss you dearly. If you would like to talk to us, just say the word, and we'll figure something out.

Triumphantly, Jessica pressed *submit*. "There. That's it. Done."

Then she stood up and made a big show of wiping away some ash I'd dropped on the kitchen counter.

CHAPTER 3

Jessica

Doors locked, kitchen clean, clothes in the dryer, and baby's finally fucking fallen asleep. That's right—all before one in the morning!

After Nina left, I went into the bedroom with my laptop, flicked the light on, and looked at Lou, who had gathered all the covers on top of him and was pretending to snore. The whole room smelled like cough drops because he'd stuck half a jar of Vicks up his nose in order to beat his sleep apnea. Poor thing. I sat on his side of the bed and pushed his shoulder.

"Definitely one hundred percent," I told him, "without a doubt. I'm telling you it was fucking Ruthy. And I know you're awake because you snore much louder than that in real life. You're not fooling anybody."

Lou put the pillow over his head dramatically and said, "But, Jess, why are you shouting, though? It's like twelve o'clock at night."

"I am not *shouting*."

Lou buried his face further into the pillow. "Use your inside voice, baby," he mumbled. "Your inside voice."

"This is my INSIDE VOICE," I whispered loudly.

That got him to take the pillow off his face, real quick. He popped up in bed. "You're going to wake up the baby, Jess. You realize that, right?"

"What do you care? I'm the one that put the baby to bed, Mr. Concerned Citizen. And if she wakes up, I'm the one who's going to end up getting her to fall the fuck back to sleep, while you lie there finally snoring *for real.*"

He put his head back on the pillow and closed his eyes. Every day the little red veins on his eyelids grew longer.

"Some of us wake up at five thirty in the morning," he said.

"And some of us never wake up, because we never even get the chance to sleep."

I sat down on the bed and pulled a *Catfight* video clip up on the screen of my laptop. "Look."

"It's already midnight." Lou turned his head into the pillow. "I gotta get up in five hours, babe."

"And I gotta get up in six." I pushed the screen in front of his face. "Just one minute, baby, please. Look, Lou. I need an outside perspective."

He groaned but finally opened his eyes.

"Thank you, booboo." I moved past the section of the video where Ruby/Ruthy was sliding down a stripper pole installed on the counter in the kitchen that blinged with silver appliances—even the toaster seemed to have been Bedazzled with rhinestones. Then I stopped four minutes into the episode to the part when she was sitting in the confessional. In a purple velvet throne-like chair, Reality TV Ruthy began to fake-cry. A tear sat on one of her synthetic lashes. "What these bitches don't realize though is that I'm classy."

There was a red scratch mark on her skin where somebody had clawed at a piece of her neck during a brawl she had at the bar, after she kissed someone's boyfriend.

"You see it?" I said. "Look at the beauty mark."

I paused the video, put the screen real close to Lou's face.

"I can't see the video when you put the computer that close to my face," he said.

So I pulled it farther away. "Now do you see it?"

He squinted at the screen. "I don't know, Jess. It's been a long time. I don't remember her face so well anymore."

That squeezed all the air out of my chest, and I got up to walk out of the room.

"Aw, baby. I'm sorry. I didn't mean to make you cry." Lou sat up and put his arms out. "I didn't mean it, Jess. Come back."

It was hard for me to remember the particularities of Ruthy's face, too.

There was the red hair, of course, and the beauty mark. And I could always look at the old pictures hanging on the walls at Ma's place. The ones of eight-year-old Ruthy faking an evil grin on Christmas morning while smashing her new action figures against each other. Or my dad and mom smiling in the hospital the day she was born. My father's short beard touching Ruthy's chin as he bent to kiss her wrinkled forehead. There were Easter pictures of us from the early nineties with matching blue gingham skirts from Caldor, all looking like we belonged to some super-religious cult.

Still images. Frozen expressions. That's all I had left.

What I had forgotten was how Ruthy's face naturally moved.

In all of these pictures somebody had asked her to stand up straight, to pull her shoulders down from her ears, to pick her chin up.

And stop frowning, nena, God.

Somebody had asked her to smile.

"I'm not crying," I told Lou, then turned off the light.

Fully awake now, Lou reached his arms out for the laptop. "You want to show it to me again? Come here, baby. Don't go."

"No, it's all right. Go to bed. You gotta get up soon."

In the dark, I put my hands out in front of me to look for pajamas. "You just watch, though. Me and Nina are going to find her," I told him before closing the bedroom door. Then I went into the bathroom with the laptop to hide from the baby, so the little dictator wouldn't smell me and wake up, demanding to be fed.

Sitting on the bathroom floor, I pumped 120 ml of milk and watched the *Catfight* clip over and over again for another half hour.

The next day, I was so tired, it was like my eyes were full of soap. Worse, my back was misbehaving. An ache beneath my left shoulder never fully went away after Julie was born. In fact, over the past year, it managed to spread because I was constantly bending over to feed her, and it vibrated every time that she cried. I woke up late and had to book it to my mother's place by bus with the baby, then drag the stroller up to her apartment, up three flights of stairs.

"This is why I told you to keep wearing the faja," Ma said, shaking her head, as she greeted me at the door with Tylenol and a cup of coffee. "If you would have listened to your very intelligent mother, your back wouldn't be hurting you so much right now."

She was talking about the belly binder the hospital gave me, which I promptly threw out once they sent me home, because after ten hours of labor and an emergency C-section, I thought no additional torture was needed.

But by the time I clocked in to work, I regretted not keeping the faja. The pain was pulsing with a vengeance, even after two Tylenol, and I was trying to breathe deeply into its center, to stretch out whatever force had greedily knotted itself into my back.

When the pain finally subsided, I pulled out my phone to text Nina to see if she'd found out anything else about Ruthy, but then my boss snatched me up and sent me over to old Mrs. Ruben to draw her blood. I tried to be quick, but it took me a straight five minutes just to find a vein. Her skin was so old and slippery, I had to stretch it over and over again. Then Mrs. Ruben got so nervous, she threw her arms up and almost knocked the fucking butterfly needle out of my hand.

I wanted to slap her.

I admit it.

I'm not going to lie, when a needle comes that close to your forehead, your automatic reaction is to survive. But, instead, I held her wrist gently, put my face next to hers, and said very softly, "Mrs. Ruben. You have got to relax."

"Oh, to hell with it. You can't find one, can you?" She shook her head with her little brown Judge Judy bob and kept on moving her mouth as if she were chewing on something invisible. "Just let me die."

On top of the lung cancer, Mrs. Ruben had dementia, so come five p.m. she'd sundown and start spitting on the other PCTs, calling them thieves and rapists—"Gang bangers," she growled; at night, she enjoyed becoming extra difficult, which was hard to imagine, considering she'd spent her whole life playing hard-ass, finding creative ways to discipline decades of "at risk" kids, depending on whatever new educational trend was popular that year.

I had known Mrs. Ruben for a long time. She had been the principal at Curtis High School when I went there in the nineties, and she was just as no-nonsense about dying now as she was back then about keeping our asses after school in the one un-air-conditioned classroom in the basement for detention. She had loved especially to lecture our parents about being "fit." To gossip about them in staff meetings behind their backs, especially the mothers, who she enjoyed making fun of—their accents, their long nails and cheap perfume, their absent husbands.

I know all of this because being frequently in trouble as a teenager meant I was in that office a lot, and when people think you're nobody, they'll say all types of stupid shit in front of you as if you aren't there.

"Nobody wants you to die, Mrs. Ruben," I said. "Should we try again? You ready?"

The lines around Mrs. Ruben's eyes had finally relaxed, and she stuck her skinny arm out for me again. Very carefully I found the vein and angled the needle against her skin. "That's it. Almost there."

This is when I felt the most tender towards Mrs. Ruben, this woman who had ruled our lives for years, humiliated our parents. Here she was only an old woman afraid to die. And she would pat my arm gratefully when the needle did not hurt her.

But then some kids outside, waiting to be let into the school, started screaming out of nowhere. We could hear them clearly from the second floor through the window. They were pretending to fight, whipping each other with their bookbags, the way that teenagers invent excuses to touch each other because they can't just admit, *I really like you. I wish you would hold my hand.*

Mrs. Ruben lost it. It was like she was having PTSD from her tenure at Curtis High School. She stood up, opened the window, and shouted, "Will you fucking be quiet?"

The kids paused their fight so that there was just the sound of traffic and one bird chasing another in the tree outside.

"Finally," Mrs. Ruben said.

In this new quiet, I reached for her blistered hand one more time. "All right, let's try this again."

She was calm now and had already picked some new topic to complain about: a nurse, who she'd accused of trying to break into her room and hide in her closet to see her naked.

Then one of the teenagers threw a cup at the window screen, and it burst into the room, spraying the both of us with orange soda.

It took me at least another fifteen minutes to wipe the trails of Fanta off Mrs. Ruben's face. She shouted through the window at the kids running away from the hospital's security guard until, finally, I calmed the viejita down all over again and refound the vein.

"No, no. Here it is. Strong and green," I whispered.

Mrs. Ruben had that stubborn blood, slow and thick, but eventually it filled the tube in my fingers.

Afterwards, I patted her hand and she looked up at me and said, "I remember you."

Her face was pinched with suspicion, but I was honored.

I'd wondered if any of our lives ever stayed with her, the way I remembered certain patients and what pain did to them, how it shifted the shape of their bodies. How it could change someone's face forever. We'd had a long history, me and Mrs. Ruben, many afternoons of staring each other down in the principal's office, way after the well-behaved children were dismissed. Back then, all the kids had nicknamed her Penguin, because she resembled the breathless Danny DeVito version in *Batman Returns*. Pale skin and graying hair weighed down by grease. Pink bags that stretched underneath and around her eyes. But up until that day I wasn't sure if she'd remembered me at all.

"You do?" I asked her.

Mrs. Ruben concentrated on my name tag now, nodding in recognition.

"Yeah, I remember you, Ramirez. You were always hanging out with that kid Dominick and his cousins and that little shit Louis Amato." Then she focused on my face. "You were a *fast* little girl, weren't you?"

I couldn't help it—right there in front of her face I busted out laughing. *Fast!*

Shaking her head, Mrs. Ruben rolled her eyes and looked away, then clasped her hands together as if I were the one who had offended her.

"That's very kind of you to remember," I said.

I couldn't wait to tell it to Lou.

He always loved the Mrs. Ruben stories.

When I went to high school, after Ruthy went missing, Mrs.

Ruben had been one of those nosy adults; she'd summon me into the office so that I could sit in front of her dusty jar of peppermints while she grilled me for information, the way white folks talk about the disasters that happen to Black and brown people for entertainment and applause. I could imagine her recognizing my sister on TV and laughing, maybe turning to her husband and saying, "Look, I always said that girl ran away. What a strange family." Before reaching into her crusty bowl for more popcorn.

I sealed the Vacutainer and bandaged her up as a group of boys began singing a Soulja Boy song outside.

"Every year they get worse," she said. Not to me, but to an invisible audience living inside her. A hundred thousand Mrs. Rubens nestled inside her body like a Russian doll.

"You have a good one," I said, waving goodbye.

Mrs. Ruben responded by grunting, which I ignored because *You ain't hurting my feelings, viejita.* Instead, I made my way to the front desk, grinning, because I had become better at drawing blood than any of the other first-year PCTs.

Sometimes the wrong people remember you.

A few years ago, I bumped into an old middle school math teacher named Mrs. Wagner at the Staten Island Mall, buying a stack of turtlenecks in three different types of green. Mrs. Wagner had been a favorite teacher of mine because in sixth grade she'd defended me at a parent conference, after my moms was ready to whup my ass for failing another math test that year for the fourth time.

"Tell me the truth. Is she not paying attention in class? She got a problem with talking?" Ma asked.

Mrs. Wagner studied our faces, calculating the importance of her response, before saying, "Jessica is a wonderful student who is really trying. Mrs. Ramirez, this is just a hard math class. But she's getting better every week."

The next day, when Ivan Maldonado tried to play Mrs. Wagner in the middle of class, I kicked the back of his chair so hard that his friends busted out laughing. "Shut the fuck up, Ivan. Some of us aren't trying to spend six years graduating junior high school, like you."

A wonderful student.

Nobody had ever said that about me before.

But at Lerner's, when the twenty-year-old version of me came up to her in line and said, "Hi, Mrs. Wagner. How you doing?" I could tell by the way she raised her thin eyebrows that she couldn't quite place me. She'd turned red and started to smile frantically.

I never held it against her, though. I knew how easy it was for teachers to forget, all of those students, hundreds of them, sometimes thousands.

Instead, I gave her an easy exit from the conversation and said, "All right, Mrs. Wagner, you have a good one."

I waved goodbye like I hadn't noticed she didn't know who I was.

Then I put down the red dress I'd been looking at and left the store.

I placed the Vacutainer on the counter. Then one of the nurses, Karen, walked up to me and quickly but gently whispered, "Jessica, room two-forty-four passed." Which is how we usually referred to the patients: by their room numbers, for the purposes of confidentiality, and because it was simple and efficient.

"I need you to get in there," she said.

Karen had already sent in Allen and Carlos—twenty-one-, twenty-two-year-old guys—who sometimes showed up to their shifts still smelling like whatever they'd smoked that morning. Sweethearts in real life, but on the job, they stayed fucking up. One PCT after another started to notice that their measurements of the vital signs were off, until that was it. Karen pulled Allen and Carlos into the break room one day for a come-to-Jesus moment, the Jamaican in her accent eclipsing her Brooklyn one. She smacked the back of one hand into the palm of the other, saying: "This is the last time I am telling you. I am so serious. I am not playing around with y'all no more. Do you understand?"

The rest of us were watching through the glass windows laughing…Poor Allen and Carlos. The boys' days were numbered, and they knew it, so they had already started applying for jobs at Foot Locker and FedEx. The other day they'd asked if they could put me down as a reference and if I could pretend I was their boss, which I was like, "Uh, yeah, that's not fucking happening. Do I look stupid to you?"

Karen didn't say it, but I knew she was sending me in there to supervise them. I wasn't much older than the guys, only twenty-seven years old, and I had just started at St. Lucy's Hospital a few months ago. But the thing was (and Karen knew this, too) you could send me into any room, and trust and believe I'd make sure that the job got done right, because when it came to my money, I did not fuck around. No way. I was the type of person who liked to do things correctly the first time. Because when you don't, that's how you slip up—end up working twice as hard to fix some original mistake you made trying to get out of work on time to catch the bus.

Some of these other bitches working at that hospital were straight-up lazy. Didn't wipe the patients right when they took them to the bathroom or disappeared for twenty minutes when it was time to empty a bedpan. Then they'd turn around and be like: *Oh, I didn't know it was my turn.* Bitch, please. Everybody knew it was your turn.

Sometimes they got away with it, though.

Which is all right because I'll tell you one thing, you might be able to dupe the boss, but karma is elegant, and God sees everything.

And trust and believe he does not forget.

"Make sure the boys don't do anything stupid, all right?" Karen said. The skin underneath her eyes had purpled over the last month.

She was probably on the tenth hour of her shift, thirty-three years old and so pregnant she couldn't bend down to pick anything up.

I loved Karen because she had gifted me an old pharmacology textbook, even though I'd never completed more than twelve credits of college. When I was recovering from giving birth to Julie in the hospital, stunned from constantly being turned over in bed—pulse and temperature checked, incision inspected, blood loss monitored and tracked ("In case you hemorrhage"), the belly pushed on to check if my uterus was descending—my body felt irredeemably fucked up. Bloated. Stripped and cut. I had told Karen how a nurse had caught me crying in the middle of the night because I couldn't get Julie to *please-just-fucking-latch* and how the nurse asked for permission to touch my breast as she gently taught me how to shove it quickly inside the baby's mouth before Julie could clamp down on the nipple. "Don't be so precious about it," she said. "You can be a little rough. Infants are a lot tougher than you think." How when Julie finally latched without making my back shrink in pain, it was like a fucking revelation. I told Karen how I said to the nurse afterwards, "I'm not usually like this," and her response was, "Girl, you don't have to feel any type of way. A lot of women cried in this room trying to feed their children." How I felt like I had entered an invisible kingdom of motherhood (whether I liked it or not). Now, I finally understood what it was like to be a mom, a universe I never cared about before. The long nights. The private pain. Jesus, I was such a little badass growing up. And now maybe God was punishing me with 422 days without sleep.

I took Karen's old book home and studied it sometimes at night, while Lou and the baby snored in the bedroom. Behind the front cover Karen had slipped a brochure for the nursing program at the College of Staten Island with a note scribbled beside the picture of some nurse holding the hand of a dying child. *This is you*, she'd written next to the nurse's curly brown hair.

One night I showed the brochure to Lou, and he laughed. "That's depressing as fuck."

"Right?" I said.

I had not told him that I'd called to get more information.

Karen reached over the front desk and lifted the phone receiver. "Go, Jess. I'll call the morgue."

The stretch of hallway to room 244 looked like it had been decorated in 1986 by the Golden Girls—soft teals and pinks streaked with white and gold, twenty-five-year-old pictures of oceans and trees dotted with dust. There was a middle-aged white woman in a long trench coat and scarf whisper-shouting into the phone, "Why am I the one who has to take care of everything? Huh?" She looked sharply up at me as I passed, and I pretended not to hear her. "You're so fucking cheap. You can't even pay for a flight to attend your own mother's funeral. Ridiculous."

When I walked in room 244, Carlos was sitting in a chair in the corner texting someone, while Allen was telling a story in vivid detail about some poor girl from West Brighton that he was fucking and planning on ghosting next weekend.

"You guys are kidding me, right?" I smacked them on the backs of their heads.

Allen put his hands up in the air and said, "Karen told us all we had to do was come to the room and wait for you. She was all like, 'Don't touch anything until Jessica gets there.'"

"Okay, but I'm pretty sure that's the daughter outside the room right now. And nobody wants to hear about this chick's toto. If that was your moms right now, would you want somebody talking like that over her dead body?"

Then Carlos tried to imitate me, weaving his head from side to side, then squeaking out in a Minnie Mouse voice: "Hi, my name is Jessica, and I'm fucking annoying."

He got quiet after that, though, and gently removed the blanket from the bed. For a moment, we all stood still looking at 244's dead body. Then we closed her eyes.

We washed her arms and legs.

We tagged her.

We wrapped her up.

And the boys moved 244's body as carefully as if she were still alive.

I went to the bathroom and spent fifteen minutes scrubbing my hands. It was not so much the deadness of the body, but the sudden weight of it, emptied of breath.

Gone.

One moment you could be sneezing or laughing or screaming out in pain for more meds, and then the next second, how was it that everything inside you could just disappear?

Karen poked her head into the bathroom, while I washed my hands.

"Thank you for taking care of that, Jessica. I promise you, I will not forget."

Then she was off to whatever next patient needed her the most.

The whole rest of the day was like that, one small crisis after another, until I found myself with about ten minutes to switch from scrubs to slacks and drag some eyeliner along my lids before Lou came to pick me up. And the whole time Nina was blowing up my phone with texts...

Did Fake Ruthy write you back yet?

Fake Ruthy cannot be Real Ruthy. Just looked at a picture of her face up close and she looks 42 underneath the make-up.

WHY DO YOU NEVER TEXT BACK???

Is it because you no longer LOVE ME???

"Jesus Christ," I said to the phone. "No wonder those girls at Mariposa's hate you. You're just sitting there texting all the time."

Though I had to admit, now that the shift was over—the drama done for the day, the boys sent home, time card punched out—I wanted nothing more than to get back to my computer to see if Ruby/ Ruthy had responded to our note on the message board. I rushed to the staff room and was trying to get my stuff together so quickly that when I pulled my purse out of the locker, the strap got caught in the door and the whole fucking thing ripped apart. I had to cradle the bag underneath my arm like a football.

My phone buzzed again, and I tapped out a response.

Not now, Nina, I will call you later. I just got out of work.

By the time I caught the elevator and said my goodbyes to the United Nations crew at the front desk—three ladies: Puerto Rican, Russian, and Chinese—it was already 8 p.m., and Carlos and Allen were smoking on the benches in the dark next to the parking lot.

Allen was sitting on the back of the bench with his sneakers on the seat, a short Irish kid who looked Puerto Rican because he had this long dark curly hair that he wore slicked back and tied up. He had grown up in the South Beach projects and was talking to Carlos about a kid who had just gotten shot and killed in New Brighton.

"Shit, imagine you're just walking? Minding your own fucking business. Bam, that's it. I'd be tight."

"Motherfucker, you wouldn't be nothing," Carlos said, laughing, "because you'd be dead."

Carlos moved over on the bench so that I could sit down next to them to smoke. Floor after floor of the hospital's white lights glowed around them, while they imagined better jobs than this one. Someone was getting paid twelve dollars an hour to work stock at the new Best Buy. Someone was getting paid more in unemployment

34

than what they were when they worked. A union job, that's what they needed. Carlos said, "Man I could do a lot with twelve dollars an hour, though."

As I lit the cigarette, Lou pulled up to the front of the hospital. For a second, I sat there quietly as he leaned out the window, because I liked to watch him look for me. The angle of light from the streetlamp fell into his car so that you could see clearly that Lou was white. Immediately, Carlos and Allen stopped talking with each other and looked up at him, mad nosy.

"That's your man?" Allen asked.

Grinning, Carlos said, "All right, I see you, Jessica. That's how you like them, huh." Then he turned to Allen and said, "Look, you just might have a chance."

When Lou made me out in the dark laughing with the guys, he shouted from his rolled-down window, "Jess, come on." Irritated.

"All right, all right." I flicked Carlos on the back of his head and walked over to Lou. "I'm coming. Geez!"

When I got into the car, he pressed a quick kiss on my cheek, then turned the wheel to pull out. Julie was cooing in the back seat and wiggling her arms.

"Hey, baby girl." I reached behind me around the car seat and caressed her cheek.

"I hate that you work such long hours."

I didn't say anything.

I'd been mad at Lou for the past week because his ex's name kept popping up on his phone, and I hadn't decided yet what I wanted to do with his stupid ass. I just looked over at him, the wrinkle that had curved quietly above his lip for the last three years, against a face that had mostly stayed the same since high school.

But then I couldn't resist. "You know what Mrs. Ruben did today?"

Lou shook his head. "I can't believe that old woman is still alive."

"So, I finish taking her blood, right? Then she looks at me,

Lou. She goes, 'I remember you.' And I'm all nodding my head like, *Aw, that's so sweet, Mrs. Ruben.* Then she goes, 'You're the one who used to hang out with Dominick and his crew and that little shit Lou.'"

"Damn, she said all that? I haven't thought about Dominick in a minute. What happened to that kid?"

"I don't know. Probably fucking dead somewhere." I rolled down the window and let the cool black air rush into the car. "But listen, then the old woman turns around and calls me a slut."

"No!" Lou's whole body shook with laughter.

"Yeah, she was all like: 'Oh, you was *fast* ass.'"

Lou sucked his teeth. "She did not say that, Jessica. Why are you lying?"

"Yes, she did."

"She did not call you fast ass, Jessica. That is not in Mrs. Ruben's vocabulary."

"All right. But she did call me *fast*. That's what she said: 'You were fast.' Literally."

"Aw, baby, you weren't even that bad. You were just a little annoying, always over there talking so much shit, in the mirror gluing those little curls to the side of your face." He imitated a thirteen-year-old version of me sliding gel along my edges.

I went to hit his arm, but Lou grabbed my hand and held it there between us all the way back home.

Later, in bed, I told him about 244 as I looked up at a footprint on the ceiling I'd left after killing a spider with my sneaker.

"A white lady. It was so fucking weird, Lou. Spanish people, you know, it's like we're very, very emotional. I don't care if that sounds racist because it's true. When we lost Ruthy, you could hear all of us wailing at once on top of each other inside the room. A white family, when somebody dies, they all start talking about money. I was running over to the room, and I bumped into one of the woman's daughters, all business, arguing about who was going to pay for what."

Lou said, "Why you always gotta be so mean to white people for? Leave us alone. You're just as white as me." Which for the record I am not...I'm just the lightest skinned in my family.

Then Lou tried to lift his arm up for comparison.

But Lou was like super-unambiguously white. Blond hair. Blue eyes. He looked like he belonged on *The Sound of Music*, Mr. Lou Amato von Trapp singing about how alive the hills were. I turned to him very seriously and said, "I'm not white. Don't fucking insult me like that."

He popped up on one elbow. "What the fuck do you know about Puerto Rico, anyway? You went there once when you were like five."

"Actually, I went twice. And the second time I was eight."

But I should have never told him that shit to begin with. He'd been holding that tidbit of information in his secret arsenal against me for the last five years, and every now and then when he was losing an argument he liked to sling it at me. "You sound more Staten Island than I do."

"Personally, I like to think of it as Brooklyn," I said, "my accent."

"Buuuullshit," he said. "Brooklyn, my ass. You sound like Olive Oyl working the Piercing Pagoda at the Staten Island Mall."

I got up from the bed. "I'm going to forget you said that and go outside and smoke."

"Fuck it, just open the window and smoke in the kitchen," he said. "But you know, Jess. I hate it. I really fucking do. It just sticks to you, the smell. And it's not good for you."

This from a man who chugs a two-liter bottle of Coke in the morning for breakfast, and still buys purple and blue quarter waters from the corner stores like he's in the sixth grade.

"Oh, reeeeally? Well, you know what I can't stand? When your ex's name keeps popping up on your phone and you text her back, like I'm fucking stupid and don't notice. So?"

"Jesus Christ, Jess. She's friends with my mother. I told you. She grew up with my sisters. She's a family friend." And then when that didn't work: "Jessica, she's redoing the upstairs, so she needed someone to look at it. I was just giving her one of the guys' numbers, all right? Okay? My mother told her to call me." He was sitting up in bed now, waving his arms around in the dark for emphasis, like that was going to make any fucking difference.

"Your mother can go fuck herself, too," I said.

"Why you gotta talk like that, Jess? Come on. Do I talk about your mother like that?"

"First of all, you better not talk about my mother like that. Second of all, my mother loves you. Like her own son. Like her own flesh and blood. And third of all, your mother's mad fucking racist. I don't like her ass. That shit she said the other day about Obama?"

Lou stood quiet.

"Yeah, you thought I didn't hear that shit, right? And I know she's rooting for your ex." I lifted a cigarette to punctuate my point and said, "She's putting thoughts into her head, Lou. I'm telling you. And I don't like it."

He turned on the light. All of his hair was sticking up on one side, like a wave, and he was grinning. "Look at you. You're jealous."

"Shut up."

"Yeah, you are. Go ahead, go," he said quickly, waving a hand at me. "Smoke that cigarette and then get your beautiful behind back in bed, before I go call her. But brush your teeth first."

"Shut the fuck up, Lou," I said as I moved out of the bedroom.

But even from the kitchen window, over the sounds of cars splashing through the street, I could still hear him laughing.

*   *   *

38

After Lou fell asleep, I went into my closet and pulled out an old photo album. There was a page from Ruthy's diary that I had ripped out in 1996 before I handed over the journal to the detectives. I'd folded up the entry and hidden it away for years.

Ruthy and my moms were always arguing about stupid shit, whether or not she could go to a sleepover or the mall or across the street to Yesenia's house or the pizzeria after track practice. Ruthy was always trying to go somewhere else instead of home, a thought that made me flinch.

The day after she went missing, the detectives had asked us questions. "Think carefully," they said. "Who could possibly hurt her?" And immediately, a name surfaced in my chest, then pressed itself against my tongue. But I couldn't bear to name him. I couldn't do it. And now the regret curdled in my chest like spoiled milk.

If I had told them, those detectives, would things be different? Would Ruthy be here?

I couldn't, not even for Ruthy, say the name that could have possibly saved her. And that thought made me hate myself, until I remembered he could not have possibly hurt her. He had already been gone, had left the city, had been missing for years before Ruthy disappeared in 1996. He was probably dead somewhere, the motherfucker, thank God.

In big electric-blue letters, Ruthy had entitled the entry: *Things I Would Never Tell My Mother*.

1. Dad makes better yellow rice than you.
2. I never threw out that shirt you hated. I just keep it in my locker.
3. I know when you are sad. I just pretend not to see it.
4. I love you. (I just would never say it.)
5. I miss being in fourth grade and you taking me to the zoo.

She was always writing little stuff like that in the journal, melodramatic poems or raps. It was a harmless entry, nothing that would help the cops track her down, and it felt only appropriate that Ruthy's secrets stay her own—even if she was missing. Nobody needs to know everything about everybody's life. Besides, the entry would have probably just hurt my mother's feelings.

I traced my finger along the indentations Ruthy's pen made over a decade ago, feeling the relief on the page where she had lifted her hand and the blue ink where she'd angrily pressed down.

CHAPTER 4

Ruthy

First of all, if you really want to know what happened to Ruthy Ramirez, then you got to understand what happened that day at school. But maybe people don't really want to know what happened that day. Maybe people don't really care. Most adults already have their own ideas about the type of girl Ruthy is, that is because everybody's always running their mouths about her. And people like that, they're more interested in the type of little girl who one day rides her bike down her suburban block and disappears, only to show up later portrayed by some B actress on *Unsolved Mysteries*. Or they greedily watch the news, obsessed, as they guess who killed JonBenet Ramsey.

So what? Most people are followers anyway. They don't know how to form their own opinions but somehow still think that they're like special. That they are better than me. Inside their head, they think they got it *all* figured out, about who I am and what happened.

Whatever! Who cares?

Not me, I promise you.

I'll tell you that much.

Let them continue to play themselves.

I can tell my own damn story.

Maybe let's start the story *this* way: There is a girl. Her name is Ruthy Ramirez.

You are that girl.

You have two sisters. You live on the north edge of Staten Island with your crazy-ass moms, your sisters, and your dad in a little pink town house. And after you turn thirteen, nobody can control you.

The whole day since homeroom, Yesenia (your fake-ass former best friend) is walking around school like she's never borrowed your lip gloss after track practice, like she ain't the only girl in eighth grade who hasn't gotten her period yet, and like you hadn't helped her lie to everyone to pretend that she did. You say to yourself, *That's all right, though. See what happens. See if I care. Keep it up,* while she acts like the two of you didn't used to sit together every day during lunch in sixth grade, reading the Say Anything section in *YM*, contemplating the various philosophical questions of sixth-grade girldom: Would you rather shit yourself in front of a boy you liked or unexpectedly bleed through your white skirt during Social Studies?

Which is worse:
   accidentally farting while laughing at a joke
   OR
   blowing snot out through your nose?

Then at lunch in the cafeteria, Yesenia, for no good reason at all, says some slick shit like "Oh, look at Ruthy's shirt," to this girl Angela Cruz (who by the way isn't even in the eighth grade). Still, Yesenia is stupid and trying to impress her. For what?

What is so special about Angela Cruz anyway? She can barely jump in during double Dutch without getting hit in her big-ass

forehead by the rope. Food clings to the rubber band
when she talks shit. And she's not even that pretty. J
little bit in the eyes. But not really, though.

In fact, you should know that there is nothing sp
at all. That is, if you really want to know my opin

But this is the problem with Yesenia: she's
homework or her hairstyle or her opinions fro'
of person Ms. Ellen in Life Skills calls a
scared to make their decisions by themselves

"You gotta be a leader," Ms. Ellen alwa   .ile
passing the cookies around the circle during G..   ｘing
references to the different outcast characters turned h.   n *The
Mighty Ducks*, while the boys in the corner break out singing "We
Are the Champions" like the real losers they are.

Now, in the cafeteria, you turn around and look straight back at
Yesenia, the way her long hair makes her look a little bit like the
Little Mermaid.

Your sister Jessica told you once, "If you're fighting, don't ever let
no bitch make you look away. You understand me?"

So, you shout at the table in Yesenia's direction, "Well, that's cool,
then. Nobody wants to be your friend anyway. Stupid." But that
sounds real little-girlish coming out of your mouth, so you imitate
your moms and add "Pendeja," for good measure.

Unfortunately, though, class 802 steps into the cafeteria prematurely
for lunch and the combination of their voices and bodies slamming
against each other—their LA Lights slipping on the floor slick with
the residue of spilled milk, their collective clowning on the dude with
the messed-up fade—eclipses your voice, which leads to the following question: If a thirteen-year-old girl screams in the middle of a
cafeteria but nobody hears her, does it really even fucking matter?

The shirt in question, the one Yesenia rolled her eyes at, is a
cropped halter top, almost identical to the one T-Boz wore when she

was dancing on top of the ocean in the video for "Waterfalls," which is by far your favorite *CrazySexyCool* track (I mean, obviously). You bought the shirt yourself, off the three-dollar rack at G+G, while your mother was looking for size 8 wide flats for work at Payless. Not that you would ever actually admit aloud that you and your family shop at Payless, but, anyways, that's beside the point. Back to the story, you see: your moms with her rosaries and turtlenecks and unlimited statues of santos and orishas would probably kill you if she ever saw you wearing that crop top now, even underneath your overalls, whose straps you let dangle to reveal your perfect thirteen-year-old stomach.

Ugh, your mom loves you, but she's like…God…TOO MUCH. For no reason at all.

Doesn't she even realize that there are girls literally giving head and smoking in the stairwells? Just because some stupid older girl dared them, and they were too afraid to say no.

Followers. All of them, just like Ms. Ellen says.

And all you do is go to track after school and get into fights sometimes, which really means you were just defending yourself. That's the real unfortunate tragedy of it all. In reality, you are the good girl, and nobody knows it.

But that's also besides the point.

That morning you hid the shirt in your book bag before you ran out of the house in your track hoodie. But once you landed at 61, you went straight into the bathroom during breakfast and changed, because you're smart like that, you see.

Duh.

The whole bathroom, it smells like straight-up doodoo. There is an un-annihilatable scent of turd stuck to the walls, every yellow stall. The smudged mirrors are so small that you must stand on both your book bag and a stack of Regents textbooks to inspect your belly button, which has turned red and started to peel where you pierced yourself one night with a safety pin that you cleaned with your mother's lighter while everybody was asleep. A lot of the other girls have tried to pierce themselves before, but they always punk out once the needle starts to break the skin, because, at the end of the day, all of them are truly and sincerely weak.

But not you.

You know that the trick with pain is to not acknowledge it.

After you find a spot to sit in the cafeteria, on the way back up to the lunchline, you spot Yesenia with her long, straight light brown hair looking up from a tray of gray broccoli that she is spinning around on the table. With what?

What is this stupid fucking look on Yesenia's face? Is she jealous?

Well then, good.

She fixes her black eyes on you and doesn't blink.

And, lately, it has been harder for you to understand what is going on in Yesenia's head. She has a new boyfriend now, who is in high school, named Ivan Maldonado. But secretly you like to call him Igor. And now Yesenia thinks she is better than everybody, just because of some stupid boy.

Not that this matters much. Yesenia with her fake-ass Filas and ninety-nine-cent-store smiley face T-shirts. ("Everybody knows you didn't get that shit from Wet Seal, Yesenia. Stop lying," Jennifer Martinez had said to her last year. And since you were Yesenia's best friend, you punched Jenny on the side of her forehead and said, "Shut up. Wet Seal is corny, too, bitch." For that they suspended you for one week.) And this is the thanks that you get.

You're about to go up to Yesenia and say something about it, too, but just as you walk by the table, you notice that they are serving grilled cheese today, which is like an eighth-grade miracle.

Oh my god, grilled cheese! If you have to eat another wet cafeteria hamburger, you're going to Promise Up to God puke everywhere. You wave at the new crew you sit with now, some girls who live on your block, as you shift along the metal counter. Today, the lunch ladies are taking their time and you rub your free lunch ticket hungrily as you wait, also thankful for the dollar in your pocket that Jessica gave you that morning for an AriZona Iced Tea.

And that's when the trouble all happens. While you're just standing there, innocent, minding your own business, out of nowhere, somebody touches the back of your head. You spin around and see that it's Angela's Ninja Turtle–looking ass creeping up behind you on line. She is bigger than you, wider and taller. You can see the blue rubber bands connecting the braces of her lower and upper jaw when she smiles. At what?

"You laughing at me?" you ask her.

But instead, she goes, "Naw, I just like your hair."

Your heart's already pounding the way it does whenever you know that you're going to need to fight. You reach for the back of your head where Angela touched you and can feel it, sticky but firm. Already you know that the gum will be tangled there in your crunchy red curls for a long, long time. And right away, your first reaction is to lift the tray and smash it into Angela's fucking face. But she punches it out of your hand first, and the green beans go flying.

The lunch ladies adjust their hairnets and start to shriek, "Stop, stop it! You stop it now! Jesus Christ. Mr. Callahan!"

This pale trio of women remind you of the black crows who sit on the wire between the street posts, squawking in the gray distance of morning.

While the seventh and eighth graders circle around the fight, forming a barrier between your bodies and Mr. Callahan's, you grab somebody's fruit cup and pelt it against Angela's forehead so that little pieces of peach slide down her freckles. Then you grab Angela's hair and lift your fist high, planning to let it drop against her temple. But then Mr. Callahan, the social studies teacher, a chubby, short, usually gentle guy, reaches you first, grabs your arm, almost lifting you off the floor by your elbow, and shouts: "What the fuck are you doing?" Accidentally, you punch him in the face.

Immediately (you might even say *conveniently*) Angela Cruz becomes somebody else. She's clutching her face innocently and picking a piece of peach from the cleavage of her 34B breasts, forcing a tear down her cheek until it stops for a second and trembles by her earlobe.

Pause. But maybe you are not the type of human who would have tried to smash Angela Cruz in the face with a tray. Maybe you are the type of person who would have walked away crying, which is completely fine, okay. No judgment here. We're all different. It's cool. Maybe you're the type who would have tugged at Mr. Callahan's arm and pointed at Angela to snitch. Or maybe you would have preferred to stay quiet and pretend not to notice that Angela had even been the one to stick gum in your hair in the first place. Fair enough. We can't ultimately decide who we are or the people we become.

Perhaps you are not even Puerto Rican.

Maybe you are not even a girl.

In any case, most likely, you are probably not like Ruthy Ramirez. Which is fine. It's okay. Not everybody can be like Ruthy.

So, let's try this again:

There is a girl.

Her name is Ruthy Ramirez.

She lives in Staten Island with her father, mother, and two sisters.

You are not that girl.

Ruthy Ramirez is in the eighth grade and likes to fight. (There's nothing wrong about that, okay? Sometimes you have to fight. So, get over it.)

During lunch Ruthy gets into a fight with stupid ugly Angela Cruz because of her fake-ass former best friend, Yesenia. Afterwards, security drags Ruthy down the brown and green hallways into the downstairs office, where the dean, Mr. Delvecchio, awaits.

And the whole time Ruthy shouts, "Why aren't you taking Angela to the principal's office? Take her. She's the one who started it." So that all the adults and kids in the hallway straight-up stop to look at Ruthy, which makes her grin. An audience. If she could, she'd wave her hand and blow a kiss at them like Mariah Carey.

In the office, Ruthy repeats her question to Delvecchio as he pushes a stick of blue gum in his mouth and answers, "You tried to assault Angela with a tray, Ramirez."

Delvecchio is a former cop, so that's how he talks, you know . . . kind of stupid.

"That's not how it went!" Ruthy says, then cringes, disappointed at how her voice sounds at that moment, like she is just some stupid little girl, when she is not *just some stupid little girl*, do you understand?

She is so much bigger than a little girl.

Then this terrible fucking weight in Ruthy's throat starts to just push all of her voice down into her chest. She keeps shaking her head and bringing both hands up in the air to explain, "That's not even how it happened, you see."

Then Mr. Delvecchio, who is always telling people not to roll their eyes, rolls his eyes. "Enough."

Which is actually the problem: the teachers always think it is Ruthy's fault, you see. Before she can even defend herself, they always assume that she's the one in the wrong. And at the end of the day, she can only hope that they will not call her mom.

Delvecchio has a smell about him, a combination of CK One and Hamburger Helper. His office is a dull beige with D.A.R.E. posters taped to its walls. The basketball trophies of the team he coaches are lined up on a shelf above his head.

"I don't know who you're shouting at, young lady. Lower your voice," he says, even though at any given moment throughout the school day Delvecchio can be caught screaming at some small, undeserving kid who others have scapegoated for talking.

The light that shines through the one gated window in the office is so strong that it illuminates the whole room. Good, Ruthy thinks. It won't be cold after school when she runs.

If she runs. Now Delvecchio is threatening to talk to the track coach, and if Ruthy's behavior continues, "No more track team for you, young lady. No extracurriculars." Then he laughs at her and tries out some Spanish. "Nada."

Ruthy's whole body tightens as she forces herself to look past Delvecchio's very stupid mouth, through the window at the orange branches of a tree swaying outside.

Yes, maybe it will be warm after school. It is a possibility. Hopefully.

The thing is that the cold makes Ruthy's chest ache, her lungs sore, and sometimes after about a mile, the pain will arch into her throat, as if yawning. Sometimes, too, she gets this really weird headache when she runs, and the taste of ammonia presses against the back of her tongue as if she's accidentally swallowed too much pool water.

"It's because you're breathing wrong, Ramirez," Coach explains.

"In through your nose, out through your mouth," she says, pacing back and forth in her white turtleneck and fuzzy green vest, a whistle dangling around her neck: Coach's uniform. (Once at an awards assembly the whole girls' track team gasped when they saw Coach walk into the auditorium in heels, her bangs pushed aside to reveal freshly tweezed eyebrows. Until that moment, they had never seen Coach's forehead.) "You have got to learn how to breathe, Ramirez."

But the problem is that Ruthy has asthma. And sometimes it surprises her out of nowhere: an invisible hand will tighten inside her chest and hold her whole body hostage. But Ruthy has been working on it, slowly, teaching herself to control her lungs. If only...

"Are you listening to me?" Mr. Delvecchio raises his voice now. "If I find you do one more thing. Just one more thing this year, Ramirez!" He lifts one finger and jabs the air in her direction.

Idiot.

Moron.

Pendejo.

"But you're so stupid you don't see the gum in my hair?" Ruthy shouts.

She wants the question to sound mean and forceful, but instead her voice breaks, and now there are tears, God. Tears! Why does Ruthy have to cry in front of stupid Delvecchio? Why? She looks down at her cropped shirt and the tiny little roll of flesh sticking out above the waist of her overalls.

Stupid.

"Okay, okay, okay, Ruthy," he says. "It's okay."

He plucks a tissue out of a pink flowered box on his radiator and extends it to her. Ruthy looks at the tissue in his hand and debates whether to accept it, because Ruthy knows for a fact that Delvecchio does not like her.

Which is like whatever, she doesn't fucking like Delvecchio, either, anyway.

Once she overheard him telling an aide, while pointing at her, "That one, it's like she's already forty-three, has five kids and been to prison."

So, this type of sympathy Ruthy finds highly fucking weird, to sit there in the smelly old-man office of this fool. But there is also snot running down her lip, so she accepts Delvecchio's pity Kleenex.

And now Ruthy has to cry in front of him.

Probably nobody has cried in his office in a long time because the tissue is dusty, and it makes Ruthy sneeze.

Delvecchio lifts a bloated red hand and dials for one of the office aides, "Kamila. Can you come over here for a second?"

An old Dominican lady who Ruthy recognizes as the Late-Pass Woman walks into the office. She clasps her hands in front of her as she waits for him to speak to her.

"Could you take care of this?"

This.

He points to Ruthy.

Later, in the bathroom, Kamila repeats, "All right, cálmate. Stay still," as she lifts her perfumed fingers to tease gum away from Ruthy's curl. The old woman is pretty, proper, and polite. Her white hair pulled into a bun. Red lipstick as if she's about to go to a wedding. And an ugly mustard-colored school shirt.

Ruthy winces. There's a piece of gum clinging stubbornly to one long red curl, and it stings when Kamila pulls at it with her long natural nails. No tips.

"Ay, Dios," she says. "I have to get the scissors. Wait right here, mi amor."

Kamila leaves, heels echoing in the hall. Ruthy looks at herself in the mirror, bunching up her lips, trying to turn her face into a stone. She swears never to forgive Yesenia. Not even if Yesenia apologizes, not even if she says please, not even if Yesenia curses out Angela and says, "Ruthy, but actually you are my best friend."

Never, okay? Never.

In fact, today after track practice, Ruthy decides, she will not take the bus with Yesenia. Instead, after Coach dismisses them, Ruthy will flat-out leave her there and walk to another bus stop four blocks away from where they practice. Sitting on the windowsill, next to the warm radiator, Ruthy tries to imagine the look on Yesenia's face when she leaves. Maybe the top of her cheek will twitch a little like the way it does when she's about to cry. Maybe she'll end up getting stuck at the bus stop sitting next to stupid Ricky Diaz, who will try to talk to her about the many details she's missed about the *Mighty Morphin Power Rangers*.

Oh, she'll really miss Ruthy then, won't she.

Oh, boy, will Yesenia miss her.

I mean, you think, she probably missed her, right?

CHAPTER 5

Dolores

Nope!

It never fucking failed.

Dear Lord, no matter how early I caught the bus, no matter what time of the day, everybody and their mother would pack that S48. And I'd be stuck underneath somebody's armpit holding on to the pole for dear life every time the bus driver braked. Then, when I got to the Pathmark this afternoon—a mess. I tell you, Dear Lord. All of the cabdrivers were already lined up along the curb in the parking lot, holding their cigarettes out their windows, begging for folks to get in their car, "Hey, Mami, come on. I got you." And in my head, I was like, You don't even speak Spanish, why you calling me Mami for? Then another one honking: "Taxi. Taxi."

Yeah.

Right.

How am I supposed to tell if these guys are legitimate drivers or serial killers when half of their cars are unmarked? Just the other day, NY1 had a story about a woman in the Bronx who was kidnapped by a fake cabdriver in broad daylight in Bay Plaza, on her way back home from working a shift at JCPenney. Minding her own damn business, too. Just trying to make a living. And I'm telling you right now, if she hadn't been studying tae kwon do during her lunch breaks, God forgive me, that sick motherfucker would have killed her right there in his car, chopped up the body, vacuum-sealed the pieces, and stored her in his refrigerator for later. Chacho. He would have turned that poor woman into soup.

That's why I always, Dear Lord, I *always* order my own cab from the same company. I tell Jessica and Nina the same thing, too, though God, you already know those girls don't listen to me. Especially Nina now that she's returned from college and all of a sudden has come to believe that she knows everything about everyone. Anyways, I tell my daughters (though I don't know why, because they don't listen to me), I do not like any surprises. If I call Angel Lakes I get the same driver: Mario Nuñez. Seven years, and it's never been a problem. Right away, the dispatchers, they recognize both my name and my number. And, in less than ten minutes, Mario pulls up in his old brown Toyota and shouts out the window, "Dolores, you want me to open up the trunk?"

Always gets out of the car, too, and places the bag with the eggs in the front so I can hold it on my lap.

Granted, he's a little bit of a flirt. But respectful. He'll say, "You know, Dolores, soon you're going to get married again, and you'll have a husband who will drive you places. You won't need me anymore, and I'll have to go home and weep." His black rosary dangling from the rearview mirror and swaying from side to side the whole time, next to the Bugs Bunny–shaped car deodorant stinking up the front seat like a wintergreen-scented fart.

Yo le digo, "Mario, I got married once. That was the love of my life. Never again."

I say this not out of hard feelings, or even because it is true, but in order to remind him that we are only friends.

Always, I give him a four-dollar tip, and always he carries the bags from the trunk to my front steps. If I open the door to the apartment, he never tries to walk in.

They don't make them like that anymore.

You remember pobrecita Maribella the other day, the little redhead in Proper Parenting, the one whose boyfriend's been dodging child support for the last two years? That story about how her fifteen-year-old son came home high after "basketball practice" and called her a bitch. Let me ask you something, Dear Lord, what exactly are we supposed to do with children like this? And what do we do when the men disappear and we have to raise them ourselves? You tell me, Dear Lord. Do we beat them? And if so, how hard? How long? And how can we stand the weight of our own hands on our children's bodies? And what do I say to the young women when the city gets greedy? When it opens its mouth and tries to snatch our children away? "You should have put your kids in time-out." Ha!

In any case, you already know, the only reason why I went to that Pathmark in the first place was the oxtail was on sale for six dollars a pound. And it was a good thing I made it there before two o'clock, because otherwise this beast of a woman would have gotten to the last three pounds of meat before me. From the opposite direction of the meat aisle, I saw her booking it away from the bread, using her green-and-pink flowered umbrella as a crutch. So, I rolled down the aisle with my shopping cart at high speed to the meat fridge, reached down, and grabbed the last package of oxtail, before she got there, her hair still pinned around bright green and purple rollos, with a hairnet keeping them in place. She stood over me, as if I was supposed to be scared about it, then said, "Pendeja. I was reaching for that."

"You were reaching for nothing," I told her. "You were over there by that tower of Fruit by the Foot."

The butcher, bald, white, and nosy, poked his head out over the meat counter to raise one invisible eyebrow.

"You lucky I don't smack you right now," she said, lifting her umbrella like she was about to do something about it.

But I just smiled at the woman very politely, full of love and said, "That's why the Lord breaks the teeth of the wicked."

In other words, I'm not going to say it, because I'm a Christian, but, *Cuidao, bitch.*

"I don't need the Lord to break the teeth of my enemies. I'll do it myself," she said, because some people, ese tipo, tú sabes, they don't got any type of manners.

But God, you would be proud of me. Instead of getting angry, I focused on staying blessed and imagined the smell of rabo filling the kitchen, the way the air starts to smell like butter when the band of fat around the oxtail finally breaks down, how the soup thickens the third hour in the pot. If I started cooking at three, everything would be done by the time Nina got home from work.

I could watch my shows until ten o'clock and then get a good seven hours of sleep before waking up to head to the church again. On the contrary, I imagined this other woman unpinning her rollos in the mirror as a gray-ass pollo guisado bubbled on her stove. I imagined her plátanos maduros tasting like ash because she'd peeled and fried them too soon. And I saw crystal clear, as if you'd given me a vision, the brown insides of the avocado she chose to split open, too late.

Which satisfied me enough to ignore both the bitch and the butcher.

"You have a nice afternoon," I told her. Then I very kindly made my way to the register to call Mario to pick me up.

I was blessed with a short line. The cashier at the register was a genius. She could ring a whole carriage full of groceries up in less than four minutes. Then while waiting, I noticed a *Christian Women Warriors* DVD for self-defense hanging off the sales rack on top of the conveyor belt. Four women squatted on the cover with their fists raised, a crucifix hanging behind them. Somebody had stuck an orange $2.99 discount sticker next to Jesus's head.

Now, at first, I admit, I thought, What type of foolishness is this? These people, always trying to make a buck off of God with their thousand-dollar Christian worship retreats and their Jesus paraphernalia. Because you already know, I don't fall for false idols. But in the back of my head I could hear my doctor complaining about how much I weighed, and I remembered watching a Richard Simmons *Party Off the Pounds* video with my good friend Irene. And if God wants to give me a discount, then who am I to disagree? I put the DVD on the counter and bought it.

Outside, patiently I waited for Mario to pull up in front of the Pathmark. "Dolores, you want me to pop open the trunk?" He started to get out of the car.

"No, no, no. This is good enough. I can hold the bags up in the front." It was unusually hot for November. I wanted to keep the oxtail on my lap, right in front of the AC.

"All right, come in."

In the car, I pulled out the DVD and used the key to tear off the plastic.

Mario, nosy as per usual, looked over and asked me, "What are you doing with that mierda, mujer?"

I told him, "Any of these crazies try to come after me, I'm going to learn how to punch them in the throat."

That old man went and laughed at me like I was joking.

"I'm serious," I said. "In the name of the Lord Jesus Christ." And then I winked at him. "Pa' que tú lo sepas."

"Dolores, you're not going to be able to learn how to defend yourself from a video."

He rolled down the window, then pulled out two cigarettes from the soft pack of Newports sitting in his cup holder and offered me one. "But if you want, I'll teach you. I used to box back in the day. Shit, you couldn't tell me nothing."

Then he let his finger linger a little bit too long on the inside of my wrist when I accepted the cigarette.

"No, I'm good. I got it," I told him. I put the Newport in my purse. "So, you had a boxer name, too?"

"Oh, I had many names," he said, turning onto Castleton Avenue. "I was Madman Mario, Mario the Magnificent, Mario the Machine. Around Bushwick, they used to call me La Mano."

"Oh," I said sarcastically, messing with him. "Mira eso."

"Shit, you think I'm kidding?"

"No," I told him. "I could see it: young Mario running the streets of Brooklyn."

"I mean, if you're not so convinced, I could show you." He turned to look at me, grinning.

"Put your eyes back on the road, all right."

"I'm serious, D. I'm telling you." He took an extra two beats to smile at me at the red light.

"Eyes back on the road, mister," I said again.

Then I sat there trying to think of something to change the subject.

If I were to be honest, I would have told him I needed the video to help me get back in shape. I had spent the last decade dieting. There was that two weeks of Jenny Craig before I realized she was going to be too expensive. Then that year I ate rice cakes for breakfast and lunch every day, until I felt like the inside of my mouth would be forever coated with dust. Then SlimFast because it was on sale at the A&P that month, until I drank a couple of expired cans that gave me gastritis. And the South Beach Diet and the Atkins, and then for a while I was doing whatever Oprah was telling us to do on the TV.

The whole time I stood approximately 240 pounds. Sometimes 235. No matter what, my body wanted that weight. Got used to it. For a while, honestly, I couldn't bring myself to care. Only, every time at the doctor's office, it was Dolores, this. Dolores, that. "Dolores, we need to have a serious conversation. Your heart cannot take this many pounds. Dolores, let me set you up with the nutritionist?"

And then finally, "Do you want to die? Is that what you want?" Dr. Kastellanos lifted his hands up, and for the first time ever, I saw that he was angry. The light reflected on top of his head, which over the past few years had started to bald, and his face was bright red.

"Bueno, fíjate," I said. I laughed at him and shrugged.

It wasn't until I started going back to the church that the weight finally began to come off. First, it was helping set up for mass, then it was volunteering at the Saturday pre-K, running after the kids, taking them to the park, cleaning the tables at the end of the day. Then it was walking to the church on Sundays, to save a little money instead of taking the bus. A few years ago, I met my good friend Irene at Mujeres de Cristo, and it was a wrap. We got a membership at a Lucille Roberts with a coupon we found in the *Advance*; then, *bam*, forty pounds later, Dr. Kastellanos was practically kissing me, he was so proud.

When we got to the house, I pulled Mario's fare out and placed my hand over his. "Thank you, my friend."

"You good getting those bags up, Dolores?" He opened his door and the car started to beep.

"Oh, I got it. There's only two of them. Besides, I need the exercise." I lifted my arm into a fist and flexed my biceps.

"Not at all," he said, laughing. "You been looking good, D."

He wasn't lying about it, either. I had a nice shape to me, even if it was thirty pounds too heavy. And, anyways, I had decided that I never wanted to be skinny again; what I wanted was to be strong.

I waved goodbye to my good friend Mario, then made the long dark way up to my fourth-floor apartment. Carefully, because the stairwell was a death trap. The carpet on one of the steps had come loose, and already I'd fallen down twice running to catch the bus.

Now I took my time. Nothing was worth a tumble down those dark stairs.

Three flights later, I opened my front door, and the apartment looked a mess. Nina had left a pan of oil on the stove from the fried eggs she made that morning, even though I specifically told her to always wash the dishes because the people upstairs brought roaches when they moved in. They leave their garbage in the hall overnight instead of going downstairs to put it outside. Worse, I can hear their elementary school children laughing well past midnight, watching inappropriate TV when all five of their crusty culos should be in bed dreaming about *Dora the Explorer*, not watching *The Dark Knight*. I have spent three years in this apartment insect free and worked too hard to welcome any six-legged company into my kitchen, especially if they're not paying rent.

I swept the coffee grinds off the counter into my hand. In the bathroom, I found that she didn't even bother to pick up her underwear from the bottom of the tub. *Puerca.* I didn't dare look inside her room.

Instead, I put on the radio and started chopping up the vegetables. Browned the oxtail. Threw in the onions and the garlic, poured the broth in the caldero, and then, *bam.* The heat from the stove warmed the whole kitchen. And the smell rose from the pot, traveling in waves towards the living room. Once the onions got soft, I added a cup of water and let that sucker sit on the stove for three hours. And maybe it was some type of sinful vanity, but I imagined the neighbors smelling my soup outside as they walked home from work. I imagined them, Dear Lord, looking admiringly at my front door, wishing that they were coming home to my meal.

The clock on the stove said it was five p.m., at least two hours until Nina got home. So, I decided to incorporate some of that *Christian Women Warriors* DVD into my nightly routine of fifteen and a half sit-ups, because at forty-four even my fajas are failing me.

I fast-forwarded through the first ten minutes of all that prayer bullshit, until I reached the fuzzy image of a white woman standing in front of the camera with her fists raised in the air. She was rotating her arm away from the cameraman, mimicking an elbow strike—whack! Somewhere an invisible man fell.

This was how it worked: Say you're walking down the street, which is your God-given right; say you're finishing up your groceries or coming home from work, or you're returning from a Christmas dinner at your cousin's house with your child holding your hand, and a man comes up behind you and wants to take what he has no right to. Say he lifts you up from behind and out of nowhere you feel the surprise of your feet dangling above the concrete: just kick backwards into his groin.

Or maybe he doesn't lift you up.

Instead, he decides to drag you by your waist. That's when you elbow the motherfucker in the throat.

But you have to put your whole body into it—not just the weight of your arm. Gather every inch, every pound, and aim it at your attacker. I pushed so hard that at one point I tripped on the sofa and fell backwards. You already know though, I got up and tried again. And by the time Nina walked into the apartment, I had moved on to practicing groin strikes.

She put her keys down and squinted. "What you doing over there, fighting in the dark, Ma?"

"You should be learning self-defense with me, too," I reminded her. "And fix your face. Don't think I don't see you rolling your eyes."

"Yeah, yeah," she said, moving into the kitchen.

I tell you. Dear Lord, I used to have so much more power than this. My daughters, they used to respect me.

"You in a bad mood?" I asked her.

"No, Ma. I'm not in a bad mood." She put something down on the counter too loudly for my taste.

"Because you sound like you're in a bad mood."

"I'm not in a bad mood, Ma."

"If you're in a bad mood, I don't know why you would take it out on me. I'm just saying you've got to learn to defend yourself, Nina. You work late at the mall and wait for the bus at eleven thirty, sometimes twelve o'clock at night," I told her.

But, God, you know how these young women do. The way they walk down the street thinking nothing in the world can happen to them.

Obviously, this is my fault. I take responsibility for it, Dear Lord. Me and my husband, we spoiled our girls. Protected them too much. Didn't prepare them. How were they supposed to learn? How were they ever supposed to understand the way somebody else's body could overwhelm them? My own mother once dragged me out of the shower naked and beat my ass because I'd lied and said that my sister was at tutoring with Ms. Alexopoulos at the Brooklyn library when in reality she was at Deandre Rosario's house, taking her shirt off. For that, my mother beat me harder than she did my sister, because what she was trying to teach me, what she was trying to say every time she lifted the belt, was that a lie is a failure of respect. Because she knew she had to make me more afraid of her than of what was outside. But me, as a mother? I never wanted that for my girls—to experience that type of violence, because sometimes getting hit like that made you think you didn't deserve to fucking smile.

All right, so here we are.

So what?

I gave my daughters too much freedom. This one could go to the mall. That one I let go on a school trip to Washington, DC. And Nina, even though it broke my heart, I stood quietly and watched her move away to college. And when she asked me if it would be okay, I said nothing. I let her go. And the worst of it all, I let Ruthy take the bus too young. I was wrong, and I'll live with that forever.

Granted, there were some things that were simply off the table. None of this strutting around wearing that porquería with half your ass hanging out. And I didn't let my daughters sleep over at other people's houses, because I'm a sweetheart, okay? Not stupid. But I gave my daughters certain liberties. ¿Entiendes?

In the kitchen Nina laughed again, but from the living room I could hear her spooning the soup into her bowl, unaware of the amount of work it took to buy the oxtail, to wrestle the woman at the Pathmark, to wait patiently for hours for the fat to break down.

And I wanted to remind her that:

Little girl, I fed you.

Taught you how to speak, how to count. In ones, then in twos, then in threes. I taught you how to tell time.

When you shit yourself, I wiped your ass. After I gave birth to you, for months I lost chunks of my hair in the shower. Don't look at me like I'm stupid; I fed you.

But any of this do I say, Dear Lord? No.

Then my daughter, she slammed the microwave door shut too loud, came into the living room with the bowl of soup, spilling over the brim onto the same fucking floor I mopped yesterday. I stared at the spill while I practiced my side kicks.

"But, Ma, can we turn this off? Can I change this?" she asked, to which I did not respond.

Let her see how it feels when people don't talk to you. Besides, there was an invisible man I needed to hit in front of me.

"Ma, come on. Please?"

My daughter, she sat down and ate with her feet propped up on the couch. Then left the house.

To go where? Who knows! You think she'd tell me?

Please.

*   *   *

That night I drank a whole pot of coffee by myself, even though the doctor's always saying, "Dolores, you gotta find a way to fall asleep, all right? Work with me, D."

I been drinking coffee before bed since I was six years old, I tell him. Before you were born. Okay? It's not the coffee that's keeping me awake.

Though he's right. I need to find a way to turn my mind off, otherwise I sit there going crazy, thinking about the same thing over and over again, on repeat. Once, Isaiah, a little boy I work with at the church kindergarten, told me that when he couldn't fall asleep, he'd imagine a blank white page. And since then, that's my new method. I picture bright, clean paper and try to keep my mind from scribbling in it.

In bed I watched three reruns of *Law & Order* in a row because Nina doesn't know how to call home to say she's going to be late. Then I sat there in the dark with only the television set on, crocheting the blanket for one of the ladies at church who's expecting. No light necessary, my fingers knew what stitch needed to happen next by memory. Tugging the yarn through each knot, feeling the pull and then the release as the next stitch came together. Even when the upstairs neighbors started arguing again about who was supposed to pay for what bill.

A psychic hotline commercial came on and some wannabe Walter Mercado white woman wearing a leopard-print blazer started chanting, "Confused about your future? Trapped in the past? Want to contact a loved one from THE OTHER SIDE?"

These people.

I dialed the number and listened to the recording, "This phone call will cost forty-five cents a minute. Please say yes if you accept the charges."

"Yes."

"American Psychic Hotline." It was a woman's voice. Southern.

And I asked her, "Does it bother you that you pretend to be able to help people reach their dead loved ones?"

"Aw, honey."

"Don't you 'Aw, honey' me," I told her, because *not a word from their mouth can be trusted; their heart is filled with malice. Their throat is an open grave.*

Then I hung up before the call could reach four dollars and switched the channel to *Caso cerrado*.

All I want to know though is how am I supposed to sit here warm in bed, raise the remote off the nightstand to click off the TV, then close my eyes and dream? Wake up in the morning. Turn on the coffeepot and the burner. Pry the refrigerator door open to look for the eggs behind last night's leftover rice and beans. In the bathroom, how do I wash my hair or turn on the faucet to take a bath, slip the MetroCard into the bus, and travel to the church, knowing the whole time that my daughter is missing, that in some other city, some other country, she can be hungry, that someone can be hurting her, can be doing terrible things to her, unspeakable things, that she cannot stop?

Am I supposed to forget that this is a possibility, Dear Lord, that this can be happening right now? They tell me I am supposed to smile, but what normal person is ever able to hold a happy thought in their head beside that knowledge?

How am I supposed to laugh? Or anything? Anymore.

When I got into the church, I crossed myself and thanked you, Dear Lord, because you woke me up this morning and kept me here for this work. Somehow, I am still alive. Then I went straight into the rec room to plan the Mommy and Me activities for this week's parent workshop:

Fun crafts to do with your child! Make a treasure chest: Get an old cigar box, tape pictures of you and your child together full of happy memories on the inside. Decorate with ninety-nine-cent glitter and stickers, ribbons, and buttons. Make your own T-shirts. Make a Mommy and Me Diary and write letters to each other back and forth.

I stood there like that by the computer for hours, until the leftover chicken I ordered from the Dominican spot turned cold. I divided the stars, the pipe cleaners, and the glitter into little plastic bags for each mother. Then waited another couple of hours at the church for the high school kids to finish chasing each other in front of the bodega and go home. Today I was not playing around; I wanted to get a seat on the bus this time with zero screaming children around me.

Later, on the S48 back home, I spotted two teenagers, beautiful girls, just standing there with half a shirt on and little shorts at eight o'clock at night at the McDonald's on Bay Street. When I looked closer, I realized that one of the girls was Veronica's daughter Ana acting foolishly, chasing some boy down the street, spraying him with a bottle of soda, and I made a note to tell Veronica about it during the next Proper Parenting workshop, privately, of course. Not to embarrass her.

Veronica out of all the mothers was the shyest. She worked as a secretary at a community center, entering in data and picking up phone calls. The first parenting workshop, Veronica had shown up dressed in slacks and a blazer, clasping her hands together in front of her purse, politely asking in Spanish if I needed help serving the coffee.

"I can't control Ana anymore," she'd said during last week's class.

When she bent her head down, I saw that she was beginning to lose her hair.

"If I tell her she's punished, she doesn't listen. She'll look me right in my face and tell me no. She goes and does what she wants. And then what am I supposed to do? How am I supposed to stop that?"

Child services had sent Veronica to me after Ana had run away a third time.

"If she does it a fourth time," Veronica said, "I don't care anymore, they can just take her."

She was ashamed as she said it. Ashamed that she couldn't control her daughter. Ashamed that she had given up.

"No, no, you don't want them to take her," I'd promised her.

Trust me, you do not want that, I repeated to myself on the bus as it passed this tall series of stone steps carved into a hill, surrounded by weeds and trees, so that there was no way to tell where the stairs would end up.

A little bit later, Ms. E, who taught ESL at the church, came on. "Dolores! Now, what you doing on this bus so late?"

"Oh, you know how it is. I just got out of the church," I told her.

"Don't let them work you like that, D. They see you doing a good thing, they'll just ride you harder."

"Not very Christian of them, is it," I said.

"Nope, not at all."

The bus stopped and a man came on, probably in his thirties. He sat down, I thought too closely, next to Ms. E. And he was closing his eyes and nodding off next to her. I didn't like it, and I pointed at him and moved down so that she could sit closer to me.

But before Ms. E could shift down the seat, another woman stood up, placing most of her weight on a cane, and walked shakily down the aisle to the bus driver. "Is this Victory and Austin Place?" she asked in what sounded like a Liberian accent. The North Shore is full of folks now from everywhere: Liberia, Sri Lanka, Mexico.

The bus driver, tired, said, "Yep." And opened the door for her.

Then the old woman stepped down from the bus with her cane slowly, into the night.

The bus driver was wrong, though. It was not Austin Place.

And when he started to pull out of the stop, Ms. E noticed it and shouted, "Stop the bus, this ain't Austin. This is Cebra. You gotta stop the bus now."

The driver stepped on his brakes, opened the door, and called out to the old woman who had paused at the corner, confused, before making her way back to the 48.

Meanwhile, that thirty-year-old good-for-nothing nodding off next to Ms. E started to shout at her, "Jesus Christ, why don't you mind your own fucking business, lady?"

Ms. E spun all sixty-two years of herself around and said: "Mind my own business? That is my business. That woman can barely walk and you going to have her hobbling on her cane that extra block in the dark? That's a sister. What's wrong with you? She could be your mother."

Which must have finally put the guy to shame because he turned around and said, "You right. You right, miss."

"Mind *my* own business. You better mind *your* own business."

And that's how Ms. E kept going until the guy went, "I said *all right*. I apologized, miss, I said, sorry."

"Raising your voice at me!" Ms. E sat down next to me and rolled her eyes.

By that time, the viejita had made her way back onto the bus.

"Thank you," she said to the driver.

Ms. E patted my knee. "Go on, baby. What were you saying?"

CHAPTER 6

Nina

It wasn't even Thanksgiving yet, and the stock boys had already started hauling in red and golden bows to attach to the registers for Christmas, boxes of thongs with literal bells hanging in the center of the waistband twinkling against their black velvet hangers. Somebody had sprayed the whole damn store with the new Thanksgiving perfume. And that Limited Edition smell of cinnamon hung in the air so long that you felt like you were swallowing synthetic pumpkin every time you greeted a customer. Better than any political science class you could ever take in college, a place like Mariposa's really taught you how deeply patriarchy was linked to capitalism. But what good was it, really, to know about a thing, to attach a name to its invisible force, if, regardless, you were gonna constantly be stuck in it?

The whole shift at Mariposa's, I kept imagining what type of lingerie Ruthy would buy. The flashy push-up bras hanging in the front display? Or the silk ones with no underwire that Savarino instructed us to carefully fold into the drawers?

When Ruthy was eight years old, she stood in the kitchen with her hands clasped as if in prayer, while my mother banged some frozen chicken against the counter. Ruthy begged Ma for a bra, "Pleeeeeaaaaaaase," her voice increasing in pitch with each new appeal for my mother's sympathy.

For no reason at all!

That girl had been flat chested and all muscle up until the very day she disappeared.

But that was what Ruthy was like, always tiptoeing to the edge of my mother's nerves. Sneaking drugstore makeup in her pockets. In the bathroom at school, sliding on lipstick in the morning. After eighth period she'd rub it off with scratchy gray DOE-issued toilet paper.

When Ma refused to buy Ruthy a bra, she'd made one out of a belt and buckled it around her itty-bitty chest. Upstairs, she jumped on the bed, pretending it was a catwalk, and got so excited that she slipped on the comforter and fell off the mattress with one resounding thump. Forever the clown, Ruthy made her body bounce when she hit the floor, then shouted, "I'm dead. Please, my sisters, help me." Eyes closed and grinning, she crossed her arms against her skinny chest, and me and Jessica lifted her stiff dead body onto the mattress. We could not stop laughing, as our mother screamed upstairs for us to keep it down. Because Ruthy was goofy like that; this fact people often forget about my sister, how freaking funny she was.

And I wish they would remember it more.

The Grown-Up Ruthy I was imagining in my head—the one who, in an alternate universe, never disappeared, who came home that day in 1996 and stayed with us—would probably walk into the store to pick up a couple of sports bras for a run and then some of the silly lingerie as a gag. She'd be annoyingly confident, a former college athlete. Maybe basketball. Or track. I tried to picture her as one of the girls who played at my college, the girls who guzzled a gallon of water a day, who monitored their sleep, who refused to drink before a game. I tried to juxtapose this image of Ruthy I had just conjured with the one I'd seen on Ma's dusty television set. The TV version was like a Ruthy who had walked into a fun house full of trick mirrors and come out broken and distorted—a Ruthy drawn in exaggerated lines.

I knew Jessica would buy the romantic bullshit, the simple silk and lace we sold in the back. On her way to the register, she would scoop up two nursing bras, *buy one, get the second half off,* because Jessica, she imagined herself to be some type of classic, modest beauty, with her little white town house and her boyfriend who had a pension and a 401(k) now working for the Department of Sanitation, this despite the tattoo of pink roses creeping up her ass.

Me? I couldn't afford Mariposa's. In general, I wore whatever was on sale and am only slightly embarrassed to admit that I was guilty of buying packs of underwear at the pharmacy when I'd forgotten to do laundry.

We sold the younger, hipper lingerie in the front of the store, though some of those panties were terrifying: thongs cut into triangles of glitter and mesh that I couldn't imagine any woman wearing without a good piece of her toto hanging out. These thongs were the hardest to fold because the strings popped up even when you pressed them down upon each other.

Closing time, managers assigned girls to that section during cleanup as punishment. Whoever came in late, whoever forgot to wear their blazer, whoever decided to wear flats—"Oh, so your feet are more important than mine?" Savarino barked—found themselves in what I had come to nickname the "sucia" section.

And guess whose ass was stuck there now?

All because I had clocked in half a minute late.

There I was, innocently standing by a rack of neon green baby doll slips, when Savarino crept up behind me to whisper in my ear, "I pay you to sell, not just to stand there, Ramirez."

Now, I'm very particular about germs, and I have a thing about people disrespecting the air between us, unnecessarily, with their funky breath. So, I turned around and looked at her like, *Bitch*.

And as if Savarino were reading my thoughts, she said, "Don't daydream on my dime. Work the room." Then she left the Sucia Section.

The room—I would like to emphasize here—was absolutely fucking empty.

I looked around to see what she was waving at, but there were no customers inside my section. It was one thirty in the afternoon on a Wednesday; everybody was at work. Except for a vaguely dressed mannequin, the room was deserted. A soundtrack of Christmas music echoed against the glossy pink drawers, as Mariah Carey pleaded, *All I want for Christmas is you*, which made my stomach turn. That song always reminded me of my fifth-grade holiday concert and not being able to keep up with the dance steps of the rest of the class. All I had wanted for Christmas that year was for my own legs and arms to blend in with the other girls' limbs. By that time, Ruthy had already been one year gone, and I couldn't help but connect my inability to keep up with the other girls' natural movements onstage to that loss, because I knew (correctly) that if Ruthy had not disappeared, she would have tutored me until I nailed every single one of those stupid fucking steps down. And it seemed to me then, and still does now, that I could have become a completely different girl, a completely different woman, if Ruthy had never gone.

"Okay, fine, whatever," I said.

Savarino popped her head back in the room. "Excuse me?"

"I said sure! No! Fine!" Putting on an innocent face.

Then Savarino let out one long, Staten Island–inflected *mmm-hmmm* as she departed the sucia section.

The hardest part about working at Mariposa's was just waiting for it to be over. You'd stand there in your heels for what felt like a half hour, then look down at your watch with hope—only to find out it had been a mere eight minutes! You would try to keep your mind occupied by spying on what was happening in the rest of the store because a fight at the register with a customer could turn into thirteen minutes of entertainment.

Mariposa's was pretty dead today. Though I spotted one of the other salesgirls plotting by the fitting room: Alexis, seventeen, her black hair tightly slicked back, a row of diamonds studded along the top of her ear. She was helping this mother find bras for her thirteen-year-old girl, who you could tell was just *so* excited at last to grow boobs, an easy mark. You could see the gears turning in Alexis's head as she hovered over the mother and daughter like a pterodactyl about to land on its prey.

The little girl kept on shyly looking at the lace shit, while her mother steered her towards the racks of sports bras and cotton double-lined cups: "Déjalo eso. Over here, mija."

And Alexis was meaningfully smiling at the girl and winking as if the two were sharing some gross and magical womanly secret.

"I got the perfect thing for you," she told the little girl. Then she pulled out a soft training bra with scalloped edges, white lace, and a small pink bow stitched between the cups. "Isn't that beautiful, sweetheart?"

I grimaced.

Alexis had the stupid habit of calling me sweetheart, too, but in a "fuck you" sort of way, as in: *Why don't you fold these bras, sweetheart? You're in the fitting room today, not in the front, sweetheart. You look like you just rolled out of bed or had electric shock therapy or need a couple of painkillers to put your face out of its misery, sweetheart.*

Secretly, I was hoping Alexis would fail. Last time I checked, that bra was thirty-two dollars, and I could tell by the mother's Jessica Simpson–brand purse she wasn't going to dish out that type of money for her thirteen-year-old daughter's size A boobs. But

Alexis had found a marked-down version in the clearance section for fifteen bucks.

I shook my head.

"One more thing," Savarino shouted as she walked back into the sucia section to spy on me, and I noticed for the first time that even though she was ladylike and pretty, she assumed an athletic swagger when she gave directions, like a football coach.

"This month we're really trying to sign people up for these credit cards. So each girl's got to get at least four people to apply by the end of her shift." With that, she gave me a stack of blank applications and a pen. "The girl who signs up the most customers by Christmas gets a raise."

Ho, ho, ho, ho!

"Imagine that!" I said. "A raise."

"Don't be a wiseass, Ramirez. Make it happen." She walked out of the room, the swagger now even more exaggerated. "You got this."

Savarino had recently started taking these supervisor workshops that were supposed to be teaching her how to empower her employees while improving their productivity. So she whipped her head around, the red hair turning pink underneath the neon light, then in one horrifying moment smiled, winked at me, and said, "I believe in you."

On the bus ride home, I tried hard to think about who Alexis reminded me of. There was something so familiar about her face, like I'd known her before—that smugness twinkling in her eyes.

I was too old to have gone to school with her, so I couldn't have met her at Curtis. And she didn't take the same bus home as me, so she didn't live in West Brighton. For a while I couldn't put my finger on it, but, as the S61 rolled down Bradley Avenue, I finally realized what it was. The way Alexis moved around Mariposa's and patronizingly smiled at everyone, she acted like this one girl in Organic Chemistry from freshman year named Kelsey.

Kelsey looked nothing like Alexis. She had the type of blond hair I'd seen only in movies, so pale the strands looked white—*Lord of the Rings* elf-queen blond. Alexis's hair was the polar opposite—dark, black and wavy. But both these girls had the same exact fucked-up way of smiling at you, like they'd just found you hanging off the discount rack with a red sticker stuck on your forehead.

Freshman year, in group projects, I'd watch as Kelsey knocked down everybody's suggestions for a presentation—"I really don't think that's a good idea." She'd shake her head no with each syllable, as if she were the one and only gatekeeper of good judgment. Looking at a girl like Kelsey, you could tell she'd never been beaten in her life. She was too satisfied with herself. She had zero humility, which had the effect of making her face look kind of stupid. I just nodded and took notes, and laughed one weekend when on the way back to my room late at night I found Kelsey vomiting in the foyer of the dormitory in front of her clearly very grossed-out boyfriend.

To be fair to Kelsey, Organic Chemistry had been a very particular type of hell for me. One of those bad dreams in which you walk into a room naked and everybody is looking at you like you owe them money.

I hated all of those students, not just Kelsey. Every single one of them with their North Faces and their four-year stints at Exeter, and their daddies who were CEOs, and their mothers who donated to charities to fund scholarships for "at risk" kids like me. When Kelsey learned that I was there on scholarship, she turned to me and said, "Do you know how lucky you are to be here? This is like a really, really good school."

In the chemistry lab these students moved around the room quickly picking up whatever flask or funnel the experiment required, knowingly reaching for whatever knobs on their gas burners. Somehow they already knew the names for everything—*this is a Buchner funnel, this is a Pasteur pipet, clearly this is the Scoopula*—while my public-school ass was still trying to understand the difference between ionic and covalent bonding. The worst part—and this was the thing that really fucked with me—was that if I asked anybody for help in the lab, they looked at me like I was an alien extra from *Star Trek* and then continued whatever task was at hand.

At first, stupidly, I thought they'd not heard my question. So I would repeat it, this time a little bit louder. Still nothing. They turned their faces down towards the glass instrument they were carrying in their hands, and I stood there dumbfounded and invisible. Though the more painful truth was that I knew that those kids saw me. They heard me ask the question twice; they just didn't think I was worthy of a response.

One day the lab assistant held us after class so that we would individually show her that we could perform a liquid extraction, and while trying to tighten the clamp around the funnel I started to cry.

"I'm sorry, I just—" And I couldn't get the words out after that.

"It's fine, you're good, please, don't," she said, and sent me out of the room, saying not to worry, that I had passed.

A few weeks later, I was invited to an event for minority kids interested in science and technology, hosted by the Biology and Chemistry Departments. There was a brief lecture to the students and a long table of hors d'oeuvres afterwards. Slivers of electric-pink salmon folded on crackers and white shrimp hanging off a giant bowl of ice like commas. Pinwheels of white bread wrapped around cream cheese and dill. I crowded the plate with food and started to shove one cracker after another in my mouth so I wouldn't have to talk to anyone.

The chair of the Chemistry Department was laughing so loud you could hear his voice throughout the whole room, even over the music. At one point, everybody looked up, startled, as he coughed up a piece of shrimp that had gotten lodged in his throat, which was how I met Dr. Wilkins. He was standing next to me, watching as one of the other professors patted the chair's back.

Wilkins whispered to me, "So unfortunate. The man's a genius but still cannot figure out how to eat and talk at the same time."

The name Wilkins was easy enough to remember, but for some reason all his students called him Dr. W or Professor W, with no acknowledgment that the initial had more syllables than his full last name. Me, I always called him Dr. Wilkins, or to other people just Wilkins, behind his back.

Dr. Wilkins was already in his midforties but was still the youngest of the faculty. And he wore his brown hair long, below his chin, his shirt constantly untucked. A little nauseous, I was pulling a toothpick out of a bacon-wrapped date when he sat down next to me and stuck his hand out to introduce himself. "Hello there."

The bacon had slicked my fingers with grease, and worse, I suspected there was cream cheese streaked somewhere across my face.

"Nina Ramirez, right?"

And I offered him the cleanish pointer and middle fingers of my right hand to shake.

"I've heard *so much* about you," Wilkins said, making my stomach seize.

All I could think of was my hands fumbling with the funnel and the mortified lab assistant sending me crying out of the room. I didn't know what to say to Wilkins, so I nodded and looked at one of the servers who was circling the lobby with a tray of balled-up crab cakes. When she moved away, I saw a reflection of myself in one of the room's five-foot gilded mirrors, my hunched shoulders and sloped back, the frizzed hair and glasses.

Why had I shown up to this stupid fucking event, anyway?

I'd been so close to staying in bed and sleeping until lunch, and now I wanted the darkness of my dorm room, which, though constructed of ugly cinder block, felt infinitely safer than the crystal chandeliers and long bay windows of this pretty lobby.

But then Wilkins went on, "So, how are you liking chemistry, Nina?"

I could have lied and said that I loved it, then recited that minority scholarship kid mantra I'd heard so many of my other peers perform before: *My dream is to become a doctor, a scientist, an engineer, to return to my city, my village, my barrio* (and always articulated with the brilliant minority student's knowledge of how those words would land on the ears of seemingly progressive white folks); but then I would look even more pathetic if the lab assistant had already told Wilkins the truth. *Much better to be honest, Nina. Much better to own it.* Maybe joke about chemistry class to act like I did not care.

Or I could leave if I wanted to.

I could stand up right there and go.

But nobody had taught me how to manage and negotiate the conversations of white folks, how to make an exit, how to say no. So I gave in.

"Everybody knows so much more than me."

Wilkins tilted his head back and laughed. "Nina, that is actually a very smart thing to say."

And a wave of relief pushed out any leftover sarcasm from my body. For the first time since Jess and her boyfriend had driven me up to campus and moved me into the dorms two months ago, I had said the right thing. And now Wilkins's validation made me feel bold enough to be even more honest. "Yeah, but half the time I don't even know what I'm doing. I'm sitting over there flipping through the lab binder looking like SpongeBob. Then I'll ask one of the other kids for help, and they'll turn around and straight-up ignore me."

This made Wilkins laugh even louder. "Well, there's a very simple explanation for that, Nina."

I didn't know if he was laughing with me or if I should be offended. So I was just like, "Oh?"

"The reason why they don't answer you," Wilkins said, raising a pointer finger in the air between us for emphasis, "is because they don't know what the hell they're doing, either."

This made me grin. I hadn't thought of that possibility.

Why had I just automatically assumed that these kids were some-how better than me? In fact, now I remembered that sometimes I caught them looking down when the lab assistant asked a question during class. How could I have not seen that, just like me, they were trying to avoid being called on?

"It's true," Wilkins insisted. "Without curving the grades, half of Organic Chemistry would fail. Very few freshman students actually know what the hell they're doing in there. They just have more practice pretending at it than you, Nina. In any case, if you need help or are confused, you are welcome to come to my review sessions." And with that he stood up, wiped some crumbs from his lap, stuck his hand out again, and said goodbye.

Wilkins's review sessions were held on Monday afternoons and crowded with other students, many of them on scholarship like me, working class or poor, brown or Black. At times, the professors or other students couldn't quite place me. I had a Spanish last name, but my hair was thick and tightly curled and my skin was dark brown. And the only pictures most people had of Latinas at that time were straight-haired Salma Hayeks and Jennifer Lopezes. The diversity curriculum was still trying to parse out the difference be-tween being Central American and Mexican, let alone being both Latina and Black.

I learned that one of my biggest challenges was this anxiety that I carried with me that clouded my ability to even understand what was happening. Anytime a teacher spoke, all I could hear was my body prickling with heat as I desperately tried to remember a concept. A word.

I took my next two science classes with Wilkins. When I was stuck on a specific unit, I'd climb the three flights of the science building to his office.

Often, he'd say, "You're thinking too hard about this."

And then with one turn of phrase or a mark on the board, all of a sudden, the concepts clicked into place like Legos. I understood. By senior year, I was feeling myself; at group study sessions sometimes the white kids had to reluctantly admit that their answer to a problem was wrong and that mine was right. And some of the incoming scholarship kids would randomly knock on my door, introducing themselves before asking for help with their biology homework.

Senior year, the department had a holiday party for the graduating science majors at Wilkins's house. There was wine and champagne this time, in addition to the hors d'oeuvres, and the faculty let the seniors drink.

My friend Matt from biology was very pleased to find out that the wine was better than the dusty jugs of Carlo Rossi he kept underneath his desk. He walked into Wilkins's sitting room grinning, expertly holding three glasses by their tiny stems without spilling a single drop on the floor.

I was sitting with Matt's boyfriend, Evan, who studied film ("An imposter, shush," Matt had whispered dramatically at Wilkins's door), discussing his dreams for grad school in New York City, which he mistakenly assumed I knew all about. "I didn't grow up in Manhattan," I told him. "I've never even been to the Museum of Modern Art."

Evan clutched his chest and pulled his face back, appalled. "But how, though, Nina?"

"I mean, I don't even want to go anyway. I don't think I really care."

It was like the time our middle school forced us to visit the Statue of Liberty and Ms. Dudley pumped the class up by waving her hands in the air when she announced the trip, as if we'd won a prize. But when the whole sixth-grade class actually got there, we realized the climb up the stairs to Lady Liberty's crown was a slow forty-five-minute-long hike behind one tourist after another, drenched in New York City June heat. Suckers! Ms. Dudley, with all of her kind smiles, long gemstone earrings, and end-of-the-month ice cream parties, had played us. After that, I distrusted anything touristy, especially elite New York City landmarks and cultural institutions.

Matt knelt down to pass us each a glass of wine. "Enough about graduate school! It's so boring in here." Which was easy enough for him to say. Matt was going to attend whatever school he wanted for absolutely fucking free. Later, we'd learn that he was going to be valedictorian, a detail he happily hid from us until the very last moment. (From Matt, I learned that truly smart people did not walk around constantly insisting on their intelligence, because there was nothing to prove; Matt knew he was a genius, and it was a fact that mostly bored and embarrassed him, a fact that had gotten his ass kicked enough times growing up in Newark, New Jersey, for him to learn not to show off.)

The night went on.

With each drink, heat spread from my stomach to my chest, gathering in my throat, where it surfaced on my neck like fingerprints. Evan and Matt were edging close to the beginning of an argument, and before they could ask me which one of them was right, I made an excuse and escaped to the kitchen to pour a fifth glass of wine, where I caught my reflection in Wilkins's long dark window that faced the beginning of campus. The tall library. Its bell tower. Unlike the first day I met Wilkins, my hair was slicked carefully back into a bun. I'd replaced my glasses with contacts. And in the reflection, my face looked unreal. Pale and heavy. And, at that moment, I knew I would be sick. I had been doing so well, laughing and lovingly making fun of Matt with Evan, and then all of a sudden it was like somebody had spun me around three times and kicked me in the stomach.

I would have to get home quickly. Somehow.

I remembered the sound of Kelsey retching on the rug in the dorm and her boyfriend's face wrinkled with disgust.

Please, please, please don't puke in front of everyone.

In the bathroom I tilted my head to the faucet and drank. Then I sat on the toilet and breathed. Deeply in. Very slowly out. Too scared to face what I looked like. Finally, I braved the mirror. The skin around my mouth was still red from the water I'd splashed on my face five minutes ago, and I had to scrub the purple stains away from my lips with my index finger. But otherwise my face didn't look too bad—clearly drunk, but not smashed.

When I walked out of the bathroom, I found Matt waiting. "You okay?" He bent his tall body down closer as if to inspect my face. "We're about to head out and Evan is going to drive. We can give you a ride?"

"We should go," I told him.

Matt laughed. "You were puking, weren't you?"

I shook my head. "But oh my god, does it look like I was puking?"

"No. You look beautiful. And we will whisk you away before anybody suspects anything. Meet us outside at the car."

Then Matt pointed at the guest bedroom where all the students' coats were piled on top of a bed.

It took me some time to find my own, but there underneath a leaning tower of peacoats I spotted the strip of fake fur of my hood. I pulled the coat out from the bed and checked the time on my phone. It was almost eleven thirty. How long had I been drinking? How long had I stood there talking to teachers and other students, not realizing that I was drunk?

Behind me somebody opened the door and I turned around, surprised to find it was Wilkins.

"Nina, you're leaving us already?" He threw his arms up in the air. "Too soon!" Then he started making fun of the chair of the department, who was pressuring the faculty into karaoke. "But we're going to start a fire outside," he said. "You'll miss the fire."

"Matt and his boyfriend are going to give me a ride, so I figured I'd head back with them."

"All right, well, I'm so proud of you, Nina," he said, clasping my hands and nodding. "You've done it. You've made it. One more semester and you're out of here."

He was staring so directly at my face that I got shy and looked down.

It felt like a gift to hear someone like Wilkins say they were proud of me. For so long I had doubted myself.

"Now, you can write your ticket anywhere. Trust me."

"I don't know," I said.

I never knew how to take compliments like that. It seemed arrogant to agree, but also rude to contradict a professor and say no.

He shook his head. "I'm telling you, it's true."

I shrugged as a way to respond.

"You don't trust a lot of people, do you, Nina?"

I didn't consider myself to be somebody who did not trust people, but I liked Wilkins so much, I wanted him always to feel that he was right. I wanted especially for him to be right about how smart he thought I was.

So I said yes. "I don't trust a lot of people."

"But you trust me, don't you?" he asked.

He was nodding his head because he already knew the answer.

And for the first time that night I noticed that his cheeks were flushed. And I realized—like all those times that I had been in his office and suddenly understood a complicated concept or idea—that he had been drinking too much as well. The smell of it had widened his pores. His breath hung in the air between us. And, oddly, this comforted me. Made me feel less stupid.

I wasn't the only one who had overcelebrated, who had over-estimated how much liquor they could hold.

My arms were in front of me, clutching my coat, and I looked down, surprised to see that he was holding my elbows.

When had he reached over to touch my elbows?

I couldn't tell.

I looked down at his hands as if they were small miracles.

"Yes," I said. "I trust you."

And I did. He had been the one person who'd helped me out during those four rotten years in the middle of nowhere, in the cold.

Wilkins stopped smiling. And I could see him consider my face. And then gently, very slowly, he leaned forward to kiss me.

Immediately, I pulled my mouth away. And then I just stood there blinking.

"All right. Thank you so much, Dr. Wilkins," I said. "You're the best."

Because my first reaction to anything fucked up that happens to me is to pretend it never existed.

Then I ran down the stairs into the cold, where Matt and his boyfriend were waiting in the car.

"Where were you?" Matt asked, leaning out the window, laughing with a cigarette in his hand.

I opened my mouth, but I couldn't speak.

"I told you," Matt said. "She was throwing up!"

"Leave her alone, you bully," Evan answered. "Our poor Nina."

I stood quiet in the car and let them think one fucked-up thing had happened to me instead of another.

Months later, I would email Wilkins for a letter of recommendation, and he would answer, *Hello Nina, My apologies for the late response. I'm sorry but at this time I cannot recommend you.*

If Ruthy was taken, it's possible it could have been someone she knew, I thought as I pressed the yellow tape for the bus to stop in front of Ma's building. It's possible it could have been somebody she loved and trusted.

Me and Jessica closely watched the *Catfight* message board for one week, but Ruthy/Ruby never replied. Several of her fans did, though.

VanillaSkI wrote:

These Bitchez are crrraaaaaazie.

ThikMike3 said:

Word Bella, I'm your long, lost sister, too. Want to come over?

But the webmaster had deleted his comment before Jessica could see it, which was a good thing, because she was already pissed off about what VanillaSkI wrote.

And I had to get her to sit down by saying, "Maybe it's just not Ruthy."

I tried to point out to Jessica the various ways in which it did not make much sense. How could a thirteen-year-old girl just disappear like that and survive this long undetected, only to surface on a reality TV show more than a decade after she went missing? "It's impossible."

"What are you talking about? It looks just like her," she said. She was getting the milk bottle out of the pot on the stove and testing it on her hand to see if it was too hot.

"I'm saying, she's got her face all fucked up. Her hair's bright red. Bitch looks like Elmo. You know, we've never even seen this woman in person. We don't know who she is in real life. I don't think it's her."

The top of the bottle must have been loose because when Jess tipped it over to test the milk, the nipple came off and hot milk spilled all over her and onto the floor.

"Goddammit." Jessica waved her hands in the air, then rushed to the sink to cool her fingers underneath the cold water.

"It's Ruthy," she shouted over the sound of the faucet.

Then she turned around and looked at me. "Why are you like

this? Why do you always have to play devil's advocate for? It's annoying."

So that I had to argue with her for half an hour until we agreed to watch a few episodes that night for further investigation.

Jessica put the baby to bed, brought some sheets down from the linen closet. We wrapped ourselves in the blankets on the couch, and I called Ma to say I'd be staying over there for the night.

"Está bien," she said slowly. "You girls have fun. Be careful and kiss the baby for me. Tell her Mama loves her."

And there was something unfamiliar about my mother's voice that I couldn't place right away. She sounded aware, as if she knew exactly what was going on. And I winced, thinking about my mother like that, picturing her praying, then lying there in bed alone, the sound of the heater ticking as it dried out the room, fully aware of all that had happened to us.

CHAPTER 7

Ruthy

In order to really understand Ruthy's story (if you still care enough to hear what happened to me), you should know it had not always been like this. I mean between Yesenia and Ruthy. Because Yesenia and Ruthy used to be tight, ever since third grade at PS 45. When they were younger, they would visit each other's houses and invent games with complex monsters they were always trying to escape from. One they called the Rat King, who would invade their villages to steal their children at night. In this game, Ruthy and Yesenia would ask Jessica to hide one of their baby dolls in the house and then the two of them would travel from room to room in search of the missing toy. The other monster they called Mr. Slug, who slithered quietly in their made-up houses to spy. You never saw Mr. Slug, just the residue he left behind, a slick trail of sadness that stank up the air, after he inched away to report the details of our lives to the Rat King.

When they got older, Yesenia and Ruthy stopped playing imaginary games. Instead, they would make fun of each other's moms and sisters, their curves and accents, the way they snapped their gum. Yesenia had even mastered an impression of Jessica, in which she would stuff her bra with toilet paper and walk in the hallway to the bathroom, poking out her chest. They had a running joke about Jessica: "Miss Pointy Titties," they'd whisper behind her back whenever she would try to boss them around.

One time in seventh grade, it was New Year's and they were sitting in Ruthy's room, bored. They had both turned twelve, and all of Ruthy's family was dancing together, laughing in the house. Someone was checking the pernil. Mom was smoking in the kitchen.

On the radio, they were playing that Frankie Ruiz song, the one that everybody loves, and Ruthy's dad was singing along and dancing downstairs, you know the one that goes, *Quiero cantar de nuevo y caminar.*

But Ruthy and Yesenia were upstairs, hiding from all of them.

Yesenia sat on the bed, pulling down her skirt. Ruthy was hanging random shit up in the closet, saying things like: "Why didn't you tell me?" Though it was true that somehow Ruthy knew about it all along. Because Yesenia was the first person who taught her how, and all the other girls at school didn't really know as much as they did.

This is how you do it in the water, Yesenia said. This is how you do it when he is on top of you. Yesenia had shown her when they were ten.

Yesenia stood up and helped Ruthy hang up the clothes, then said, "Me and Ana"—Ana, her best friend in third grade—"used to hide from him in the bedroom and lock the door. Then he'd bang on it and tell us to open."

This made Ruthy jealous. Ana had been friends with Yesenia longer. Ruthy said, "You should have told me."

But Yesenia didn't trust anyone. "Okay? You have to understand."

Then she explained how she couldn't bear to be in the same room with other men.

"Even your grandpa?" Ruthy asked.

Yesenia's grandpa who went to church and used to pick them up from elementary school sometimes, in a long old green Cadillac.

"Even Grandpa."

This made Ruthy think. "What about my dad?"

Yesenia stood quiet for a second and considered it while Ruthy's sisters were downstairs screaming about something that one of them had taken from the other.

"I don't worry about your dad," she said.

And Ruthy smiled, relieved because she loved her father. She didn't want Yesenia to believe he was capable of doing anything wrong.

She put down the laundry and turned to run back down the stairs to the party to sneak them some cups of coquito before the ball dropped.

But then Yesenia said, "There was so many of you girls."

Ruthy spun around and looked at Yesenia, confused. "So many of us?"

"I thought, your dad don't need to touch me," she explained, "because he's probably already touching you."

And Ruthy felt surprised and maybe a little bit angry, not only because she felt defensive of her father, but also because she realized in that moment that Yesenia could live with Ruthy being hurt as long as Yesenia wasn't the one being touched.

Things were different after that.

No matter how many experiences they had shared, how many years they were best friends, Ruthy suspected there was a part of Yesenia that Ruthy could never understand, a part of Yesenia that could very easily turn cold and sacrifice Ruthy, if pressed, to one of their childhood monsters.

But look at me getting off track.

My bad. I'll take you back to the story.

First-floor bathroom of IS 61. Staten Island, New York. November 1996.

After Kamila does what she can with Ruthy's torn hair, she returns her to fifth-period Earth Science, where they are reviewing questions about Jovian planets and the extinction of dinosaurs.

Ruthy's stomach growls so loud that the boy sitting next to her, this really goofy-looking kid named Doug, can hear it. He laughs and waves his hand in front of his nose, pretending that the sound was a fart. Ruthy ignores him because if she were to clap back it would be too easy to hurt his feelings; Doug still does things like eat his boogers in math. One "your mama" joke and two well-landed comments about his Keds looking like they're from Wal-Mart, and Ruthy could easily make him cry. Never mind the fact that her family also shops at Wal-Mart, but whatever.

There are much bigger things to think about than Doug Luciano. Even though Ruthy missed lunch and her stomach is moving noisily, she does not feel exactly hungry. Her body still vibrates with the memory of the fight. And the gum is still stuck in her hair. Ruthy can't see it, but she can feel it. And every time she lifts a hand to try to tease a piece of it out during Earth Science, she catches Yesenia looking at her, not exactly angry. She's pursed her lips and tilted her head to the side.

In fact, you might say it is almost as if Yesenia looks sorry.

Pause.

Out of curiosity, if in fact you are still listening, let me ask you this question: Would you rather walk out of the bathroom with the hem of your skirt accidentally tucked inside the waist of your stockings, or would you rather accidentally miss a big patch of hair on the back of your leg while you were shaving?

Me, personally, I don't really care about the hair.

The stockings, though!

That would be so freaking embarrassing, oh my god. I would much rather somebody see my hairy leg than my underwear. But then again maybe you're the type of person who would rather vomit Jolly Ranchers and macaroni and cheese than cafeteria broccoli.

It's okay. I'm not judging. I strongly believe that we all should be able to choose our own ways to be ashamed.

CHAPTER 8

Jessica

I paused Ruthy/Ruby's face on the TV, turned to Nina, and said, "Why you got to hog the damn popcorn?" Ever since Nina was a kid, she was always so possessive over the bowl; she'd be sitting there, ten years old, and actively counting how many kernels were left after you took a handful. "Like we don't have a whole box in the kitchen that we can microwave."

Nina grinned like a Disney villain. "Fiiiine." And pretended to reluctantly pass the bowl back to me. "I'll trade you," she said, reaching for the baby.

Little Julie, the traitor, happily accepted her arms.

"Good," I told my daughter. "The feeling's mutual."

I rolled my shoulders back and cracked my neck. Ever since giving birth, I felt like my whole body was caving in, shifting permanently into the most convenient shape to hold, feed, and comfort Julie. We had at least four hours of *Catfight* episodes to catch up on, and the stupidity of the show was slowly melting my face off.

Originally, *Catfight* season four had started with a cast of six women. The first was an Indonesian girl from Miami called Gem, a bartender—they all had, at some time, worked as bartenders, party promoters, video girls, or strippers. All had some type of personality disorder, except for a Black Dominican girl named Lulu who went to Harvard and was very religious. Lulu was the wild card. Apparently she was some type of badass geek who spoke five languages, including Latin. On the show, Lulu would like to walk around and say things like, "I got God on my side, so you don't scare me." Or: "I go hard for Christ, I don't care."

Nina laughed. "Doesn't she remind you of Ma, though?"

The third girl—Kelly, an Italian from Chicago—would constantly imitate Lulu, until one day she said some wild racist shit about Lulu only getting into Harvard because of affirmative action, so Lulu popped out of her seat and with the full force of almighty Jesus, smacked the shit out of Kelly, and slammed her face against the counter.

The directors showed the takedown again and again, sometimes with flashes of pink and blue emanating from the collision of Kelly's face against the white marble, like a comic book.

After that fight, that was it for Kelly in the *Catfight* house. If you lost a brawl, you got kicked out; it didn't matter if you were the victim of a sucker punch or if you got jumped. Rules were: No losers allowed in the *Catfight* house. No exceptions. No returns.

So that brought the cast down to five.

The next girl was a debutante, a sorority girl named McKayla from Alabama, and she fit her stereotype perfectly: a southern accent, an overuse of pearls, an occasional homophobic or racist remark. At times during the show, if she seemed to move too far away from the stereotype by saying something reflective or smart, she would self-correct and say some shit that would automatically assure you that she was just a dumb blonde...the show, it seemed, loved for the girls to live up to their stereotypes, maybe even encouraged them. It was hard to tell. But Nina kept pointing out how the directors would selectively make certain cuts or obsessively repeat clips of the girls saying the same dumb shit on purpose.

Episode after episode, Nina kept shaking her head. "This show is so fucking problematic. The way they depict women or talk about sex workers." And then to me, "Ew, stop licking the salt off your fingers and then dipping them back in the popcorn."

"Shut the fuck up."

"I'm serious. Now the popcorn's going to taste like your breath."

"Go make your own damn popcorn, then," I told her.

There was a Black girl from the Bronx named Ariel who basically ruled the house. The other girls didn't do shit without first looking at Ariel to see what she thought about it: What club to go to? What restaurant to eat at? What dress to put on?

Ariel and Gem and Ruby were a clique, though they were flirting with letting Lulu in, thereby completely alienating McKayla and eventually planning to jump her. But Gem argued that at least McKayla was fun to tease, while Lulu was always saying that she was classier than everybody else just because she went to Harvard. Ariel hadn't decided yet in favor of McKayla or Lulu and argued that they should just wait it out and see if eventually they would fight each other—it would be easier to eliminate one of them. "As opposed to two bitches at the same time."

And of course, there was Ruby, who said she didn't care what anybody decided to do.

Ariel could kick McKayla's ass, or she could let McKayla rock.

"Either way I really don't give a fuck. I'm just here to have a good time," she said in the confessional, grinning. "But for real, seriously, sometimes these girls do too much."

I paused the TV. "You heard that, right?" I asked Nina.

Growing up, Ruthy was always saying *But for real, though*. Or *For real this, For real that*.

But Nina only looked at me with pity. "Come on, Jess...that's not unique to Ruthy. That's not special. Everybody said that in the nineties."

I couldn't argue against that. She was right; I was reaching. Maybe too hopeful. I pressed *play*, and we continued to watch.

On *Catfight*, Ruby played the role of the clown…always drunk in the morning or acting foolish at the club. Drinking beer with cereal for breakfast. The directors liked to show blurred-out clips of her crotch every time she bent over in a short skirt to back her ass up when she danced, which made some of the other girls call her dirty.

A slut!

"Ew, don't drink from her glasses, unless you want to catch something," McKayla said.

Nina shook her head. "The respectability politics here are out of control. And wasn't McKayla's ass doing the exact same thing at the club last week? Just a total lack of self-awareness."

Right away, Ruby and Ariel had become allies because they were both from New York City, which I quickly took note of and pointed out to Nina as further evidence that this could be Ruthy. Although Reality TV Ruby always claimed Brooklyn, during one odd episode she started spitting a lot of facts about Staten Island, telling stories about how she used to chill with Method Man in Stapleton. True, she could have been some Wu-Tang Clan superfan, but only Staten Islanders really know that much about Staten Island.

The rest of New York City usually stayed the fuck away.

We sat like that on the couch for a while watching previous episodes on TiVo, studying how the cast moved on the set, how they played each other, how at times they reached tenderly towards one girl who was crying, pretending to be her friend, while they bashed another's face against the toilet as she was throwing up. How they figured out ways to torture or bully each other, carefully watching the other girl move in order to identify her weakness or a tragic flaw, so that they could later stick a knife inside of whatever vulnerability and rotate the blade in the wound as the girl squirmed.

That felt very Ruthy-like, too. She had an incredible talent for sizing people up in a matter of minutes. Once, freshman year of high school, I brought home my friend Amanda, this shy white girl, who had been experimenting with silver eye shadow that just left her eyelids looking greasy. While we were in the kitchen searching for something to eat after school, Ruthy went up to her and looked closely at her face. Underneath Ruthy's gaze, my friend began to visibly squirm, and I got scared my sister was going to clown on Amanda's makeup. But instead, Ruthy, seeing the way my friend shrank, was like, "Girl, your eyes look nice!" Immediately Amanda's face lit up; you could literally hear her breathe again. And I looked at Ruthy gratefully. Later, I'd gently tell Amanda that the silver color was too light for her skin.

On the other hand, if Ruthy did *not* like you, it was a wrap; she'd find whatever comeback made you hurt the most and use it repeatedly, afterwards figuring out new ways to sharpen the insult for future fights.

Nina was shaking her head again. "Man, this show is *truly fucked* up. This is like a microcosm of all the worst parts of America. I'm telling you. You got racism, sexism, capitalism all in the same house. Somebody could write a whole paper about this show. 'Thirteen Ways to Look at an Episode of *Catfight*,'" she went on.

Until, finally, I couldn't take it anymore—the commentary. Nina was always trying to analyze some shit using whatever new word she learned in college. Then worse, she'd pause the TV and spend ten minutes explaining some clearly obvious shit that you already knew, as if she was some type of professor. I rolled my eyes and told her to shut up.

"What?" Nina said. "God! You're so dramatic."

95

"Can we just watch the damn show, please? I would like to watch the show in peace."

"Yes, fine, let's peacefully watch all these women pull out each other's extensions."

She wasn't wrong, though—the show was truly vile. You sat there watching hour upon hour of these girls jumping each other, and it made you think of all the other fights you ever had in your life, the ones where you came out victorious but especially the ones you lost, the ones that made you silently mouth a comeback as you reenacted the fight in your head, five years too late.

And watching these women brawl made you want to return to those moments to deliver whatever punishment you thought some previous ho from another period in your life still very much deserved.

And sometimes it just felt good to watch these women argue, when so much of your day-to-day life consisted of nodding politely or biting your tongue so that you would not be fired, so that you could buy groceries, so that you could pay rent and take care of your family.

Four weeks after Ruthy disappeared, Mami held a vigil at Titi Monica's house in Jersey because her place was nicer than ours. Titi Monica was not really a titi, but an old friend from way back in Mami's past, when they used to live next to each other in the same building in the Bronx and their mothers would not allow them to go to the bodega or a school trip without the other one in attendance. They'd grown up so close that sometimes people mistook them for sisters. Twins, even, with the same dark skin and tight black curly hair.

Titi Monica had "made it," my dad liked to joke (maybe a little meanly), with her husband the banker, an Italian man who fell in love with eighteen-year-old Monica in the eighties. He'd offered his sweatshirt when he heard her teeth chattering next to him in a gray BMCC classroom with a broken-down heater.

Monica's living room was full of church people. There was old Ms. Denise, who only spoke Spanish and demanded the children respond back likewise, even though everybody knew Ms. Denise was fronting; that old woman understood every single word of English. She just liked to fuck with you. Nina would scramble away from Ms. Denise every time she saw her, because Nina knew about ten real words in Spanish and half of them were curses. For this reason, Ms. Denise especially loved speaking to Nina in Spanish.

Thirty-year-old Sofia, who lived in the Bronx, brought her six-foot-tall teenage son, who was not afraid to make it known that he was very unhappy to be there. Rolling his eyes, he sat his long ass down in the corner and managed to stare at the wall during the whole two-hour vigil without saying much. People forget that in the nineties kids didn't have cell phones like that. So this was an incredibly impressive feat—it took a great deal of teenage asshole commitment to publicly disengage for that long. All the Puerto Rican mothers in the room glared at him, their palms itching to just reach across the kitchen and hit the boy with un cocotazo.

Missing was anybody from Ruthy's crew of friends at school, including Yesenia, who Ma called the night before and offered to drive to Jersey. But Yesenia's mother had explained that her daughter felt too sick with grief to come, a lie that did not escape Ma, who hung up the phone with one long eyebrow raised; it stayed stuck there on Ma's forehead as she tapped a cigarette out of her pack of Newport 100s.

After that vigil, I decided to conduct my own investigation. The cops had done shit, found nothing. And they'd act like my parents were a nuisance whenever they called the precinct for updates. I knew for a fact Yesenia was seeing Ivan Maldonado, the same fool I had to put in his place in Mrs. Wagner's class. Ivan was nice enough to *me*, but he was always lying. About stupid shit, too, that didn't matter…whether a bus had come or gone, or what day the math homework was due. It was unnerving to be around somebody who seemed incapable of telling the truth. You never fully knew what he was about, which, come to think about it, might have been purposeful; the pathological lying gave Ivan some power in his crew. Also, Ivan was mean—he enjoyed humiliating girls he found "ugly," even though homie legit looked like a Puerto Rican Frankenstein, with monstrous breath to match. Word was that his friends had taken advantage of some middle school girl in September and I'd told Ruthy to stay away from his ass when she told me Yesenia had started dating him.

For a full hour, I waited at the park on the swings by that old McDonald's on Forest Avenue where Yesenia hung out with Ivan on the regular. I waited there quietly until Yesenia saw me and it was too late for her to turn around. Then I walked straight up to her and said, "You weren't at the vigil."

She rolled her eyes, sucked her tongue, and opened her mouth to try to say something cute, but then creepy-ass Ivan swooped in and had the nerve to put an arm around my waist. "Jessica! What you doing here?"

I pushed that motherfucker off me so fast, he almost fell over.

"But chill," he said, holding on to the swing set to regain balance. "What's wrong though?"

I turned to Yesenia. "I thought you'd be at home, sick with grief."

She scoffed and sucked on her fountain drink, so I knocked the soda out of her hand.

"Where's Ruthy?"

At this point Ivan and his friends Isaiah and Ricky had surrounded me. "Yoooooo, chill, Jessica. She's like in middle school." The irony of this last statement lost on their predatory high school asses.

"Where is she, Yesenia? Where's Ruthy?"

"I don't know where your stupid sister is," she spat.

And that was it for me. All those boys had to pull me off her.

"I know you, Yesenia," I said. "I know what you're about. And I know you know something. I'm not stupid."

After all, why had she not visited the house when Ruthy went missing? Why didn't she show up to the vigil?

"I'm watching you, Yesenia. Tust and believe. Know that."

Then I pushed Ivan's nasty ass off me and walked those long cold twenty minutes home, instead of taking the bus.

We watched TV until Lou got home, only taking a break to eat some pizza he picked up after work. Then he went upstairs, and the baby woke up, and we watched again as I laid her down on the coffee table and changed and fed her. By the time we got to episode six Julie was knocked out again in my arms, and my shirt was stuck to my back with sweat. When I stood up, my legs felt like a Barbie doll's, like they might pop out of my pelvis if I walked too fast.

I put Julie to bed, then went back downstairs and turned the TV back on, because I was hooked. Was Lulu going to win the fight with McKayla?

Probably.

McKayla couldn't fight for her life; once Ariel caught her tucking her thumb into her fist when she was trying to punch someone. Still, I wanted to be sure; I was sick of all the unchecked racist shit McKayla got away with saying, and ready to see Lulu send her packing, like she did when she whupped Kelly's ass.

I could see it on Nina's face, too, her cheeks puffy with salt and soda. "Hurry up. Put it back on."

Anytime a new argument broke out, the adrenaline in my body surged; the alliances in the house were slowly shifting, and it seemed that Ruthy/Ruby was beginning to fall out of her clique.

All of the *Catfight* women, except Ruthy/Ruby, were sitting around a pink marble kitchen island, microwaving a box of Hot Pockets. The sorority girl was so hungry, she continued to eat hers even though it was still frozen inside.

"I'm tired of all of Ruby's drinking," Gem said after Ruby had gotten into a fight with a girl at a club for kissing her man. All of the *Catfight* girls had to jump into Ruby's fight, too. "I'm serious; don't you ever just want to go out, no drama, and have a good time?"

Gem was secretly displacing Ariel as queen bee in the house, which did not escape the ever-faithful Ruby, who screamed down from the upstairs loft, "I can hear you [*bleeeeep*] talking about me behind my back, Gem. I can smell your nasty-ass breath from upstairs. You snake. You're so two-faced. Don't think I don't know what you're up to in this house."

Then: "I can't stand none of you anyway," Ruby said, walking away, to which Ariel stood up and screamed upstairs, "I know you're not talking to me."

Ruby came out with her toothbrush. "I said GEM. GEM."

"You said *none of you*," Ariel shouted back upstairs.

Ruby clicked her tongue. "Whatever, you know what the hell I mean."

Then she disappeared to talk shit to the producers.

"So," said Ruthy/Ruby in the confessional booth, a small closet-sized room with walls insulated by purple velvet. "One thing you gotta understand is that I'm from [*bleeeeep*] Brooklyn, and I don't gotta take shit from *no* one. So, any of these bitches get in my face, I mean I can't promise that you're not gonna get snuffed…"

She laughed, her lips bright red. And it's the laughter that gave her away, the laughter that made me certain.

We paused and replayed the same scene five times in a row.

"See," I said to Nina. "I told you so."

She stood quiet, which was how I knew I'd won—those thirty-two seconds of radio silence vibrated between us. And let me tell you something, getting Nina quiet is no small feat. She sat there, staring at the TV, covering up her mouth with one hand.

On the screen, we'd paused Ruthy/Ruby one more time to inspect her face more closely. Her mouth so wide open, we could see the metal filling in the back right molar, her eyebrows raised as she was about to unleash one more tirade into the empty confessional room, as she flexed and posed for the camera.

"Maybe," Nina said quietly. "Maybe it is her."

She squinted at the screen as if she were studying for an exam, then picked up the remote and rewound the scene again.

I'm from [bleeeeep] Brooklyn, and I don't gotta take shit from no *one.*

Once more she pressed *rewind* and Ruthy/Ruby's face scrambled and rearranged itself backwards in time.

I'm from [bleeeeep] Brooklyn.

Nina tossed the remote control on the coffee table in front of her. "I mean, I see it a little bit. The way she kind of shakes her head there sort of looks like Ruthy."

Nina had to admit it. That woman didn't just look like Ruthy, she moved like her, too.

"Sort of?" I said. "That's her spitting image, Nina. Look." I fast-forwarded to the part where Ruthy/Ruby laughed. "You see how she throws her head back and then shakes her hands out, like that. You can't tell me that's not Ruthy."

Whenever our sister found something funny, the laughter would knock around inside her like a pinball, until she'd end up practically rolling on the floor, tickled by the force of her own glee.

We plotted.

How far was the drive to Boston? What if they'd recorded the show months ago and the cast didn't live on the same street anymore?

What if the production of the show was over, and all the girls had already moved out of the Catfight Condo and disappeared back into their real lives?

"Nope, it's still in progress," Nina said. She had been following a celebrity gossip blog that faithfully gave behind-the-scenes details.

They released each episode a week after it was filmed. And Nina found out on the show's website that there was going to be a *Catfight* cast appearance at a club called the Balloon Factory in Boston on Black Friday.

"So, we have to get out there now before the season ends," I said.

It was already almost Thanksgiving, which the Ramirez family didn't celebrate much anyway. Nina thought the holiday sucked, and for years after Ruthy disappeared, my moms frequently wondered aloud, "For what am I supposed to be thankful for?" Most years she spent Thanksgiving helping the church cook a big meal for families in need.

But in the world of retail, Black Friday was holy.

Nina shook her head. "I don't know, Jess. I don't even know if I can get off of work that day."

"We got to, Nina. This might be our only chance."

Still, how could we travel to Boston without tipping Mom off? And who was going to take care of the baby while we drove out there?

"Doesn't Lou work?" Nina asked.

"Ma will take care of Julie," I said. "Look, this is what we're going to do. Tomorrow, I'll take her to that church. Butter her up. Say you're a changed woman and that you and me are taking a women's retreat to Maryland or something. Make it a Christian Thanksgiving workshop. Something like "United Sisters of the Holy Spirit." She loves that Hallmark shit."

"But then, watch," Nina said. "She'll ask why she can't come."

"That's all right. I'll tell her it's for women under thirty."

We stayed like that, huddled in the dark on the couch, cross-legged, searching for directions on the computer, mapping and remapping the route to Boston, until Nina fell asleep.

That night Ruthy would not stop showing up in my dreams. Every time I thought my nightmare ended, I found another world hidden inside it like a Russian doll. In one of the dreams, there was a four-year-old Ruthy trapped inside a crawl space underneath our old house. I could smell mud and trash everywhere. Cereal boxes, baby bottles, and diapers. Ruthy's red hair stuck to the sides of her dark face with sweat as she screamed.

I was six, quiet, and determined. "Hold on, Ruthy. You got to stay still. Stop moving. Let me get Ma."

But she wouldn't stop fidgeting. "Don't go. Please don't go."

"I'll be right back, I promise. Just stay still," I said. "Don't move."

But the house was starting to crumble, as if it was going to cave in. Her foot was stuck, she said. It was sinking into the ground underneath the house. The earth was pulling her little body down. And I couldn't find Ma anywhere.

I held my breath and made myself small so I could fit in the crawl space to drag myself over and pull her out. Already the weight of the house pressed on my back, snapping the bones. My body was being split open, yet somehow I was still alive. "It's going to be all right, Ruthy. I'm coming."

But then the house collapsed around us, and all we could do was call out to each other from underneath the debris.

Nina woke me up in the dark, whisper-shouting, "Yo, Jess, can I borrow some pants?" I'd fallen asleep beside her on the couch.

She'd already gone into my room and torn through my dresser looking for something to wear, with no luck because I hadn't worn a real pair of pants in a straight year. I'd put those shits away after Julie was born, and it was sweatpants and scrubs ever since.

"Wait, are you wearing boxers?"

Nina rolled her eyes. She was tossing random clothes out of her book bag, searching for a bra. "They're boy-short panties. And before you say anything, I happen to know that they're in style right now at Mariposa's, so clearly you're the one who's behind in fashion. Now, can I get a pair of pants?"

"I didn't need all of that background. I was just asking a question." I pointed to the coat closet, where I'd put a bag of small pants that I was going to donate. "Check the top shelf all the way in the back. They might be a little bit big on you, though."

She pulled my pre-baby slacks up her little hips and tightened a belt around her waist so that they wouldn't fall.

"Don't forget to talk to Ma," she said.

"And don't forget to brush your teeth," I shot back.

Nina rolled her eyes before opening and shutting the front door, not even bothering to zip up her boots.

The sound of crickets came in through the door, and the sun was starting to come up.

When I couldn't fall back asleep, I walked into the bedroom and put my face real close to Lou's, examined the way the sunlight fell on his razor burn, the places he dragged the blade against his skin. Then I poked him in the cheek until he woke up.

Lou groaned a little bit but kept his eyes closed.

He was pretending to be asleep and started to dramatically snore, as if to prove it.

But when I put his hand on my boob, he twitched his eyes open and smiled, falling for the bait.

"Sucker!" I mushed his face. "Listen, can you drive me and the baby to my mom's, then drop us off at the church?"

He groaned, pulling the pillow over his face.

"Pleeeease," I said.

"All right. But like, you guys gotta come down quickly, Jess. Don't leave me downstairs waiting in the parking lot forever. You know your moms. She's going to be up there changing her sweater a dozen times and offering to cook you bacon and eggs. Then she'll be like, 'Tell Lou to come up.' Meanwhile, I'll already be twenty minutes late for work."

"I promise," I said. I placed my hand over my heart. "Up to God, baby. I will be in and out."

In the next room I could hear Julie's waking-up noises, her voice bobbing up and down in the air as she tested each note in her gray room. She only started crying when I opened the door to the nursery to tell me that it was time for teta. Seeing me in the doorway, she grabbed the bars of the crib and shook them dramatically. Julie's hair was a hundred percent mine. Black and wavy, it stood up in every direction. She was all the good parts of me, and sometimes I felt the heftiness of the fact that she had materialized inside my body, from scratch—like she was always waiting to happen, a girl from me, of me, but untouched by my past.

She looked up and smiled as I fed her. "You want to wear the yellow dress today, I can tell," I said. "Right, mami?"

She giggled, and milk squirted all over her face.

We drove out all the way to West Brighton to my mother's, where the elevator didn't work so I had to climb three flights of stairs with the baby, who I decided to bring up there as bait. The whole time up Julie decided to wriggle in my arms, because climbing the stairs was her new obsession so she wanted me to put her down. And when I wouldn't, she started to do her little baby protest by wailing and smacking her cheek against my chest, as I nearly fucking went into cardiac arrest on the seventy-second step.

The familiar smell of both bleach and coffee hit me when I opened the door. Julie seemed to sense we were at Grandma's, too, because finally she stopped crying and sort of drooled happily when we walked inside the kitchen.

There was not much in the sink, except for a bowl that held on to a few soft fragments of ramen. My mother liked to keep a clean home. For us, cleanliness always was a type of safety against the outside that she was forever resisting, the bullshit fighting, some couple yelling at each other for no good reason, some poor kid getting jumped. We knew Ma was not doing well if we walked into the house and found dishes in the sink or smelled the remnants of a cigarette that had turned the air stale. When our mother was doing okay emotionally, she only smoked outside, even when the temperature dropped to single digits.

The radio was on in the living room, playing Gilberto Santa Rosa's "La agarro bajando."

It had gotten to the chorus now and my mother was singing out in her low scratchy voice, "Todo lo que sube tiene que caer."

I followed the song to the bedroom, where steam rose around her hands as she slid an iron against the blue blouse she was planning on wearing that day.

"Hey, Ma," I said, smiling.

She only had a light blue bra on, and her soft belly was pinched inside a pair of black pants. That was my mom—always matching the color of her shirt to the color of her bra. Always trying to press a fold down the front of her slacks. Tidy, precise, and bright, she had already slicked her curly hair into a clean bun and blown out the bangs. I could smell the VO5 from the door.

The baby called out for her attention, swinging away from me as if she were trying to dive to the floor and commit little-baby suicide.

My mother's face lit up. "Oh, you brought my baby," she said, blowing kisses to Julie. "Mama loves you, yes she does."

"She didn't want to stay in the car with Lou," I said.

"Of course she doesn't. She wants to be with Grandma. I didn't even hear you walking in!"

The ironing board barely fit in the room, but she had managed to wedge it between her massive vanity and unnecessarily king-size bed. In the vanity's mirror, I could see my reflection between the pictures she'd taped around its frame of me and my sisters as little girls. At least two dozen of them: graduation pictures and class photos of Nina in her uniform. One old picture of Ma leaning on Dad's car in the late seventies, another one of her mother in Puerto Rico, nose turned up, looking almost resentfully at the camera, daring whoever took the picture to judge. At the top of the mirror, she'd taped a picture of us three girls from the eighties, all under the age of seven, our hair sticking up everywhere. Ruthy, four years old, standing on the couch, grinning with her brown cheeks and red hair, arms open, ready for a hug. I am holding Nina, who is just a little over one, the darkest of all three of us and the most beautiful, her big shiny eyes intelligently sizing up the person behind the camera, smart even then. My mother's vanity—full of perfume and oval-shaped cardboard boxes of Maja powder. A small porcelain dish with the words, *There is no crying in Grandma's house*, beside a stack of rings she removed before her shower. My father's old golden box chains hanging from the hooks inside one of the mirror's side panels.

Between all of the pictures, I noticed a long, thin lonesome-ass wrinkle stretching across my forehead, like the indentation you get along your hairline after you take off a shower cap. But, mostly, I was surprised at how pale my twenty-seven-year-old skin had turned. It never failed. Being at my mom's house always made me feel like expired milk.

"Jesus, Ma. You walk up those steps every day?" I collapsed backwards on the bed with Julie sprawled on top of me.

"I mean, I must," she said. "You think I have wings?"

I put Julie on her stomach on the bed and rolled over. "You headed to church?"

She looked up at me, and then right back down at the iron, then said, "Claro." Which was basically Spanish for: *Yes, dumbass.*

She picked up the shirt and inspected it closely, the tops of her eyes peering over her glasses at the collar. Now she speed-walked from one side of the room to another, looking for a scarf, opening a drawer to pull out the same gold teardrop earrings she'd been wearing since we were kids. She used the earring's hook to search her earlobe for the hole. Then she sat on the bed and smiled at me while putting on her little high-heeled boots.

"I was thinking me and the baby might join you at church this morning! Then we could go take a trip out to the mall. Go to Applebee's. My treat. Lou could drive us to service today, all right?"

The smile on Ma's face widened.

"Oh!" she said. "Lou's coming to church!"

She loved Lou. Ever since we were kids, he had this talent of conning old people into liking him, into thinking he was a respectable young man.

"No, he's gotta work, Ma. But I'll be there."

She nodded and said, "Good, we can pick up Irene, too."

Irene was my mother's sixty-year-old church "friend," who blew her hair out like Whitney Houston from the *Bodyguard* days and still rocked her Rum Raisin brown lipstick like it was 1992. Irene wore power suits to church, the type of joints you'd see on the sales racks at JCPenney, and everything that she touched—everything—afterwards smelled so unfortunately like Skin So Soft.

Inspired by a new diet, Irene had started eating seafood three times a week to lose weight. I was not excited about the idea of paying for her entrée of Applebee's salmon and orzo.

"Irene doesn't drive?" I asked, because I distinctly remembered her pulling up one day in a bright red Kia with a Jesucristo bumper sticker so that she and my moms could go watch *The Changeling* together half-off using Irene's senior citizen discount.

"¿Cómo?" my mother shouted, pretend-innocent from the bathroom over the noise of the blow-dryer, like she hadn't heard me the first time. She'd wrapped her bangs around the brush and was lifting them up against the heat. Her face was flushed, and her cheeks had grown damp from the effort of retorching her bangs for good measure.

"I said, Irene. She doesn't drive?"

My mother shut the blow-dryer off, walked out of the bathroom, and slammed the door, making one of her Franklin Mint collectible plates rattle against the wall. "Ay. Jessica, what's the problem here? Her car broke down! We can't help somebody else out?"

"All right, all right," I said. "I'm sorry, I didn't know."

"And usually, she's the one that takes me every Sunday, since you don't never want to go to church," my mother kept on.

This line of conversation was about to become a thing if I didn't stop it, I could tell. But also, I saw the opportunity.

"Actually, Mami, I was thinking that I wanted to start going to church more, you know." Which stopped my mother in her tracks.

"Is something wrong? Are you okay?"

"No, I'm all right, I promise. I was just thinking it's probably good for Julie, too, you know, to expose her to that stuff young, so she grows up with it."

My mother looked pleased at this, but also suspicious. "Are you sure everything is okay? You're not having those heart troubles again?"

Growing up, I'd had some issues with an irregular heart rhythm— nothing fatal, but my mother loved to tell anybody she could about how fragile my heart was.

"I'm fine, Ma."

"Cause you should be going back to Dr. Woods. Remember, you always had that bad heart."

"Ma, I'm telling you, I'm fine…I just been thinking a lot about it. And I was even looking at this Christian retreat they have coming up."

"Ha," my ma said, but she was all smiles. "That would be beautiful. I love a retreat."

"It's for women under thirty," I said quickly. "And you know, Nina wants to come, too." Which made my mother jerk her head back in disbelief, so I added, "I mean, I'm trying to get her to come, and I almost got her committed to it—"

My mother raised an eyebrow and stood there quietly.

"—but we just need somebody to take care of the baby because Lou has work, you see?"

"Aha! So that's where this is going." My mother laughed. "Listen, you don't ever gotta ask me to take care of my own granddaughter. That's my baby, too. You leave her with me. We'll be just fine. And you two go and build your relationship with the Lord."

I cringed inside hearing that Lifetime Christian talk but went over and gave her a big hug.

Meanwhile, Lou had begun to honk the horn outside, while simultaneously calling me on the phone. His ringtone—the chorus of Destiny's Child's "Bug a Boo"—played on repeat, until I gave in and finally picked up.

"Jess. Come on. I'm going to be late," he said. "What are you guys doing up there?"

He was still going on and on when I hung up on him.

"Ma. Lou's going to lose it downstairs." I stood by the door and opened it loudly, jiggling my keys. But she had already disappeared with a tube of lipstick to the back of the apartment. A minute passed as she rummaged through the vanity. And now she was on the phone telling Irene that we were going to pick her up.

Finally she stepped out of the bedroom with her royal-blue shirt on and calmly pulled the strap of her purse over her little shoulder. One room after another, she shut off all the lights, but not before spraying herself with some CK One.

"Ma, please. I'm begging you."

"Ya, nena, oh my god. I'm coming." She put a hand in the air. "All right, let's go."

I grabbed her coat and mine and ran down the stairs. But when I got out of the building, the car wasn't where Lou had parked it. I looked around at the empty lot, the anger multiplying inside of me. Cold wind dragged pieces of a newspaper along the ground. *If this motherfucker left...* But then there was a honk, and I realized that Lou had just pulled up to the curb on my left.

"Jessica," he said, holding both of his hands out in a question.

Then my moms, she finally opened the building door behind me and tottered in her heels towards the car, went straight up to Lou and said, "Hi, papi." She reached through the open driver's window, touched Lou's cheek, and then tapped it twice. "Such a good boy you are."

"How you feeling, Dolores?" Lou said.

"Very *good.*" She sat down in the back next to the car seat and folded her hands over her little blue purse.

And me? I'd barely gotten the baby buckled in the back and sat my ass down in the front seat before Lou started pulling out of the parking lot and speeding off. I put one hand up in the air and told him to relax. "Okay?"

My mother, she started making louder baby sounds in the back, then broke out into song: "Qué linda manita que tiene bebé..."

"Don't tell me to relax," Lou said.

But before I could respond, my mother protested from the back seat, "Oh, NO, Louis. You're going the wrong way!"

Lou turned to me. "I'm dropping you guys off at the church, no?"

I cringed.

I had forgotten to tell him.

Behind us my mother shook her fist at me. "We have to pick up *Irene. Bruta.* You didn't tell him?" The five golden bracelets she always wore jingled against each other, making their own noise.

"Aw, Ma. Look, just tell Irene to take a cab. Lou's going to be late. I'll pay for it. I'll give her the cash when she gets to the church."

"I already told her we were going to pick her up. If you didn't want to pick her up, Jessica, you should have told me. Now you got her waiting outside. She doesn't live too far away." My mom paused, then said, "Lou?"

And the combination of the way she said his name in a super Spanish accent and the way Lou's face tightened as he tried to fix the anger on his face into something kinder made me laugh.

"I'm going to be late. But this is funny to you," he said to me in a whisper, as if my mother would not be able to hear it. Then he looked back at my moms. "All right, D. I got you. Where does Irene live?"

"Prospect Avenue. Just a few blocks away."

Lou shook his head. That was four minutes backwards from the direction to the church. He made an agitated U-turn into the grocery store parking lot, and we all stood quiet in the car until we got to Irene's little blue house.

"Isn't that beautiful," my mother said.

And it was.

Irene's place stood out on the block because she kept the front yard immaculate, while trash littered the bushes and grass in front of the other houses. She'd done the town house up with Christmas decorations. Shiny red plastic bows hung on her fence, where she stood now with her "I Will Always Love You" hair, looking from side to side down the block. When she recognized my mother's face in the back of the car, she lifted one finger as if hailing a cab.

My mother rolled down her window. "Vente, mujer."

But when Irene opened the door, do you think she even said thank you? No. "Estás tarde," she said to my mother but loud enough for me to hear.

I sent my mom a look like *Don't let her say that shit in English in front of Lou. Or else I'm going to have to hear about it forever.*

My mom's pupils, despite her suspicious grin and various

medications, twinkled knowingly, and she turned to Irene. "Ay, did you hear about what happened to Luz's daughter?"

"The fat one or the one with the lazy eye?"

"La gordita."

I closed my eyes, relieved, and then looked over at Lou, who was now hunched over the wheel practicing his own type of secret and deeply petty language.

The church was not really a church. It was a gym that had formerly belonged to a community center. Every Sunday they put the teenagers to work dragging hundreds of metal chairs to the floor and rolling a dusty blue runner between the aisles up to the podium, where the musicians were already testing the timbales. Banners with proverbs written in Spanish and decorated with hearts and Jesus fish hung from the metal rafters like boughs of flowers. But you could still see a basketball hoop hanging behind the altar, where Pastor Richie (this twenty-eight-year-old green-eyed Puerto Rican, who I knew was definitely cheating on his wife, because I saw him once palming his side chick's ass in the cereal aisle at a CVS) was standing, his arms stretched to the sides, singing, "Querido Dios, gracias por tus bendiciones," as if he were Marc Anthony. Outside the building you could hear his voice—so loud that it reached the parking lot of the Western Beef across the street, rattling against a row of shopping carts locked into each other.

Service, obviously, had already started.

As soon as Irene and my mother pushed through those double doors, they put up praise hands like a couple of scarecrows, which made them look even guiltier as they squeezed themselves down the aisle searching for three empty chairs. I followed them, holding Julie in her car seat, trying not to hit anyone in the head. When Mom and Irene finally found their seats, they closed their eyes and moved from side to side with the music, multiplying the energy of their worship by how many minutes they'd showed up late. The lights and the thumping bass had stirred Julie awake and she was twisting in the car seat, trying to look away from me to the front of the church, where Richie was singing, "Con brazos abiertos, Señor." My mother picked Julie up and started swaying with her, one arm in the air.

In the front, by the altar and the microphones, Mr. Rafael was killing it on the congas, slapping the edges of the drums and ending with a resounding echo from the note he struck with the heel of his hand, while the pastor lifted his voice, chanting a prayer in Spanish: *Señor: Sin ti, nada podemos hacer.* And a viejito on the guitar was strumming and rotating his head, the sweat trickling into his collar, the top of his bald head glistening underneath the fluorescent lights—Mr. Ruiz. During the week he delivered pizza for Little Caesars. On Sundays he made hundreds of people bend at the waist with one hand raised towards the ceiling, their hearts softened by the sounds he conjured with his guitar.

I'm telling you, some of these old Spanish dudes could really play, and I wondered if they were so good because of God, or if they played at church because it's where the most people showed up. At one point the combination of congas and the guitar and the drums and the piano shook the whole fucking building and the baby started to cry, agitated and frightened by the sound of all of these strangers and their sorrow.

I took Julie and touched her face. "We're going to get outta here soon. I promise," I whispered.

But two hours in, we were still there. Way after John, chapter 16, verse 33: "I have told you these things, so that in me you may have peace. In this world you will have trouble. But take heart! I have overcome the world." And way after Pastor Richie started laying hands on people and making them squirm. Irene, she passed out on the floor and lay there twitching against the blue commercial carpeting, incapacitated with the Holy Spirit.

I'm ashamed to say it, but I could feel that faith rise inside me, too, and those were the times I most believed in God, until I'd look at that two-timing pastor singing and think: *Damn, you're so full of shit. May that basketball hoop not fall on your head and strangle you with the net.*

Still, I stood the obligatory two and a half hours of Pentecostal church and behaved like the good Puerto Rican Christian woman I am not. The baby had somehow managed to fall back asleep and snore through the whole loud morning, until the music died and Richie gave up flirting with the viejitas. He was shameless, that one; a nerd who grew up to become handsome and never forgot the days the older boys shoved his face into the concrete. He couldn't completely hide the satisfaction curling up on his face whenever the grandmother of some boy who beat him up came to him to lament that her grandson was now locked up. Worse, he was always using his power of good looks on other people; the biggest victim of his charm was his wife, who seemed tragically proud of her husband, clutching her pregnant stomach even as the younger women smiled at him and winked.

I tell you, the worst type of womanizer is the former geek.

Finally, the service was over. The speakers buzzed as the musicians unplugged their instruments. The feedback stirred Julie awake and she reached her hands in the air to be picked up.

My mother made her way to the front of the church and spent twenty minutes saying goodbye. By the time she came back to me, Irene was still down lying on the floor, her eyes closed faithfully. Strangely, Irene had made sure to wrap the strap of her purse around her wrist, so that nobody would take it while she was conversing with the Holy Spirit. People were stepping over her left arm to exit the church.

I saw where this was going.

I'm no fool.

I looked at my mother and was like, "All right, Ma, let's get moving. Time to go."

She sat down, defiantly folded her hands over her purse, and pointed at Irene, who was ever so softly convulsing against the floor. "We should wait for her."

An old woman maneuvered her walker around Irene's body and nodded reverently, but I could see Irene open her eyes sometimes to inspect who was watching her. I swear, I think she even winked at me, when my mother was turned the other way.

After about fifteen minutes of this, I couldn't take it. I said, "Ma, please. Can't we wake her up? We gotta go."

Ma looked at me as if I had just suggested killing a newborn child. You could see the waxy line she drew in brown pencil underneath her scarce eyebrows lift in surprise. "Shush," she said, doubling down in her seat. She recrossed her legs to indicate that we would wait.

I had no patience for this.

Yes, I am the oldest daughter, but I am also human.

I went up to Irene and nudged her shoulder gently. But she only breathed in more deeply, as if she were stuck in a deep trance.

"Jesus Christ," I said.

"Jessica!" my mother whisper-shouted at me. Then raised one finger. "Respect!"

Which I did. Because I am a good daughter. Very respectfully, I sat back down and texted Lou: *Tell me why this old woman at Church just pretended to pass out on the floor.*

It was at least another fifteen minutes, me and my mother sitting there. By that time the gym was almost empty. Pastor Richie said goodbye to the last of the viejitos, then made his way down the aisle, at which point Irene very conveniently fluttered her eyes open and coughed as if she'd been stuck underwater too long. She put her arms up in the air.

Playing his part, too, Pastor Richie bent down and touched

Irene's face. The sweat underneath his armpits made the fabric of his shirt almost translucent; I could see the wifebeater he was wearing underneath and smell the way his BO warped the cologne.

He grasped Irene's arm and lifted her up. "You are very blessed," he said, in such a sincere way that I was about to fucking lose it.

My mother had taken the baby to the front of the church now and was showing her off to all the older women.

So I decided to take my opportunity to step outside and smoke a cigarette. It looked like rain. The sky was white but heavy. "Que Dios te bendiga," the old people kept saying to each other as they left the church.

I was sitting on a turned-over shopping cart that somebody must have dragged over from the Western Beef, finishing up the last of my Newports by the time my mother came out. When Irene saw me like that, sitting on the shopping cart and smoking, she straightened herself and dragged one of her hands down the front of her beige blazer, patting the polyester collar.

Then she said to my mother in Spanish, "Ida's daughter, she smokes crack."

I swear to God. That's exactly what she said.

I looked at Irene like *I'll hit an old person, I don't care.*

Then my mother flashed me a super-fucking-sane *Don't start, Jessica* look.

And in my head, I was like, *Great, now you're normal, Ma. When it comes to me, you're mad regular.*

When the cab pulled up, me and Irene squeezed into the back with the baby. My mom sat in the front. And I used Julie and the car seat as a buffer zone between me and Irene, who started passing out little pieces of white and yellow chicle. "Her husband could not pick us up?" she asked my mother.

It took me a second to realize that she was talking about Lou.

I looked at Irene and said, "That's not my husband. That's my boyfriend."

"But you two live together, no?"

"Yes, Irene," I said. "We have a child."

She looked at my mother and then frowned. "You give the cow away, you cannot sell the milk."

"Irene, the saying is the other way around. It's if you give the milk away, you cannot sell the cow."

The cabdriver, Mario, snorted with laughter, which pissed Irene off.

"I know what I said. And that's exactly how I wanted to say it," she said. And with that she buckled her seat belt loudly. She was the only one in the car with it on.

My mother, she reached behind her to pretend to pat my knee so that she could pinch me, and because I respect my elders, despite wanting to kill them, I stood quiet. But I swore that the next time Irene decided to be blessed with the Holy Spirit and pass out for an hour after church, I was going to "accidentally" step on one of her fucking fingers. I imagined her pulling her hand away from underneath my foot while cursing in the sacred house of God and me saying, "Oh my, how quickly the spirit has left you!"

CHAPTER 9

Nina

Why in the world would you give up months of your life to live with a group of people who were clearly fucked up and who, past seasons taught you, would eventually turn on your ass? True, there was something about the fame and attention of it, probably. These were girls who wanted to be seen, girls who had sworn nobody could touch them, nobody could hurt them, girls who said you better be afraid when I walk inside the room, you better watch your fucking mouth around me. And who the fuck you looking at? A brief internet search showed that they were getting free rent and a little bit of cash, but that money was minimum wage. And sometimes the women were rich, so it wasn't like they needed the money. Two or three of the former *Catfight* girls had gone on to have their own reality TV shows, but most of them disappeared after the season was over. To where, I wondered, and exploit yourself on TV for what? That fifteen minutes of fame couldn't have been worth getting your ass kicked.

This Ruby character...she had worked as a waitress in L.A.— briefly. Had done some modeling for a cheap brand of swimsuits back in 2006. She didn't talk about having any family, no boyfriends, no sisters or brothers, no kid. She wanted to be a model. Or possibly a singer? It was hard to tell. Online, we found a clip of her *Catfight* audition tape and replayed it over and over again, noting each of her movements, tracking each verbal tic.

The clip starts outside her old apartment building. Somebody is filming her as she opens the door, though we never find out who he is. He focuses on her lips, then shifts the camera down to the edges of her tank top, the bare line between her armpit and her breast. The hem of her purple shorts cut right above her legs.

Ruthy/Ruby bends down to pull her red hair up into a bun, piles the curls on top of her head to look strategically out of place. It is sometime in the afternoon; the sun is still bright outside, and you can hear how much she drank since she woke up, the weight of it dragging each of her syllables out. "Welcome, to my beautiful apartment," she says, sweeping an arm across the empty living room walls.

The camera shifts to a corner with multiple garbage bags of clothes, the black plastic crinkled and gleaming like winged roaches. The rest of the room is empty except for a beanbag chair, which she sits on, tapping an ashtray on the floor with a freshly lit cigarette, the smoke curling against the window's crooked blinds.

"Just kidding," Ruthy/Ruby says. "I live in shit."

Next to her pretty ankle, though, is what looks like a journal or a large planner with stars exploding against the cover's green sky, like the Lisa Frank stickers we used to beg our mother to buy, though she couldn't afford them.

"She's poor," I said.

Jessica nodded silently in agreement.

I don't know why this surprised me so much. Maybe we hadn't expected that from the episodes we repeatedly watched, the women dripping with expensive designer clothing, spending cash on twenty-dollar martinis, throwing random singles at each other as they pretended to strip.

Until then I don't think I had thought of Ruby as a real person. Just some type of B reality show celebrity. A figment of my sister's imagination. Her hope. A dream. But in just a little over a week, we would be driving up to Boston to see this woman in person, a fact I hadn't fully prepared myself for. And now Ruby looked recognizable, like some of our cousins who'd dropped out of college and couldn't find jobs. Like my Titi Ivette, who, one day, the police found dead, alone in her apartment, after she had a seizure and nobody was there to help her. Or like a warped magnified version of my own underemployment.

Next, the camera followed Ruby into the bedroom. A well-watered pot of azaleas sat on the window ledge below her crooked blinds, taken care of and loved. I imagined Ruby at night, turning on her faucet, filling up a coffee cup with water, then tipping it into the flowerpot before lying down on top of her sheetless bed, tired from whatever minimum-wage job.

"So, this is my kitchen." Small, dark, and windowless. Just enough room to stand between the buzzing door of the refrigerator and the oven streaked with grease, the oven which Ruby bumps into accidentally. (Or maybe on purpose? For dramatic effect.) Her hip presses against the dial on the stove, rotates it just enough to turn on the flame. Ruby spins around, surprised. "You see?" She smiles. "This is why people hate me." She throws her hands up in the air. "Because I can't do anything right." Then lights up with mock laughter. "But also, because I'm prettier than them."

"Who am I?" Ruby is sitting on her beanbag again. Crossing her legs and sipping a glass of wine as if she's being interviewed on *Oprah*. "You want to know what I'm about?" She uncrosses her legs. Leans forward to show cleavage.

"Yes," the man behind the camera says.

It's so fucking creepy.

I turn to Jessica. "Why does she keep on giggling like that?"

"Shush," she says.

In the video, Ruby asks, "What do you want to know?"

Off-screen, the cameraman must have made some obscene motion because now Ruthy/Ruby is laughing like a Teletubby at the joke.

I tell Jess, "I wish she'd stop giggling like that."

"Shush," Jessica says again, entranced by the audition, as if she's the one being seduced.

After all these years, Ruthy still managing to be the center of attention, even after she left us.

Each week there was a different challenge in which one of the women could win some lavish prize: a new Louis Vuitton purse, a pearl necklace from Tiffany, a two-thousand-dollar shopping trip. But at the end of the episode, only one woman could succeed. And each girl had to scheme and lie to the others in order to win.

For example, during a scavenger hunt, each of the women was given a unique clue that nobody else in the house possessed, forcing them to choose an ally to share their information with. Some chose a girl in their clique, while others purposefully chose women they thought were "too stupid" to understand their clue, which generated a great deal of distrust. In order to win, ultimately, you had to step on the other woman, which reminded me of sophomore year of college and meeting the only other Puerto Rican girl in the Biology Department and the look of hate on her face when I introduced myself.

Ariel, the girl from the Bronx, won that challenge. And at the end of the episode you saw her sitting alone at her vanity, drunk, fingering the five-thousand-dollar strand of pearls around her beautiful neck.

Inexplicably crying.

*   *   *

In another episode, a group of Christian fundamentalist men gather around the Catfight Condo with JESUS IS KING signs.

One shouts through a bullhorn: "Sluts and harlots, you are going to hell. Hell. Hell. Hell. Hell. Hell."

Ruby is tickled. She screams out the window, "No, papi, we're going to the club!"

When Gem goes down there, one of the old men tries to bump chests with her. Calls her a dyke. A slut dyke, to be more accurate, and all of the girls in the house descend upon him, livid.

"Get your hands off her, motherfucker." They've torn his sign off his neck, they've stomped on his bullhorn and ripped up his shirt.

Once he's down on the ground, Ariel walks over to him and says very calmly, "You don't touch us. You don't *ever* touch us. Do you understand?"

At two a.m., the night camera makes Gem's eyes glow in the dark, and you can hear the other girls snoring in their beds. Gem looks from side to side to make sure both Ariel and Lulu are still asleep, then crawls to the other bedroom, and startles McKayla awake. "Listen, shush," Gem whispers, and puts a hand over McKayla's mouth. "I have an idea, but you gotta be quiet."

With her mouth still covered by Gem's hand, McKayla nods her head.

"Do you really want to get revenge on Ruby? Or are you going to keep on letting people pick on you?"

McKayla narrows her eyes at Gem. Those questions were simultaneously an insult and a power play. Nevertheless, McKayla nods. She needs an ally in the house, otherwise it will only be days before she gets kicked out. In fact, she'll be lucky if she can make it to the weekend.

"All right, bitch, get up then. We got stuff to do," Gem says.

Quietly, they both crawl out the door on their hands and knees, through a long pink hallway to the dressing room where each girl is assigned a vanity. Alone now, they stand up and walk over to Ruby's space, which is decorated with various versions of the Puerto Rican flag, old selfies, a small poster of the cover of La Lupe's *La Yi Yi Yi* album, and a picture of La India, her long black hair flipped over one side of her face.

The vanity is full of small bottles of perfume, a gold heart-shaped canister of purple makeup brushes, and a large tub of edge-control gel made of olive oil. Ruby is so obsessed with her makeup that the girls have never seen her bare face. She goes to bed all made up, and in the morning scurries into the bathroom to wash up and reapply her lipstick, foundation, and mascara in private, which makes some of the girls (even Ariel) laugh: "How early do you think she gets up every morning to put it on?"

Gem slides her hand across each of Ruby's items as if cursing them, while a dissonant chord plays in the background. She picks up a fifty-dollar bottle of foundation, unscrews the top, and spits in it. Then Gem passes the bottle to McKayla, who takes off to the bathroom and returns with some Windex that she mimes pouring into the makeup as the evil music intensifies.

But in one surprising moment, Gem holds out her hand to stop McKayla and says, "No, that's too much."

That happened sometimes.

Glimpses of the girls' real selves cracked through whatever front they'd built to audition for the show, which made me wonder: Was there an alternate universe where all of these girls were actually friends, co-conspirators, in which the ultimate joke was on us, the viewers sitting on our bored asses at home? Behind the scenes, off camera, did Ruby crack up with Gem and the sorority girl like they were homegirls, laughing about how *Catfight* fans were going to go crazy watching the next day as Ruby dipped one of her fingers in the ruined foundation and dotted the rancid makeup underneath her eyes?

It was possible. I thought about my six-year-old surprise when Jess revealed to me that Hulk Hogan's wrestling was fake, the oiled-up men circling the stage, flexing their orange muscles, their arms extended, palms up like prophets, the spit that flew out of their mouths, ripping off their costumes (now it seems so obvious, but back then...)—fake, all of it was fake. And the real rage, the only real emotion, belonged to the screaming audience.

Whose design was it to choreograph such violence between these women, who was really in charge, and why could I not stop watching?

CHAPTER 10

Dolores

First, Dear Lord, I want to say that I am sorry, because I have not prayed in one whole long dark week, because I let doubt creep into my heart. I know, sometimes I allow my own desires to supersede yours, and I lose patience, like what happened with Yesenia, Altagracia's daughter, you know who she is, the one with no goddamn sense, that day when she came to the parents' workshop after service and placed that porquería of a purse on my seat while I was making the coffee, which by the way wasn't even my job, but you already know how that shit goes. If I don't make the coffee, olvídate, nobody else is ever going to do it.

That's how the church operates now, ever since they put that baby pastor Richie in front of the pulpit. And you already know my heart, Dear Lord, and that I don't question you, but I do wonder what you're thinking sending in a twenty-eight-year-old child to deal with a congregation of women old enough to be his grandmother.

I still remember Richie as a ten-year-old and how I had to intervene when a couple of high schoolers tried to jump him at a bus stop for his Game Boy.

Nice kid.

Very nice boy.

Excellent parents.

But talk to me; what type of spiritual guidance am I supposed to expect from a young man like that? It's like asking a five-year-old to file your taxes. No order whatsoever in the church right now. This one's setting up the congas too soon, that one wants to hog the mic during song and worship, and two of the women in the choir started arguing in Bible verses over whose turn it was to sing the solo. Ms. Lopez, the choir director, practically shouting across the church, "Love is patient and kind...it does not insist on its own ways." Then Ms. Ruiz, straightening herself up from the piano: "Amen, it is. But some of us seek our own interests and not the way of Jesus Christ." And that's how they kept going, talking like a bunch of fortune cookies, while Richie's standing there looking like he's about to cry.

That poor boy doesn't stand a chance.

The other day, I heard one of the younger women, Marisol, tell him, "Oh, no te preocupes, Richie. Dolores will take care of it." You hear that? The goddamn nerve of that woman.

And you know what Richie says to Marisol? "Okay."

Like I'm everybody's fucking mother.

That's all to say, God, forgive me for questioning your larger design, but I'm just wondering why we have to resort to child labor when you already know it's a recession and there's a lot of other qualified adults in need of work.

The point is I didn't mind making the coffee, but at least once in a while they can get someone to clean the pot instead of letting it sit there in the dark at night in the sink with God knows what mold growing in that black soap and water. Filthy. I mean, you already know that I don't judge—to each his own—but at least these folks should have some type of respect in the church, enough decency to keep God's kitchen clean, right? You can just imagine what these people's sinks look like at home, the various types of animals growing in their drains.

Well, I guess you don't have to imagine because you're God, but you get the point.

It took me fifteen minutes to give the pot a good wipedown, and after the coffee started perking, I came back to the little circle of kindergarten-size chairs in the rec room to sit down. But Yesenia had placed her ugly brown-and-pink purse on top of my seat, while she went to the bathroom.

Which is no big deal.

Fine.

How could she have known it was my seat?

I'm not vindictive. So, this is what I did. I clapped my hands to get the attention of the ladies who were still talking in the circle. And then I very gently moved Yesenia's purse onto the floor, which I had just vacuumed, by the way. I promise you, Lord, I did not mean anything by it. The floor was clean. But also: Where the fuck else was I supposed to sit? On the alphabet rug? Or maybe Yesenia expected for me to just stand there while her purse rested on my seat and caught its breath?

She looked at her purse on the floor, then up at me and said, "Could you not touch my stuff?"

Pendeja. I almost told her, too, If you spent more time taking care of your own son than worrying about your stupid purse, maybe then the city wouldn't be requiring for you to go to Proper Parenting in the first place.

Which then I quickly felt bad about.

I mean, I get it.

It's annoying.

Trust me. I know that a lot of those young women in my workshop felt this deep and terrible shame when ACS sent them to me. But there is no need for the elaborate attitude. I wanted to pull Yesenia aside and be like, *This is not* my *fault, sweetheart. I am not the reason why you are here.*

And also: *How'd you let Elijah miss twenty-three days of school?* Twenty-three days, and it wasn't even November yet. Instead of going to class, the boy would ride the S46 past the school bus stop, get off at Castleton, and walk over to that McDonald's on Forest Avenue. Then when the school called Yesenia at her job and made her come into the office, she beat the boy right there in front of the principal.

Which I guess that much I understand. Believe you me, I know it is frustrating. However, she should have known better than to slap the boy inside the school. You gotta discipline him at home, not in front of white folks, most of them who don't even have any kids themselves and will talk to you for an hour about time-out.

I mean, I sympathize with the girl. I do. You're sitting there in that office, you think you're doing the right thing, that you're going to scare the shit out of the kid and embarrass him to remind him that he's just eleven years old and that you are the mother. You are in charge. You're angry at the boy for lying to you, angry at the school for making you leave work, angry at your boss for giving you a hard time when you asked for the rest of the day off, angry at the principal for sitting there grinning uncomfortably and judging, nodding her head like a robot.

But at the end of the day, it's not that big of a deal.

All this girl had to do was attend Proper Parenting once a week for a month. It's not like ACS is taking the kid away, and to be honest, Yesenia could use a little help, twenty-five years old raising an eleven-year-old boy. She gave birth to him when she was just a baby herself fourteen years old.

It's not easy.

Especially now.

I remember being twenty-five, trying to survive my own three girls. A lot of my mothers, they come to me, no older than thirty, thinking that I don't understand. But I always tell them right away: I've been in your shoes. I know what it feels like to work fifty, sixty hours a week at minimum wage, having to skip paying the electric bill one month so that you can buy a MetroCard to get to work. How sometimes there's not even enough for transportation, so you change into your sneakers and walk that long, hot mile home. And at first, they don't want to be there in that workshop with me. You think I don't know?

But usually, after it's all over, the girls, they always come up to me and say, "You know what? Thank you, Ms. D. I learned a lot."

Which I appreciate. Sometimes it feels like you're getting up in the morning and you don't know why.

I guess if I were to be honest, Dear Lord, the reason why I'm so frustrated with Yesenia is I've known this girl since she was practically a baby, eight years old. She went to school with my daughters, even came over to the house every week to play. And I always knew the little girl had trouble at home, so I made it clear to my daughters she was always welcome. When there wasn't enough to eat at her house, I fed her. Once I even took the girl shopping with Ruthy and Nina and bought her a new pair of shoes for back-to-school.

So when she sat there and gave me this little fucking attitude, maybe I got a bit sensitive, because my first instinct was to turn around and be like, I know you did not just roll your eyes at me, little girl. But instead, I decided to leave it alone and forgive.

As the Lord forgave me.

I sat down next to her. I smiled. I patted her hand. And when she pulled her arm away, I ignored it. Yesenia moved her chair closer to the blue bucket of stuffed animals we kept for the kids. And I said, "All right, let's begin, then."

But she turned around in her seat, picked up her purse from the floor, looked at me, Dear Lord, and continued, "Do you know how much this costs?"

Twenty years older than this girl. I could be her mother. In fact, I know her mother very, very well. Our families go way back on the Island. But do you think she has any respect for that? Do you think a girl like that knows anything about history?

If one of my daughters was there to see it, olvídate, Jessica would have knocked her ass out right there in the church rec room, and I would have had to drag my own daughter past the pulpit, out of the building by the hair. And here is where I confess to you and ask for your forgiveness, Dear Lord, because I, too, wanted to slap Yesenia.

I apologize.

But it is true.

Forgive me.

I was vengeful. When we took a fifteen-minute break from the workshop, and everybody went into the cafeteria, I started serving coffee to all of the women. *Veronica, here you go. ¿Maribella, no quieres azúcar? Oh, okay, nena, I see you with that Sweet'n Low.* Yet I did not offer a cup to Yesenia. And as one of the founding members of Mujeres de Cristo and a state-certified instructor for Proper Parenting, maybe I should have been a little bit more Christian.

And she's not much younger than Jessica (who I know, I know, doesn't always show up to church, but my daughter has the baby now, and she just gets a little angry sometimes. It's a lot for her, entiende?).

I mean, of course you already know.

Obviously, because you're God, but I just wanted to remind you.

Not that you need reminding.

It's just—I don't know—I've lost so much. And sometimes I wonder if you are even paying attention to what is happening down here, at all?

The next parenting workshop, Yesenia came into the rec room huffing and puffing. And when she sat down, her blue bubble coat exhaled the smell of weed, which put me in a predicament, Lord. Say I ignored something like that and gave Yesenia a pass; what if one of the other girls decided to come in drunk next week, because they thought Ms. D was a punk? Or maybe they decided to miss a class or leave early or come in late?

It's a slippery slope. And part of me wanted to ask Yesenia to leave, but part of me also felt like sending her home might be a missed opportunity, you see. Like they always tell us, there is no saint without a past, no sinner without a future. Who am I? To immediately judge?

That is what they don't tell you when you get your parenting instructor license, that everything is fragile with this type of work. You can lose the trust or respect of one of these girls if you so much as look at her the wrong way.

So, all of it I ignored. I started teaching. When I reviewed the Mommy and Me activities I made sure to pick Yesenia's hand first. To praise her for her response. And at the end of the class, I stopped her and said, "One second, Yesenia."

She paused, but didn't say nothing, just looked at her phone without nodding yes. Just stood there as I signed the last of the girls' attendance forms.

After all of them left, I turned to Yesenia and told her to sit down.

She nervously smiled and squeezed herself into one of the daycare seats, because without an audience, Yesenia was the type of woman who turned back into a little girl. She didn't know what to do with her face but turn it from side to side, until finally she stared at the lipstick left on the white plastic lid of her coffee cup.

"How are you doing, sweetheart?" I asked.

She fake-smiled too widely. "I'm doing good, Ms. D." And I couldn't tell if that falseness was more of her being nervous or defiant. Then: "I just need to catch this bus, Ms. D. I'm so sorry, I gotta go."

"All right," I said. "You sure everything's okay?"

And that's when her whole face fell apart. Her chin trembled and she said, "Last night the baby wouldn't stop crying."

Soon enough her mascara was sliding down her cheeks.

"All right, sweetheart," I said.

"And when I asked Elijah for help, all he kept saying was 'I want to go with my dad.' 'What dad?' I said. 'You don't got no dad. All you got is me.' And Ms. D, it was like he hated me even more for saying that."

I passed her some Kleenex from my purse. "I know. I know, baby girl."

"Elijah says to me, I don't even want to be here no more."

"And you're the one who's actually doing everything. They don't realize."

She put her face in her hands. "I'm so tired of this shit."

"Oh, I know, baby." And then when I reached an arm around her, she started to cry so much that her words dissolved into mush. Which was all right. I'd been there.

I already knew what she was trying to say.

I got to the church early to teach and moved the small blue daycare chairs in a circle. The sky was dark by the time class began, and it had started to rain. Car lights smudged against the window as the women pulled into the parking lot.

Ten minutes later the room was full of young moms, sitting in their small blue chairs, the women's thighs too big for their seats, and all of them beautiful. Some of the most studious ones had notebooks, their blank forms ready for my signature to turn in to their case supervisors.

But not Yesenia.

I looked at the clock. It was only three minutes after six, so I decided to give it another five. Take my time pouring everyone coffee. Ask Veronica about her day. But soon it was almost 6:15, and I had no choice. The women started to look at me like, *So when are we going to start?*

Sometimes this happens.

One of the moms gets sick or there's an emergency, in which case, I have the student make up the class by meeting me on another day. So I decided that I would just arrange another time for Yesenia and me to sit down. But then in she came, forty-three minutes late, and right in the middle of my lecture about setting boundaries. She shut the classroom door loudly. "So sorry guys, I missed the bus!" Then she started to laugh and whisper in Veronica's ear as she sat down.

I stopped talking and crossed my arms in front of me.

Veronica, the quiet one from Ecuador who was here because her daughter kept on running away, was too shy to tell Yesenia to shut up. She kept on smiling and then turning her face in my direction, as if to say, *I'm here. I'm sorry, Ms. D. I'm listening.*

When Veronica stopped responding, Yesenia looked around the room at all of the girls before landing her gaze on me. "What?"

I sat down, folded my hands on the desk, then looked at my watch. "Unfortunately, Yesenia, I'm going to have to ask you to leave."

"Leave?" She jerked her head back. "You're fucking kidding me? That's a joke, right?" Her cheeks were flushed with cold, but also you could see a thin sheen of sweat on her forehead, maybe from running.

"Watch your mouth," I said.

"Okay, whatever. I came all the way to Stapleton from Mariners Harbor, okay? I waited for the S48 for twenty minutes, and it took me another forty minutes to get here. You telling me I just wasted two dollars on the bus for no apparent fucking reason?"

I stood there and just looked at her. I've had girls who've talked back before. I am aware that the secret is to not be rattled. You can't let that shit faze you. So I kept my cool and told her, "As I've said before and indicated in your contract, you must not be later than fifteen minutes or else you'll be counted as absent."

And it's not that I didn't feel for the girl, but if I'm not strict enough she'll never learn. Worse, the other girls will start getting ideas in their heads: coming in late, smoking before class, taking advantage.

Yesenia rolled her eyes. "I don't care. I'm not going. I'm staying right here, so you better start teaching."

Which forced my hand. "I'm going to say it one more time, nicely. And if I have to ask a third time, it won't be so nice," I told her.

"Or what? What's your ass going to do, old lady?" Then she got up from her seat and puffed out her chest.

I turned to the rest of the group. "Ladies, we will have to cancel this class . . . if your case managers ask any questions, you tell them to feel free to—"

But no! Yesenia just had to keep on going.

The girl walked right up to me and said, "You ain't canceling class. I spent two dollars and more than an hour getting here. You better fucking teach me."

Still I ignored it. I stepped back from her, waved my hand at the girls. "I'll see you all next week."

"I don't even know why they have you teaching these fucking workshops anyway," she said, grabbing her purse so violently from the seat, it whipped around her back.

"I said goodbye, Yesenia." I turned away from her and started to pack up my books. "And know that I will be contacting your case manager tonight. Don't you forget it."

"What a joke. You would beat Ruthy harder than I ever touched Elijah," she said.

And then before I could even realize it I was three inches away from her face.

"Yeah. You think I don't remember that shit, Ms. D. That one

Claire Jiménez

time Ruthy came in with a short skirt in middle school and you dragged her ass out the courtyard and slapped her right there in front of the car."

"You better watch your mouth," I said.

"All of you. You and Jess always looked down on me. You always thought you were so much better, like I didn't lose something also, when she left. But I loved Ruthy, too."

"Enough, Yesenia. I said enough."

But no, God, she just had to keep on pushing.

"Anyways, what do you know about being a mother?" She started to laugh. "Unbelievable. This fucked-up city sends *you* to teach *me* how to be a mother. And your own daughter ran away from you."

A piece of her spit landed on my face. On purpose, Dear Lord, I'm telling you, it was on purpose. I swear on everything and everyone I love. And that's when I swung on her. First her face, and then when she bent down to escape my hands, I pounded on her back. And it took both Veronica and Maribella to pull me off, to stop me from teaching Yesenia the lesson her mother should have.

Later that week in the office, Pastor Richie's hands trembled as he pulled the seat out for me. "Ms. Dolores, you know, you have always done so much for us. Always."

I felt bad for him. So I tried to make it easier. "Yes." I smiled and nodded to encourage him to continue.

"We appreciate everything you do for the church."

And I remembered again when the boys tried to jump him for the Game Boy, how I'd stepped outside and shouted at them and pulled him into the house. He'd sat in the seat turning pink, insisting that these seventeen-year-old boys were only trying to borrow the toy from him.

"What's this on your forehead, then?" I had asked, pointing to the bruise lifting above his eyebrow.

"That's nothing," he'd told me. "That's from before."

So I'd tried to save him some face by pretending to believe it. "Don't lend those boys shit, ever again. You hear me, Richie?" Then I called his mother to pick him up.

Now, eighteen years later, here he was, turning pink in front of me again.

"I know, Richie. It's all right. I understand." He's just a baby, after all.

"Thank you, Ms. Dolores. You don't know how hard this is."

"I know," I told him.

Because I know better than anybody else how hard it gets.

On the way back home, I called Jessica and explained how Richie'd removed me as the leader of Mujeres de Cristo and fired me from teaching Proper Parenting, because I would rather she discover it from my mouth than anybody else's. I wanted to spare her that shame.

"What?" Jessica yelled over the phone in the mall parking lot, waiting for Lou. "They been leeching off you for free work for the past two years and Richie's just going to fire you? Get the fuck out of here."

"Jessica," I said.

"Yo, Yesenia is lucky I was not fucking there. I would have knocked that bitch out for real."

"Your mouth," I said, regretting it already. I should have never told her. Now I really can't bring her to church. "Besides, it's not her fault," I said. "It's my fault. I don't want you approaching her at all, Jessica. Do you hear me?"

"Ma."

"Do you hear me, Jessica?"

"All right, but if the bitch tries..."

"Jessica. You leave it alone. Do you hear me?" I asked her. "Leave it the fuck alone."

"All right, fine, all right, Ma. Look, Lou's here. I gotta go. Let's talk about it later, okay?"

"All right, baby, I love you."

After she hung up, I gave the kitchen and the bathroom a good scrub. I took a shower and afterwards I stepped on the scale. Watched the dial slide to 155, then 160, then 198 pounds.

When Nina came home that night she found me exercising, practicing my *Christian Women Warriors* fighting moves, with just the television set glowing in the dark.

"Ma, what you doing?" she asked, throwing her keys and purse on the counter. "Ma, what's wrong?"

She moved beside me and looked at the woman on the television set, practicing a front kick. The woman's fists were raised, and she lifted her leg, curled her toes upwards, and struck a pretend man in the knee with the ball of her foot. Over the past couple of weeks my center of gravity had improved so that when I kicked my own imaginary attacker, I didn't lose balance at all.

Nina watched.

"Again, you want to hit him with the ball of your foot," the woman explained.

The ball of your foot.

Nina lifted her right knee to mimic what was happening on the screen, the TV light blinking against our bodies. Then she extended her leg and kicked with all of her might.

When she stumbled forward, I helped her.

I corrected her posture.

I taught her in the dark.

CHAPTER 11

Ruthy

In English, after talking about *The Adventures of Huckleberry Finn*, Ruthy is tasked with writing a story about her life. She begins the only way she knows how: *Once upon a time there was this girl named Ruthy.*

Then she crosses it out.

Stupid.

She rips the paper out of her notebook and crumples it, which makes the English teacher, Mr. Hernandez, say to her in Spanish, "Pórtate bien."

Ruthy rolls her eyes at him but doesn't dare say anything. He went to school with her moms back in the day, so one word from Hernandez to her mother and there will be punishments of biblical proportions.

She picks the pencil up and starts again: *Once upon a time there was a girl named Ruthy. She had red hair and two sisters, and she liked to run, because she was good at it.*

Ruthy erases the last part of that sentence and replaces the clause with: *very good at it.* Then she stares at the words on the page.

This time it all sounds boring. Who cares about a Puerto Rican girl from Staten Island on the track team? Who cares about her mother or her sisters or her father?

Instead, she writes, *Once upon a time there was a girl named Ruthy who had a friend named Yesenia.*

Ruthy stares at Yesenia's name in script, the reality of its loops and how softly she's drawn the word on the page. What if someone sees Yesenia's name there, etched inside her binder? What stupid thoughts would they have, if somebody walked by and peeped the word *Yesenia* written in that big loopy font of Ruthy's?

What if they all thought she was weird? If they all started to laugh?

So Ruthy quickly drags the pencil back and forth against the paper to scratch Yesenia's name away from the loose-leaf. As she does this the paper tears, and Mr. Hernandez comes up to her and says, "Ruthy, I'm sure it's not that bad."

From where she is sitting, she can see where he has cut himself various times shaving, the sharp black stubble underneath his chin. Ruthy turns the paper around so that he won't be able to read it.

"Come on. Let me see." Hernandez kneels down next to Ruthy and places his left hand on the paper. His wedding ring is too small. It's barely wedged below his left knuckle. Then he tries to slide her story away from her.

"Déjame verlo," Hernandez says, because sometimes he thinks that speaking Spanish to Ruthy holds some type of special power.

It doesn't.

Nothing holds power over Ruthy.

She tears the paper away from under Hernandez's hand and rips it in half and does not stop ripping it, until nobody will ever be able to read the words on the page. No.

Nobody will ever be able to read her story.

"Ruthy," Hernandez raises his voice. "Stop it."

Nobody.

*   *   *

Later, in math, Mrs. O'Brien stands at the front of the classroom, next to the chalkboard and what looks like a fifteen-year-old map of the United States. The top left cardboard corner of the map has peeled away completely from the board and droops bent toward the floor as the teacher keeps repeating, "Ruthy? Ruthy Ramirez? Is there a Ruthy Ramirez here? Where is Ruthy Ramirez?"

Ruthy is sitting right in front of this teacher in a cluster of desks that Mrs. O'Brien has labeled the Red Team. Two months of eighth grade and this bitch *still* cannot remember her name, so Ruthy rolls her eyes and decides to just sit there and watch O'Brien ask over and over again, while everybody in the class kind of chuckles.

Until Yesenia gives her away. "She's sitting right *there*."

Traitor.

The math teacher directs her attention at Ruthy, squinches her face up, and says, "Ha. Very funny."

"Ha," Ruthy says, imitating the teacher's nasal Island accent. "Maybe now you'll remember me."

And O'Brien dares not respond.

In Life Skills (Ruthy's favorite class) they split everybody up into two groups: boys on one side and girls on the other. Ms. Ellen and Mr. Andrew coteach the class, and they make everybody call them by their first names.

They're not really teachers, though. They're student teachers.

"Students just like you!" they always say, super corny and in unison.

But Ruthy likes them.

Together, they are an odd couple. Ms. Ellen is from Trinidad and wears her hair in long braids that almost reach her waist. Every day she puts on bright red lipstick and hoop earrings. Ruthy wishes she looked like her. Mr. Andrew is white and comes to class always wearing the same old dusty Mets hoodie and khaki cargo pants.

When Ruthy walks into class she sees that Devante has cornered Mr. Andrew with "So, I got this friend who's in sixth grade but he's really tall, so he looks a lot older. He's dating this girl in high school, who doesn't know he's in the sixth grade, and over the weekend we got her to take us to a PG-13 movie."

During eighth-grade Girl Talk, Ms. Ellen has all the girls write down questions and then place them in a hat, which they then pass around. Each girl digs through the scraps of folded loose-leaf and selects a question to answer, to discuss the different important philosophical issues of eighth-grade life, such as: *Suppose you have a neighbor who's your best friend and she starts hanging out with your other best friend without you, would you be mad?*

"Definitely. They should know better than that," one of the girls, Lourdes, says. Lourdes who has four best friends who are terrified of her.

When Yesenia picks her question, she gets *How can you tell when a boy likes you?*

Immediately, everybody giggles as if this question is supposed to be funny.

"I don't know," Yesenia says. "If he teases you. If he pushes you." Because Yesenia is doing this new thing now where she likes to pretend that she's more stupid than she is.

Ms. Ellen does not like this answer. She even looks a little concerned. Ruthy can tell, because when she is nervous, Ms. Ellen always blinks and smiles. The more she disagrees with you, the faster she'll nod her head.

"Oh," Ms. Ellen says. "That's an interesting way to think about it." Bobbing her head up and down. "Does everybody feel this way?"

The girls start to argue, comparing the different boys who have hit them, taking turns deconstructing their intentions, while Ruthy just sits there and snorts, until Ms. Ellen says, "So, Ruthy, what's your take on this?" Because that's the way Ms. Ellen talks to them, like they're important.

Ruthy looks at Yesenia and says, "I think this is stupid," then automatically regrets it when she looks back at Ms. Ellen's face and notices how her cheek twitches as if Ruthy has raised her hand at her.

When it is Lydia's turn she selects the question: *How do you show a boy that you like him?*

Again, all of the girls start laughing like it's the funniest thing they've ever heard. Ruthy sits there trying to figure out at what exact moment this group of girls she's known since sixth grade decided to become so corny. The same girls who once colored their Barbies' hair blue and purple and red, who severed their limbs and made their Barbies wrestle. The same girls who once circled Anthony Delgado after he hit Olivia Wright in the face with a basketball on purpose and pulled him down to the ground and kicked him in the stomach. These girls, now, all they know how to do is giggle.

Lydia answers by blinking and bringing the tops of both manicured hands to her chin to show off her new blue acrylics.

"I smile at him," she says, "like I'm the Grinch."

When it's Little Lucy's turn, she shyly picks a slip of paper from Ms. Ellen's top hat and struggles to read the question, because she only arrived here from Mexico last year: *What's the most embarrassing thing that happened to you this week?*

Lucy, who lives with her father in the Stapleton projects, whispers in Aylin's ear so that she can translate.

"Okay," Aylin says after each of Lucy's whispers, and then, "Wait, *what? ¿Cómo?*"

Luz (that's what they call her for short) hides her face behind her long black hair as she leans into Aylin's ear to try again.

On the other side of the room, the boys have all burst into laughter, and Mr. Andrew is standing up now, saying, "Okay, guys, one mic, one mic!"

The whole time Aylin chews her gum dramatically as she tries to understand Luz. Then finally, she lets out a long "Ohhhhhh." Nodding with recognition, Aylin smiles: the resident eighth-grade translator, fluent in Spanish, English, and 1996 New York City Slang. "I know. I get it now."

The circle of girls leans in.

"Luz said she got her period, and since she don't got no moms anymore she had to tell her dad instead."

Aylin says this and Luz pinches her right pointer finger with her left hand, watching them with her big black eyes, looking like Bambi. She starts to cry. All of the girls—even Ruthy—stand up to hug her, and the nosy-ass boys playing Musical Chairs stop right in the middle of "This Is How We Do It" to yell "Ew," all at the same time.

"Man, nobody was talking to you," Lydia yells back. "Mind your own freaking business."

"The girls are so gay," Devante shouts.

Which gets the boys shouting: "Ohhhh, shit."

All of a sudden, Mr. Andrew is standing up on top of a chair, waving his hands, so nervous the hoodie of his Mets sweatshirt has twisted over the right shoulder. "Boys. Boys, enough!" But they've started to inch toward the girls' side of the room, eager to hear what secret drew the girls together.

Lydia breaks away from the circle and pops her chest out at the boys, as if to fight.

"Okay, enough," Mr. Andrew says, but he's lost control and he knows it. So Ms. Ellen has to step in and shout: "Excuse me."

Immediately, Devante shrinks back toward his side of the room and the boys look up at Ms. Ellen. "Back to your side, please." The boys walk quietly to their chairs. "Thank you."

Then when the girls let go, and Yesenia's hand falls away from

Luz's shoulder, it brushes against Ruthy's. On purpose? Maybe. It's possible. Ruthy tries to look at Yesenia's face, but now Yesenia is staring at Armando across the room.

After they sit back down in their circle of desks with pale, decade-old gum stuck on the bottoms, the hat goes around the circle of girls again, and it is Ruthy's turn.

The question she picks is this: *Who do you have a secret crush on?*

This is definitely a Nicole question. She's been obsessed with the word *crush* ever since reading one of those stupid Baby-Sitters Club books.

When Ruthy brings her hand into the small metal shelf underneath the desk, she can feel a pile of wet sunflower seed shells hidden in its darkness like insects. Her fingers recoil.

"What is it?" Tenaja says impatiently. "Come on, Ruthy."

Ms. Ellen has a rule that if any of the girls don't want to answer a question during Girl Talk they don't got to. No explanation required.

No punishment.

No detention.

No demerits for your silence.

So Ruthy returns the slip of paper into the dark hole of Ms. Ellen's black top hat and says, "Pass."

Period 8: Chorus wouldn't be so bad if Ruthy weren't an alto, because altos always have the suckiest parts. It's almost like they aren't even singing but grunting out random low sounds. Like little cavemen. And for this reason, the altos have been beefing with the Chorus teacher, Ms. Marino, since September, because they think she's making them sing all the most boring parts on purpose. And every girl in the alto section wants to be Mariah Carey but ends up stuck groaning the low notes while the sopranos get to sing the melody in "All I Want for Christmas Is You."

Ms. Marino is tall and flat on all sides and wears teal and pink triangles for earrings. And Big Leslie McDonnell has made her cry no less than sixteen times since September, so that once a week, Marino, adjusting the cup of coffee stained with her purple lipstick on the top of the upright piano, looks at the class bitterly and announces, "I do not know why I am even here."

Today, though, they are singing "Siyahamba," which has a better alto section than any of the other songs, so the altos are willing to behave. After Marino makes them practice singing the scales in increasing *la, la, la*s, she stands up and strikes a chord with one hand while lifting her other arm, revealing a damp circle of sweat, and all thirty kids start singing: *Siyahamb' ekukhanyen' kwenkhos', Siyahamb' ekukhanyen' kwenkhos'*. And then in English: *We are marching in the light of God.*

Almost everybody is paying attention, except Gloria D'Alessandro, who is playing MASH with Erica Santiago in the back of the soprano section, counting the tallies on a piece of torn up loose-leaf while Devante escapes the tenors to peek at who they've listed as their future husbands.

All is well until Big Leslie decides to burp loudly in the middle of the song, so that Ruthy can literally smell the Department of Education grilled cheese she ate for lunch. The belch is so loud that you can hear it over all six sopranos reaching for that high C:

Weeee.

Everybody starts laughing until Marino bangs the piano and shouts, "Shut"—and here she almost says *the fuck*, but catches herself—"up."

"That is it. That is it. That is it!" Marino stands from the piano, points one skinny arm at Leslie, who laughs, "So what you going to do about it?" Her white face dented by acne scars like the moon.

The bell rings before Marino can form some type of threat, and all the students rush to the door, around the teacher's body crouched over the piano.

"That is it," Marino says as Ruthy runs out of Chorus to the locker room to change on time for track.

On the way downstairs, thirsty, Ruthy stops at a water fountain, takes a sip and stares at a piece of green gum stuck in the drain.

Say something is bigger than you, like much bigger, like a lot; is it really your fault if you cannot stop it?

CHAPTER 12

Jessica

Two months after Ruthy disappeared, I cut school early. In the locker room, during gym, instead of putting on my uniform, I took a left at the storage closet and cranked open the ancient rusty door that Ms. McGregor, the gym teacher, always left unlocked so she could sit outside and sneak a smoke between periods. Then, before anybody could miss me, I hustled to the bus stop to get to the middle school on time for dismissal.

I knew Ruthy'd had Mr. Hernandez for English, and right now he would be packing up his things and booking it to catch the bus so that he could make the boat to return home to his family in Brooklyn.

Mr. Hernandez was my second suspect, after Yesenia's gross boyfriend Ivan, who I had to rule out because apparently he'd had detention the day Ruthy went missing, and then work, though, trust and believe, I would have liked nothing better than to put my foot in his neck.

There was nothing wrong really with Mr. Hernandez. He'd never done anything foul to me when I was in his Language Arts class. Ruthy had never complained about him. And actually he knew my mom from way back in the seventies when they'd attended the same high school in the Bronx. But past experience had taught me that familiarity and kindness meant nothing.

And I recalled how once, before I graduated middle school, I went upstairs to his classroom to say bye, but the door was closed. I could tell Hernandez was in there, though, because I heard shuffling and the door had a very small window; I stood on my tiptoes to see through it. And there was Hernandez sitting with Gina Russo from homeroom, a very quiet, good girl, who'd speed-walk from one period to the next, clutching her messenger bag against her stomach for dear life with her head down as she dodged the attention of other kids. Everybody teased Gina because there was a peeling patch of eczema growing on her neck that would redden anytime she was nervous. And once, stupid Joey Henson left a bottle of Head & Shoulders on her desk.

Hernandez—and I had to make sure I saw it correctly—had his hand on her shoulder. And instead of cowering or crying or twitching nervously, Gina was glowing, just happy. Really happy. And I felt a smile form on my face. I'd never seen Gina like that before.

But that hand on the shoulder reminded me of how Hernandez liked to hover over you while you were doing your work, and sometimes bend his face close to yours to give feedback. What could he be saying to her? And why was the door closed? The possibilities multiplied like a virus in front of me. And I wanted to warn Gina to get the fuck out of there. But then I heard Hernandez walking to the door, and I was too much of a punk to say anything. So I ran away instead.

Not this time, though.

Here, now, he sat at the bus stop, reading the *Post*. I'd brought a switchblade I'd taken from Lou's book bag without asking, and I was handling it in my pocket. That morning I'd practiced opening the

149

blade quickly, because the lever was heavy, and it still scared me every time it sprang up.

I had brought the knife to protect me, but standing there watching him read the *Post*, feeling the cold indifference of the metal in my pocket, it became clear how simple it would be to hurt him, really hurt him, and nobody would ever suspect that the culprit was a little girl.

But then he saw me first, jerking his head back from the paper. "Jessica?"

I didn't say anything. I just stood there breathing through my mouth, unable to get in enough air. I felt like I'd been caught. How sad and small I must have looked.

"Oh, Jessica, I heard about Ruthy."

I gripped each strap of my book bag tighter, still unable to move.

"Come. Sit down," he said.

And for some reason I listened. The metal arm on the bench was cold between us.

"How is your mother? How are you?"

That simple question made me want to cry. How stupid could I be? Hernandez had done nothing to Ruthy, had done nothing to Gina, and nothing to me. What was I doing here? And how could I be so wrong?

"Oh, Jessica, I am so sorry."

His bus pulled up just then and he put a hand on my shoulder and squeezed. The departing passengers lowered themselves out of the S48.

"Are you going to be okay?" he said, looking at me and then the driver.

Was I?

I nodded.

"Tell your mother to call me, okay? And you should come back to the school tomorrow. We can talk."

The driver, now irritated, shouted, "You coming or what?"

Hernandez patted my shoulder again. "Tomorrow," he said, and pointed at me.

I nodded, even though I knew that I would never return to see him. It felt silly now, my efforts to find out what happened to Ruthy, because really what I always ended up thinking about was what happened to me, instead.

CHAPTER 13

Nina

In the store window half-naked mannequins wrapped in ropes of light were bent over, posing in the darkness. Savarino was changing the display for Christmas, her red hair arching fiercely away from her head like a flame as she pinned a Santa hat to one of the mannequins' wigs. On the bus ride to work I'd practiced how I was going to ask for the weekend off, but when I got to Mariposa's my stomach twisted in uncertainty. They'd raised the heat up in the mall and I felt dizzy from the warmth after having sat in a cold bus for so long. My skin prickled at the collar, itchy and hot. Savarino was looking away from the door. So I tried to hurry into the store without her seeing me.

No luck. She turned around, clenching a safety pin between her teeth, then said, "You're late."

And I said, "Actually, I'm one minute early."

And Savarino said, "But by the time you get to the cashier and clock in, Nina, you'll be late."

Really employee-empowering, that lady.

Rather than wait to have to engage in a conversation with her again, I asked her for the weekend off right there. It was a family emergency, I told her. Unavoidable.

Savarino looked down at me from her ladder with both eyebrows raised. "Nobody gets Black Friday off, Nina. Especially not somebody who just started a few months ago."

"I have to," I said. "My sister's sick." But the word *sick* did not feel heavy enough of an excuse. "It's—I mean *they*, the doctors, think that it's cancer."

The stink of my unconvincing lie hung in the air between us like rotting fruit and Savarino smelled it right away. "I got Christmas around the corner, Nina, and corporate breathing down my neck. We need all the girls on the floor." Then she hopped down from the platform and said, "But whatever. You go, then. I can't guarantee you'll have a job when you get *back*. But hey, you do what you got to do."

The threat was not to be taken lightly.

If Savarino didn't fire you, she'd find ways to make you quit, like she had to my only friend in the store, Meghan, a fifty-six-year-old Irish woman. A real professional, she'd worked as a salesgirl for thirty-five years.

One day I walked into the store and looked around the back section they usually put Meghan in, but she was gone. Instead, the room was empty. There were the usual black-and-white pictures of women modeling lingerie displayed on the pink walls, stretching their arms in bed or standing with one hip popped to the side. But there were no traces of Meghan left in the store, nothing that would indicate she ever existed, though she'd worked at Mariposa's for thirteen years.

"Where's Meghan?" I had asked.

"She quit," Savarino said, punching a tag loudly into one of the new midrise lace maternity briefs.

And I wondered why they called it quitting when saleswomen left their jobs and how when doctors or teachers or businessmen left, they called it retiring. It was a small thought. So thin and tiny that

I'd forgotten it by the time I started fumbling with the computer at the register to clock in.

"Move, Ramirez," Savarino called out from the window. "There's a whole box of panties in the fitting room that need to be folded."

"Yeah, yeah," I said.

The sucia section was a mess. One group of customers had flung a drawer of underwear everywhere as they looked for their sizes. That week there was a free cotton panty coupon that had come out in the Sunday section of the *Advance*. But most of the customers had not read its fine print, which clearly designated that the panty had to be cotton and white. At least five times that night, I had to argue with them, and at least five times a customer ended up telling me that I was incompetent and dumb. What I wanted to say was *Bitch, you're the one over here looking stupid begging for free panties.*

Later, at the front register Savarino was with one of the other salesgirls motioning grandly to this old Puerto Rican woman, unnecessarily stretching out each syllable in her kindergarten Spanish, "Un mi-nu-to." Then she shouted out to me. "Ramirez, can you come over here for a second? I need someone who can speak Spanish."

My heart crashed into my stomach, and a whole series of expletives burst like fireworks inside of my head. On my way to the register I tried to conjure every Spanish word I ever knew and string them together into something coherent.

The old woman had emptied her purse on the counter—a package of cough drops, a key chain, and a wallet—while looking for a receipt. In her hand she held a bra.

Quick, Nina, goddammit, think.

Perhaps Savarino was trying to figure out if the customer wanted to return the item or exchange it. But if so, how do you say *exchange* in Spanish? *Regresar* is for return? I thought, I'll ask her what she needs. Let her *talk* first. But seeing me, the customer sighed with relief and right away started talking quickly in Spanish.

I could feel Savarino watching me from the corners of her eyes, ready to pounce, and the words misshapen and soft like mud in my mouth. I smiled at the woman. "¿Con qué puedo"—*How the fuck do you say* help?—"ayudarte?"

Then the lady looked at me as if I were some type of charming but silly breed of barking dog.

Oh, that Old Puerto Rican judgment!

Yes, I have failed you, I wanted to say. *I am an imposter. I wish I weren't. Do you think I want to be this way?*

It is not my fault.

Please do not tell this white woman I cannot speak Spanish.

My job depends on it. Remember? Solidarity!

I value my culture and language, I promise, miss.

Uh-huh, yeah, I grew up in Staten Island. No, I did not forget, and I am not ashamed that my family is from Puerto Rico. I love Puerto Rico. (Although I've only been there twice. The first time I was a small, fat, unintelligent baby. So I can't remember it!)

Yes, my mom speaks Spanish fluently. My dad did, too, but he could not read it. My mother was seventeen when she started having kids. Sorry, they were so busy working hard, they didn't have any time to consider the logistics of language acquisition. In fact, my mother did not have the words language acquisition *in her vocabulary. My parents had no idea that language could disappear.*

No, I did not want to be assimilated! I already explained that to you. That was not my choice. Trust me, I don't like white people, either! I don't want to be like them. You think I want to be like this Savarino woman? She's awful!

Whatever. Okay, fine. You win.

I am a colonized subject.

Who cares?

In my dreams I say all of this in English and the woman understands.

In my dreams I say, *I can't speak Spanish*, in Spanish, and the woman understands.

In reality, she smiled gently at me and lifted the bra up for me to inspect.

"This," she said, "no good."

She placed my hand on the cup. It was one of the push-up bras. And with her hand over mine, she squeezed. And I could feel where the gel had separated and somehow broken down into strange pebble-like clumps. She was not asking for a refund. *She is not asking for a larger or smaller cup, Savarino.* She wanted a new bra in the same size because the cup was damaged.

But before I could explain this to the cashier, someone behind me said, "You don't really know how to speak Spanish, do you, sweetheart?"

I turned around, and it was Alexis, punching security tags into a stack of miracle bras with her orange talons. She had just begun her shift.

She abandoned the pile now, grinning at the Puerto Rican woman. And I wish I could say that Alexis's Spanish sucked, that the accent was awful and misplaced. But the girl spoke it beautifully. As she finished with the customer, I tried to escape to the back, to the fitting room, to hide behind a rack of discarded lingerie. There I spent the last hour of my shift hanging up bras and unlocking fitting rooms, prolonging my conversations with the customers as I helped measure their bra sizes. "Oh, so you just had a baby! How wonderful! What's his name?" Or "Yes, this bra takes off at least five pounds. More reliable than any diet. Ha, ha. Worth every single cent, I tell you." Even though I didn't own not even one single Mariposa's bra.

Still, I felt the shame prickling against my skin. When there were no customers trying on clothes, I sprayed the fitting room with our fifteen-dollar sour green apple body perfume. Gagging. Wiped the mirrors down with Windex. And dodged Savarino's gaze when she came back to return the rejected lingerie to the store floor.

But it was no use.

On my way out that night, Savarino stopped me and said, "Ramirez, after you take that vacation, don't think about coming back."

CHAPTER 14

Dolores

My daughters—Dear Lord, forgive me for saying it—good-looking girls, but not too smart, if they think I don't know what they're doing. This one over the phone saying, "Oh, Ma, we're just hanging out over here for the night," believes she is the only one in the world who knows how to use a computer. But I took a class last year in the library, so I know what's up. And Nina will never admit it, but the other day I had to teach her how to make a formula in Excel. You should have seen her face when I got all the numbers in the column to add up, Dear Lord. She didn't see that coming.

This morning I wake up and find that she's left her sneakers in the middle of the living room and a half cup of coffee right next to the TV. The exhaust fan in the bathroom was still humming and I had to turn the light off. She left footprints of water all over the floor and her pajamas twisted under the toilet.

Chacho, I was so mad I started talking to myself—"Do I look like Con Edison to you?"—washing away the blobs of toothpaste she left inside the sink. This girl could not even stop herself from wasting an expensive tube of Sensodyne.

So, I cleaned the coffee cup. I picked up her sneakers. Then there I was, Dear Lord, just going about my business, getting ready to put on my DVD for my morning physical exercise and prayer, when I almost tripped over Nina's laptop because she left it open in the middle of the carpet. So, I picked it up, very carefully, just to put it away, and what do I see?

Some porquería that at first looked like pornography. There are these girls lying in bed with each other, half-dressed. And I'm thinking, Oh my god. What has Nina gotten herself into? (I wasn't snooping, Dear Lord, I promise. I would never do that. I was just concerned.) I kept on reading until I realized it was just a web page for a television program. *Catfight*. I scrolled farther down and there it was. A picture of Ruthy, my Ruthy, twelve years older. A grown woman but looking like a clown. And I'm thinking, Why would they not show this to me?

I am the mother.

So, immediately, I sit down and dial Irene.

And she picks up the phone with an "Mm-hmm."

"¿Estás en la casa?"

"Yes, but I have a doctor appointment. For my blood pressure. God, the headaches I've been having, you wouldn't believe it."

"Irene, listen. They found her."

"¿Quién?"

"Ruthy. They found her."

"No me diga. Is she okay?"

Then it took me about fifteen minutes to walk her through finding the same web page on the internet.

"Type *channel eleven*, slash, *catfight*, dot, *com*," I told her.

"I did! I did!" she insisted. "Pero, all I get is error."

She sent me a picture of the URL that she typed.

"Forward slash," I said. "Forward!"

"Where's the forward slash?"

When she finally found it, she gasped. "Ay, Dolores," she said.

And I knew what she was thinking.

What could have happened to my Ruthy that she would be on the TV looking like this?

Just the other day we had driven out to Forest Avenue to the movies and saw a trailer for *Taken*. So I knew she was remembering Liam Neeson, that part where he's talking on the phone to his daughter's kidnappers, with his Irish accent, threatening to hunt them down.

Automatically, just from the trailer, I knew I was going to hate that movie.

It had been over a decade, and I still hadn't found my daughter. Movies like that were just cartoons, fairy tales that gave you hope that life could be some other type of way.

But now, here Ruthy was, staring at me from Nina's banged-up laptop. I clicked on one of the website's videos. At one point, at the end of an episode, they zoomed in on her sleeping face.

Until next time, the show said.

At night, I returned the computer to the floor in its original spot and turned off the light. I went to the bathroom and washed the makeup off my face, wiped the bathroom sink down, and prayed for wisdom and patience and strength as I checked the front door to make sure it was locked. In bed, something fluttered inside me, a feeling I didn't immediately recognize. It had been so long since it lifted inside my chest, like the room had been closed off and dark for years and suddenly somebody had decided to open a window.

CHAPTER 15

Jessica

Once, I dreamed I was barefoot chasing a dog down a hill of mud and metal into somebody else's house, where I found Ruthy sitting there, waiting for me on a couch, looking through a shoebox full of folded paper. In my dream she was still thirteen years old. And she'd knotted her long red ponytail into a bun.

"What is that?" I asked her.

She lifted the box and said, "These are all the letters you have sent me."

Except her voice did not sound like hers because it sounded like mine instead. She stood up to wipe a kitchen counter in wide, quick arcs.

"Shush," she whispered. "Keep quiet or else they'll hear you."

Another time, I dreamed we were all grown up. She was a mother and had a family, and we were in the mall shopping for the holiday. Her laughter felt so real that when I woke up for a second, I looked for her in the morning, before I realized she was gone.

Now, the thought of seeing Ruthy squirmed inside my stomach.

The baby screeched as Lou tried to pick her up. She flapped a red fist against his chest as if she was telling him to shut up.

"Just pass her to me, Lou. You're doing it wrong," I told him.

Then he made a show of saying, "No, no, I got her. You're tired."

But when I reached for Julie, he readily put her in my arms.

Maybe Ruthy did not want us in her life at all. If she was still alive, then why hadn't she contacted us? Why hadn't she called the police? Maybe she *had* run away, like Nina had always insisted. Had gotten tired of us and wanted something more. In a week, we would finally find out.

At work, a new patient had been admitted into room 244.

"Old bitch is frightening," Carlos said in the break room. "A fucking bruja, man." He was banging the vending machine to try to get it to give him two canisters of Pringles. "She cursed me out in Spanish for no reason."

Which was doubtful.

There was always a reason with Carlos.

"That's because you don't know how to talk to people," I said. "Also, Karen sees you banging that machine, that's it for you. It's a wrap, kid."

Carlos dismissively flicked one hand in my direction and kept on hitting. "You think I'm scared of Karen? I'm not scared of Karen. Karen does not scare me," he said. "Anyways, that old bruja, she don't like Allen's ass, either. Yo, Allen, tell Jessica what happened." He turned back to me. "She stuck her skinny old gray tongue out at him."

Allen was wearing headphones and nodding his head to music at the table next to us but perked up when he heard his name.

"What happened?" he asked, taking off the headphones.

Carlos ignored the question and just pointed at him. "Even though he got that pretty-ass ponytail."

"Man, shut the fuck up," Allen said.

Carlos pulled his arm back to bang the machine one more time, just as Karen opened the door. He paused, his fist frozen in the air.

Then Karen? She nodded silently at Carlos like he was her stepson and she was about to take out the belt. Carlos dropped his hand to the side and looked down at the peeling green tile floor.

"You've got five more minutes for break," she told the boys. Then she turned to me and said, "Jess, from now on, you take care of room two forty-four."

"Of course," I said.

Because I liked Karen.

But secretly I was kind of pissed off—now, in addition to Mrs. Ruben, I was going to have to work with this other difficult patient. It seemed that they were assigning me all of the mean old women on the floor. Which I guess is the thanks you get when you're doing your job correctly. Your bosses wind up giving you twice as much the work. I just hoped that at the end of the day when I asked for the weekend off, Karen would remember that. And I told myself, if I wanted to actually become a nurse, I'd have to learn how to manage those long workdays, the twelve-hour shifts. Karen was preparing me for a new life.

Room 244's real name was Virginia. But in Spanish you pronounced it like *Veheenya*. She was this old Puerto Rican woman in her seventies with little to no English, so Karen sent me in there to say good morning, ask her questions, take her vitals.

When I walked into the room, the lights were turned down, and Virginia was lying on her side with her back to me, a small, pale blue lump in the bed.

She turned over slowly and struggled to make me out. Wisps of gray hair had refused to fall off her scalp, despite the chemo. In the corner I saw that she had set up an altar for Saint Lazarus, one of the few santos I could remember, only because he always terrified me. His legs were pocked with red and brown sores, and he was skeletal and dressed in rags, leaning on a cane. San Lázaro, also known as Babalú-Ayé, was the orisha you prayed to when you were sick or when somebody you loved was dying.

"Aha?" Virginia said.

She had breast cancer and was on a type of chemo here that they called Red Devil, which was exactly everything you might imagine it to be. It strips away all the insides of your mouth. And no matter how hard she tried, Virginia couldn't fall asleep for more than twenty minutes at a time, she told me as I held her wrist and listened for the blood pressure—that faint knocking.

"Gracias, mi amor," she said when I stood up from the bed.

And as I left, I noticed the glass of water she kept on the floor next to the door. If one of the nurses saw it, they would surely move it away. In my grandmother's house in Puerto Rico, she'd always kept a glass just like that—full of water at the front door to prevent evil from entering. So I pushed the glass farther into the corner, to a less noticeable spot.

When I walked back into the break room, Allen and Carlos were still there, and Allen was pacing in front of the vending machines talking to himself, emphasizing each syllable, while counting on his fingers: "*To-day Miss-us Ru-ben*...Damn." He shook his head. "That's six."

"What's he doing?" I asked Carlos, who was eating a lunch of the purple Takis.

"That dumbass. He's got to write one haiku a day for his English class." Carlos leaned too far back in his chair and almost fell.

"Stop playing. This shit is hard, man," Allen said.

Carlos laughed. "Yeah, motherfucker, 'cause you gotta count and spell at the same time."

By the end of the day, Karen had demoted Carlos and Allen to bedsheet and pan duty. It was not a passive-aggressive move. It was an aggressive-aggressive move. "Think they could show up to work and not do shit. Like I don't got a child that's about to drop out of my vagina, and I got to be here and picking up after them, like they're one of my damn kids," she said to me once.

The boys were not happy. They were all like, "Naw, it's your turn, motherfucker."

"Last time the old woman tried to bite me," Carlos said. "Because she's racist. She'll like you, though, Allen, because you're as white as Parmalat milk."

Then the conversation shifted into talk about which movie they would rather die in: *Poltergeist* or *A Nightmare on Elm Street*?

"*Poltergeist*," Carlos said. "One hundred percent. I don't fuck with Freddy Krueger. That asshole sneaks into your dreams."

"What about you, Jessica?" Carlos threw an M&M at me.

"I don't even know why youse are talking about *Poltergeist*. Nobody in that movie dies, except in real life. The actors."

"Oh shit, she's right, though," Allen said, letting the legs of the chair he was leaning backwards in slam down on the floor. "The little girl. The blond one. Her heart stopped or something. The older one, too, though."

"What happened to the older one?" Carlos asked.

"Her boyfriend," I said. "He killed her."

"Oh snap!" Carlos stood up with the bag of Takis in one hand, pointing at me with the other. "That's right. That's why she don't show up at all in *Poltergeist II*. Like they don't ever bother to explain it, either."

"Woooooow," Allen said. "That's some crazy shit."

I stood up and threw out the wrapper of a chalky-ass meal-replacement bar I had been eating to lose the baby weight. I told them, "No, it's not. It happens all the time." Then I made my way to the next patient.

"So, you don't think Ruthy had a boyfriend?" Lou asked. He was always thinking Ruthy had a boyfriend.

We were lugging groceries up the outside stairs to the house.

"No, I don't think so. Ma had pretty much of a tight control over her. And she always hung out with the same annoying three girls. Yesenia, Tenaja, and this girl Angela Cruz."

In her diary their crew was forever plotting some type of prank or internal coup to unseat whoever'd ascended to queen bee of their group that week.

Ruthy was never queen bee.

Ruthy was always muscle.

She seemed to understand and accept that. In her diary entries she never tried to be anything else.

"Maybe she was talking to someone, and you didn't realize it," Lou said.

"Nah, I would've known. I would've seen it."

Still, the boys' conversation about *Poltergeist* left me walking around all day feeling like I'd grown an extra shadow, and Lou heard it in my voice.

"Come on, Jess. How much shit were you able to hide from your moms, growing up?"

"Trust me, I would have known."

This I said too loudly, and Lou got quiet.

As an apology I touched his back as he bent into the fridge to shove a cold slab of chicken onto a shelf. Sometimes still I could feel this anger surface whenever I talked about Ruthy, and I felt bad. Lou didn't deserve it. But for so much of my life, I felt like I was defending my family against other people's opinions. All those nosy-ass folks who tried to get in our business, as if we were some type of *Unsolved Mystery* they could click on and turn off when it was time for dinner.

About three months after Ruthy disappeared, I remember the guidance counselor, Mrs. Burke, pulling me out of tenth-grade math. When she saw me look around, confused, she added, "You're not in trouble at all, sweetheart. Come."

She was humming as we walked to the office, jiggling the keys that hung around her wrist, so I thought I had done something good or was about to receive some special award.

This I explained to Lou. "I mean, don't get me wrong. I knew I wasn't getting Student of the Month anytime soon."

But you know, I thought that maybe the guidance counselor had noticed how I'd started helping Elena Diaz carry her books upstairs when her cerebral palsy got so bad she had to use crutches. I was the girl who defused the fight, or made someone feel better when they heard their crush telling their best friend, "Eww, she's ugly."

I wasn't going to be salutatorian—so what? The point is that I was kind.

Maybe this was some type of Good Citizen of the Year award.

When I walked into the office, Mrs. Burke was all like, "Come in, Jessica. Sit down."

I lowered myself onto the crummy teal couch in her office. At least I was escaping Algebra.

Burke had a habit of buying her Conflict Resolution students pizza, so you know my fifteen-year-old ass had also secretly been hoping there were going to be a couple of boxes of Domino's on her desk when I walked into the room.

But nothing. Her desk was bare except for a rotating fan that made a stack of pages flutter next to her phone every time it turned in that direction.

"So, Jessica, how are you?" Burke mechanically tilted and nodded her head as she spoke.

For some reason, guidance counselors always reminded me of robots, as if they'd downloaded their gestures from a manual.

"How are things going?" The way Burke pronounced the word *things* slowly, I knew that the only reason she brought me into that office was to talk about Ruthy.

"Good," I said.

Ruthy's disappearance had helped me create my own robotic

responses to adults. I'd gotten tired of well-intentioned people asking me about my little sister, of having to artificially smile back at them so that they felt good about themselves.

I didn't want to hear another teacher's prying questions.

"Everything good at home?" Burke asked.

"Very good."

I was fifteen and could spot adult bullshit a mile away. Just that week, there had been some detectives who'd come around and basically insinuated that our family was dysfunctional. They had asked the type of questions that would suggest that maybe Ruthy ran away because our home life was fucked up. And one time when the detectives asked me and Nina what our relationship was like with our parents ("Your dad?") I put my hand in front of me before Nina could blurt out some stupid shit. Then I told them both to go fuck themselves. It had bothered me that they spent more time asking us questions about our family, as if our parents were somehow at fault, than actually really investigating what happened to Ruthy.

I was ready for Burke even though she was sitting there looking innocent with her legs crossed and her thick shoulder pads. I knew what to say.

"You know what? To be honest, I have been pretty sad."

I wouldn't give her any tears, though. Instead I asked, "Do you think we could order some pizza?"

And she did. Two liters of Coke, too.

Lou started to laugh when I told him that story. "Your sneaky ass. And those teachers thought you and me were dumb."

After my shift, I sat down with Virginia for five minutes to watch *Mariana de la noche*, though there's probably very few things I hate more in life than a novela: the melodrama, the ghosts, the psychics, the stupid weddings and mariachi bands at the end.

This particular novela was unbearable: white-ass Mariana weeping while men secretly leered at her from another room. The voice-over: "Una mujer vestida de sombras." A woman from the village runs up to her screaming in Spanish, after her third boo dies in a car crash, "You are cursed, Mariana. You are cursed!"

There were generations of women who grew up watching these stories and loving them, my moms included. And always in the shows, the woman played a victim, a martyr. The more defenseless the heroine was, the more she was loved. The wailing, the dishes crashing on the floor. The mothers and grandmothers and daughters constantly crying to each other over the same bullshit. I couldn't stand it.

There have been things that have happened to me, too, terrible things, but I don't talk about them.

And I never will.

That night I thought about Virginia.

"I feel bad for her, Lou," I said, stroking the side of his face.

He was trying to fall asleep, but I wouldn't let him. "She has no visitors. Like nobody comes to see her. At all. And the thing is, if you don't have family coming to look after you, the doctors and the nurses and the PCTs, they all start to treat you different. They pay less attention to you, Lou, you know?"

I was sitting up in bed, and he was falling asleep next to my hip, tickling my skin with his breath. His eyes were closed, so I flicked his cheek. "You listening?"

Lou nodded.

"And I'm not dumb. I saw that shit. Like one of the doctors, his mother was checked in as a patient, and everybody was fucking scrambling to make sure the woman got her meds on time, that she was comfortable, that she got everything she needed. The nurses came to check in on her around the clock. The PCTs double-checked the numbers over and over again and stayed kissing her ass. And I'm sitting there like: Are you for fucking real right now?

"I don't play that shit, though," I said. "Trust and believe. I don't care how much money you have or who's your fucking mother, or what school you went to, I treat everybody the same, no matter what."

"That's very nice of you," Lou said.

And then he yawned.

"You're drooling on my hip. And you're not listening to me," I said. "People don't really talk about this, but hospitals, they got their own hierarchy, too, you know?"

There was a way of life, a world within the oncology unit, with its own little ecosystem—the residents who slept in the back and ran through the halls, the way you could smell their tired bodies every time they lifted their arms; the nurses who secretly ruled the unit; the socially awkward doctors.

PCTs, we were at the bottom of the food chain, but we knew the most about the patients. Every day we counted how many times they breathed within a minute. We measured their pulses. Checked their teeth for rot. Tested their urine. We listened to the sound of their blood moving through their bodies, the way that it knocks.

I looked down at Lou. He was stroking my knee absentmindedly, but his eyes were closed. The Department of Sanitation had given him a promotion, but it meant that he'd have to get up at four thirty in the morning to drive all the way to the Bronx to get there by six a.m.

I bent over and kissed him on the forehead.

"You're doing a good thing, baby," he said.

Then his hand stopped moving, and he was out.

Are you awake?

The text blinked on my cell phone. It was from my mother, and she had sent it at four in the morning.

The baby roared in the next room, and I waddled in the dark over to her crying body, picked her up, told her it was okay.

Part of me wondered what it would be like to be a kid again, to not have to work, to lie in bed all day, to simply open my mouth and scream. Surely somebody would run to my side and cradle me in the dark, whisper *It's okay my love*, over and over again into my ear, until I fell asleep.

I sat on the floor with my tit attached to her mouth, considering whether or not to answer my mother's text. A message in the middle of the night from my mom could mean several things that might draw me into an hour-and-a-half-long conversation, and I had high hopes that night for an extra two hours of sleep. Already the baby was starting to nod off.

Before I could even decide whether to call her, another text popped up on the screen.

Because I would like to call a family meeting.

Could you and Nina please come to the house at 10:30 am.
Please bring the baby since I have not seen her in four days.

Always with the guilt, that one.
I texted Nina:

What do you think this is about?

To which Nina answered, at eight in the morning:

It's Mom. She knows.

CHAPTER 16

Nina

A family meeting! Taped on the chinero was a piece of butcher paper outlining an agenda with several black bullet points, the first of which was: *My Daughters the Liars*. For the last item on the list, Mom had changed the marker to red and wrote in big letters: *Get Ruthy Back*.

It was ten thirty in the morning and Jessica was sitting on the love seat, bouncing one of her legs up and down in what I had trouble distinguishing as either anger or nerves. I squeezed in next to her. In the background, the TV was playing a rerun of *The Cosby Show*, the one where Theo tries to hide his pierced ear from his father by wearing a pair of headphones and pretending to listen to music. My mother sat across from us, holding the baby in one arm while sipping her coffee with her free hand. Next to her, for no explicable reason, sat Irene. The two of them like a king and queen delivering orders from the dining room table chairs they'd dragged into the living room, the seats covered in plastic. Me and Jessica—their unwitting and unwilling subjects.

"Why is Irene here?" I asked Ma.

This made Irene turn to me and raise an eyebrow as if I were the one who did not belong in the room, in this very personal meeting about my long-lost sister.

My mother was indignant. "That is my dear friend and my confidante," she said.

Me? I was merely some chimpanzee she adopted from the Staten Island Zoo.

"Ha," I said.

Apparently, unbeknownst to the both of us, Irene had somehow reached comadre status. While me and Jessica had been arguing about the details of Reality TV Ruthy's face, the two of them had been scheming over cafecito and prayer sessions at church.

My mother lifted a marker and declared, "Irene will be helping us find your sister. Now, have some respect, Nina, please, and sit down. I raised you both better than that."

The plastic-covered love seat squeaked as I lowered myself next to Jessica. And Irene grinned at us, looking like a Puerto Rican Cruella de Vil. Maybe if we stood quiet long enough and nodded our heads with sufficient enthusiasm, I told myself, maybe, just maybe, we could get my mother to back off or forget whatever plan she'd hatched with Irene.

That was stupid of me to hope, though. I should have known better.

My mom stood up in front of the poster board with the baby, who was cheesing in her arms. "All right, let's get started."

It turned out that Ma had gotten farther than we had, with Irene's help. Irene had found the Catfight Condo's address, with the assistance of an old librarian named Mr. Alvarez, who had been trying to impress his way into Irene's Fruit of the Looms since 2003. My mother had also done significant research on the other girls living in the house.

"The Indonesian punk girl from Florida," my mother said. "Irene found out that her name is not really Gem Stone."

"*No way!*" I said. "Irene should be a detective." Then I rolled my eyes until Jessica elbowed me and whispered to stop.

Gem's real name was Martha. And she was a rich girl pretending to be poor. As a teenager she'd run away from her family a total of fifteen times before she went to college and then found a way to run away from that, too.

McKayla, the blond sorority girl, was using her real name on the show, but she had never gone to college. Actually, she was from Manhattan, Kansas, even though she claimed she'd grown up in Alabama in her audition tape. The boarding school she'd said she'd attended was made up as well.

"Now, Ruby—" My mother lifted a sheet of paper and revealed several pictures of the Ruthy lookalike that she had cut up and taped to the wall, with captions, dates, and notes. "No mention of her family, at all. But *your brilliant mother* was able to find out that she lived in a group home for girls in Pennsylvania at one point, when she was sixteen. She worked at a strip club for a few years, before she was cast on the show," Ma said, pausing meaningfully after each sentence, which made me wince. "Her dream was to become a dancer."

There was something embarrassing about this that I couldn't quite put my finger on…it felt like my mother was rehearsing a scene from *Law & Order*, as if she were some type of private investigator. And for a moment I had to interrogate why I was so embarrassed by this, my mother acting as an authority. Could this be some type of internalized colonialism? Wasn't she, after all, the utmost authority on Ruthy? Didn't she literally make her?

When Julie cried, my mother put the baby's fists in her mouth and pretended to eat them. "*Nom, nom, nom, nom, nom.*"

Crazed, Julie shrieked with laughter, and my mother started to sing: *Qué linda manita que tiene bebé. Qué linda. Qué bella. Qué preciosa es.*

It was very endearing and very aggressive, this performance of motherhood. It seemed like my mother was trying to suggest that in her forty-four years on this rancid earth she had survived two generations of children, a crack epidemic, several recessions, the death of her husband, and three bouts of circular migration between New York City and PR. She was trying to remind us that she had lived longer than any of us; there was a reason why you could find the word *grand* in *grandmama*.

My sister stood up and said, "Why don't you just give me the baby, Ma?"

"She likes me better, Jessica. Sit down."

Then my mother lifted the large white sheet with the agenda to reveal another piece of butcher paper, which looked like a map or a football diagram of intricate plays; she'd drawn a complicated web of X's, arrows, and numbers, and then what looked like a complex math equation. It seemed she had already calculated how much it would cost for gas and one night in a motel room once we all reached Boston. Irene pushed her glasses up and tapped her upper lip with her pointer finger as she squinted at the math.

"All right. First things first," my mother said. She had spent the night figuring out how to drive to Boston, devising a plan to infiltrate the reality TV show, which included a haphazard mixture of white lies and many layered prayers to God. Underneath the plan she had also listed the numbers of several Christian self-help gurus and investigative news shows we could call for help. If she had the money, I knew that my mother would have hired a private investigator from one of the true-crime shows she watched, but alas, we were just some broke-ass Puerto Ricans.

I started to say something to protest, but Jessica raised her hand for me to be quiet.

"I got this, Nina."

I rolled my eyes. *Of course, Jessica, you take the lead. God forbid anybody else say anything before you do.*

175

"Ma. I think it would make a lot more sense if me and Nina just take care of this ourselves," Jessica said, putting on her best kindergarten-teacher voice. "We'll drive out there and call you when we arrive. I swear we will let you know everything that happens." And then, with the utmost emotion and sincerity, Jessica nodded slowly as if she were talking to one of her older patients. "We'll bring her home to you, Ma. We promise."

To which my mother rolled her eyes. "Bring her home! The two of you? No. You girls can't even take care of yourselves, let alone something like this. A daughter needs her mother," she said, passing the baby to Jessica. "Irene and I will be coming with you to get Ruthy. She'll remember me when she sees me." And then, as if she were quoting a proverb from the Bible, "A daughter always remembers her mother."

"Oh, Ma," I said. "Come on."

"You just leave it to your mother. I know what I'm doing," she said.

"And we have God on our side," Irene added, clapping her hands, apropos of nothing, before excusing herself because she had an important appointment at the church.

After several rounds of hugging and kissing each other's cheeks—"Que Dios te bendiga"—Irene finally left the apartment. And my mother went to the kitchen and started banging things on top of the counter. "¿Quieren más café?"

Jessica and I exchanged *What the fuck should we do?* glances in that silent sign language of siblings developed by decades of being fed, hugged, dressed, and beaten inside the same house. I shrugged and with a flick of my hand indicated, *This is all you, girl. I'm staying out of this.*

Jessica sighed and shook her head. I could see her calculating what to say next.

My mother called out again, "¿Ya comieron? You want eggs?" She turned the water on to clean a frying pan, while we started to mouth things quietly to each other to figure out what the hell we were going to do. When nobody answered Ma, she turned around with the frying pan and said, "Helloooooo, am I talking to the walls?"

Then Jessica just went for it. "I'm good, Ma. Listen—"

My mother moved around the kitchen as if she weren't listening, but you could tell that she was.

"I'm so tired of Irene. The way she sits there and judges everyone," Jess continued.

But my mother pretended not to hear her. "You want scrambled or fried, Nina?"

Irritated, Jessica stood up and made her way into the kitchen. "It's disgusting the way Irene judges people. I don't think that she should come with us."

I peeked at them from the living room.

"Disgusting?" My mother snorted, returning to the kitchen sink.

"Yeah, and then she just like pretends to pass out in church. It's embarrassing."

My mother turned away from the dishes, the water still running, and looked at Jessica and started to laugh. "The way *she* judges?"

A tower of bowls collapsed in the sink, splashing leftover soup everywhere. She turned off the water.

"Do you two girls know what happened to Irene when she was three years old?"

I did not know what happened to Irene when she was three years old. And I did not want to know, either.

"Huh?" my mother said. "Her father used to beat her mother when they lived in Cataño. One day the mother couldn't take it anymore, so she leaves, just gets up and leaves. But the thing is, she doesn't bring Irene. And Irene, you know, was a very, very difficult child. She could not stop crying."

I nodded and shrugged. I could imagine that.

"So, one day the father lifted an iron and burned her with it to make her stop." My mother fixed a stare at us. "Three years old," she said. "You girls, you think you've got it hard? That you had a bad life?" My mother started to laugh. "Oh, you have no idea, honey. No idea. So, if Irene decides to lie on the floor because she thinks she hears God, you leave her the fuck alone. Do you understand me, Jessica?"

Then, just as Jessica was about to say something, Ma lifted a finger at the both of us. "Respect."

Fine then, that was always how it was. That was the cue to leave it alone. To shut the fuck up. My mother, she started cracking eggs into a frying pan, though none of us were hungry.

A fight had happened; now it would be necessary for us to sit down and eat. It was my mom's way of emphasizing, *Here I am providing for you again. You have always been fed. You have always had a roof over your head. Why complain now? Look at what you have compared to the rest of the world.*

"We were not..." Jessica said quietly. She was staring at the edge of the table instead of at Ma. She was carrying the baby, who had fallen asleep and was drooling on her chest. She seemed to be holding her breath.

"Irene will be coming with us. I don't care what the two of you say," my mother said. "God knows, I need at least one real adult on this trip."

"We were not," Jessica said louder now, so that my mother could not ignore it.

She turned around and looked at Jessica. "Not what?"

"We were not spoiled." The word *spoiled* came out nastily from Jessica's mouth.

I flinched as my mother leaped towards Jessica the way she did when we would talk back and quickly smack us for daring to say anything opposite of what she said.

I saw Jessica flinch, too. An old habit.

But we were grown now. My mother seemed to realize this as she took in the sight of Jessica holding the baby. We were too grown to get hit that way. Still, my mother was fuming. Her face had grown puffy and was glistening from the heat of the stove. I thought I should do something to defuse the confrontation, but I felt like it was inevitable, this scene; it would play out no matter what I did. We were not that kind of family, the type who spoke politely to each other about where and how we were in pain.

"What was so bad that happened to you? Tell me what was so bad," my mother said.

"I don't want to talk about this now, Ma." Jessica started packing her shit up to leave.

"But you brought it up, no?" she asked. "So then speak. You're all brave now. You have something to say. So what was so bad, Jessica, huh? *Dímelo.* You had a roof over your head. You had food. You got to do your sports and your little extracurricular activities. Me and your father, we protected you from everything." Ma was counting on her fingers.

Everything! Meanwhile, my mother grew up poor, rotating back and forth between Puerto Rico, Brooklyn, and the Bronx, depending on where and when her father got work. Her own family had been evicted twice from their apartment. Twice! And had to beg some distant family member in the Bronx to take them in. For three months they slept on a cousin's living room floor, until the cousin's husband got fed up and asked them to leave. ("But what would you girls know about that? The two of you never missed a real meal in your whole life. Not one single meal. Jesus. Imagine.") And then when my mother's father disappeared, she had to get a job at thirteen to help her mother with the rent, take care of her little brothers when she got home from school. Cook, feed them. Clean the dishes, put the boys to sleep, while her mother worked nights. ("The little shits, where the fuck are they now? Both high somewhere, I promise you," she said. "They would steal from their own mother. They stole from *me.*")

And what was wrong with us? Her own daughters.

After all she had sacrificed, the long days at work, so that this one could have what? PIANO LESSONS. Fucking piano lessons! And braces, Dear Lord, braces.

"A quinceañera!" she said. "We paid three hundred dollars for someone to make you that dress. Three hundred dollars!" she said, pointing at me. "You looked so beautiful, Nina. Oh my god, I can still see it."

Ha! In most of my quinceañera pictures at Silver Lake Park I stood awkwardly holding my older cousin's hand, squinting at the camera, angular and boyish in what looked like a wedding dress from the eighties.

God, please, I thought, not the quinceañera. I hated the quinceañera. But of course, my mother had imposed all of her missed opportunities and broken dreams onto our lives, as if she were forcing the pieces of one old puzzle onto a completely different other one. As a child she had surmised that the only thing needed to change her life was money. And she would find a way to make it, no matter what. At thirteen years old, after getting her first job, she promised herself that she would never be poor again.

My mother scraped scrambled eggs from the pan onto our plates and slammed the dishes in front of us.

We did not even know how to show respect, she said. The most basic thing.

My mother was spitting, she was so angry.

I tried to cover my eggs and protect them from her saliva, because I knew now, it was unavoidable, that I would have to eat them. The only way to calm down my mother would be to very appreciatively swallow every single bite she made for us. To tell her that it was delicious. To tell her that her food was the best.

"Ma, I really loved the quinceañera," I said. "Thank you."

But Jess refused to play along. "I can't, Ma. Really, I can't with the

Betty Crocker act. Just stop. And for the record, you did not protect us from everything."

I was looking at Jessica now, like: *Oh god, please don't talk about Ruthy, Jess. It's already two p.m. Let's just hug Ma, kiss her goodbye, and talk shit in the car. You know how Ma gets. Ignore her. Just leave it the fuck alone.* I touched my sister's arm.

But it was too late.

My mother cocked her head to the side. "What the fuck did you just say?"

"I don't want to talk about this now, Ma," Jessica said, drawing out each word. Then she stood up, holding Julie with one arm. Jess slid the other underneath the strap of her purse, which kept slipping off her shoulder. "I have to get out of here. Lou's waiting for us at the house."

They had to take Julie for her first flu shot before it got too cold. The pediatrician insisted, she said. Last month, Julie had somehow gotten whooping cough, and Jessica said the sound of the baby struggling to breathe still sometimes haunted her dreams at night. Jessica was always having loud nightmares; when she called out in her sleep it would wake me up. Ever since she was a teenager, she'd have these dreams where she felt that she was awake, but her body was stuck. And in this state of paralysis she could feel something stalking her.

Normally, any mention of the baby, the baby's health, the baby's things, would have worked right away to stop even the most heated argument. The three of us always managed to put our differences aside for Julie.

But this time, no.

"What exactly is it that you're trying to say, Jessica?" Ma said.

Jess pretended like she didn't hear her and moved to the door. You could see Julie's face bubbling with emotion over her shoulder. Her circles of spit shining underneath the kitchen light.

My mother caught Jess's arm before she could open the door. "What? You tell me what. Now."

And in one quick and wild movement, Jessica turned around, her face vibrating with anger. "I was hurt. I was hurt, too, Ma!"

I had never seen Jessica talk to my mother like that.

Nobody, not once in our childhood, not even my father had ever talked to my mother like that—screaming. In my head, I was like, Oh shit, this is not looking pretty. My chest tightened and part of me thought I was going to laugh. Not because I thought it was funny but because I couldn't breathe. Without thinking I touched the pack of cigarettes in my pocket, while the baby screeched in her stupid weird language between the bodies of my mother and Jessica.

"You remember Mr. Alvin, next door, huh? *Oh no* you don't remember Mr. Alvin. Because you were too busy working, but *oh, leave us with Doña Miriam. She's from the church. You trust her,*" Jessica said, making her voice high and imitating Ma's accent. "Well, you shouldn't have."

And suddenly, I knew what she was about to say, as if I had always known, after all these years.

Because I *had* always known. Hadn't I?

"No," I said. "Jessica, don't."

The way I could hear Jess crying in the bed above me at night. The way I pretended not to hear it or see it. Alvin, Doña Miriam's son, always out of work and too old to be living with her. A thirty-five-year-old man! The time Doña Miriam drifted off to sleep in front of the television. And I sat there on the floor, a bowl of cereal between my legs, watching the cartoons hit each other over the head, over and over again.

Where had Jessica been all those times, while me and Ruthy sat on the floor with Doña Miriam snoring above us on the couch? I can't remember.

I was eating my favorite cereal. It turned the whole bowl of milk bright pink. The sugar ate right through one of my baby molars that year while I watched the cartoons chase each other off of various cliffs.

Pow!

The coyote fell into the canyon; his body exploded into a cloud of dust. Beep, beep, the Road Runner said.

I was so busy laughing. I could not stop.

My mother's mouth twisted open. Horrified. In recognition. Jessica did not even have to say another word.

"Yeah." Jess nodded her head.

Then something changed in my mother's face and it became like a rock. "That is not true, Jessica. Whatever you're saying right now is not true."

"It is true," Jess said in a very reasonable voice.

"It is not true. Alvin was already gone from the house before I let Miriam take care of you."

"No, he was there." Jessica could not stop nodding her head.

"He was not."

The baby started to cry, and Jess kept pushing the bobo in her mouth, and each time her lips would open to scream the pacifier would come right back out.

Then Jessica turned to me. "All right, let's ask Nina, then."

I was surprised to hear my name. Without even realizing it, I had backed away into the small hallway that connected to the living room. I had put my hands up.

"Nina, tell her," Jess said.

To admit that Mr. Alvin was in the house was to admit that I had known all the time what was happening to Jessica. Even if I had not known. There was a stink that had grown between us that summer. And somehow, I knew that it was connected to Mr. Alvin. I knew that whatever was happening was so terrifying and gross that Jess could not mention it to me, and I could not mention that I knew it was happening to her. And we grew up that way, knowing and not knowing all at once.

But now, all these years later, how could I admit that I had suspected what happened to Jessica but never told? And what did that silence say about me?

"You know he was there, Nina," Jessica said. "Tell the truth."

Both my mother and Jessica stood there looking at me, refusing to let out another word.

Until all I could do was lower my head and say, "Yes, Mami. Mr. Alvin was at Doña Miriam's house."

My mother's face was shaking. "You girls are lying to me!" she said.

But it was half-hearted. Afterwards, her whole demeanor crumbled.

"How could you have not told me?" my mother asked. She reached her arms out for Jessica. "Baby, how could you have not told me." My mother's voice was soft now. And I hated it, hated to hear her sound like she was begging.

"What was I supposed to say, Ma? How was I supposed to say that? I was fucking ten years old, Ma!" Jess was screaming now.

And my mother's voice continued to grow softer. "How could you have not told me? Oh, my baby, how could you have not told me?"

I watched as Jess's shoulders seized before she let my mother pull her into her arms. And then my sister gave in.

"It's okay, Ma," she said. "It's okay. Please, Ma. Things were good. You were right."

"I wish you would have told me. I would have fucking killed him. I would have dragged him out the house with my own hands."

"I shouldn't have said anything," Jess said, and now she was the one consoling my mother. "You were right. We had everything. We always had everything, Ma. We always lived good."

CHAPTER 17

Jessica

The last thing I wanted to do was debrief or answer questions, but there was Nina following me out the door, unnaturally polite, carrying the baby all the way down the stairs and buckling her into the car seat while Julie assaulted her face with the pacifier. Nina didn't have to help me in the car, but she did.

All of that kindness.

It was as if this new knowledge made us strangers.

I turned the car on, and she poked her head through the passenger window and tried to make a joke. "Never a boring moment in the Ramirez family, huh?"

"Don't do that, Nina."

"Do what?" she said.

"Don't do that shit where you try to be funny when something fucked up just happened. It's just like...it's just kind of annoying, you know?"

She nodded. Opened her mouth to speak. Then shut it. Then opened her mouth again. "You don't want to talk about it, Jess? 'Cause I mean, we can talk about it. I'm here."

"No, I don't want to talk about it, Nina."

And maybe there was something nasty in my voice that mocked her concern, but as soon as Nina flinched and looked down, I regretted it.

"Look, I'm good, I just want to get home. It's already late, and I'm tired."

Mostly, I just wanted for that part of me to disappear. I wanted to forget that little girl, the way she felt after those things at Doña Miriam's house. I wanted to never think about her again.

For so long, that was the way I operated. Not Lou, not my mother, not my sisters, nobody would know. And speaking it felt like I had betrayed that ten-year-old girl who thought if she sat still enough on the couch, nobody would call her into his dark room.

Standing outside the car, in the cold, Nina somehow looked distant to me. Nothing like this had ever happened to her. And I wanted to be that person so bad. Sometimes I dreamed of a type of alternate-universe Jessica; I dreamed of her being able to walk into certain rooms without something clenching in her body, twisting my heart. At the same time I couldn't stand the type of person who never had to experience what I did. And if I wasn't too careful, the jealousy could creep up in my throat like acid.

"We don't gotta talk about it," Nina said. "I just. I just wanted to say, I'm sorry. I wish I could have done something. I *should* have done something, but I was too small."

Which irritated me.

"It's not about you, Nina. None of this is about you," I said. "Go take care of Mom, all right? I shouldn't have said nothing anyway. I just want to concentrate on getting Ruthy."

"But I'm glad that you—"

"I don't want to talk about it, all right? I love you."

And then I drove back to the house, where Lou was lying on the couch watching TV.

"My ladies! They're back! I knew you guys were going to be late coming from your ma's. Tell me at least you called the doctor?"

He jumped up to his feet and turned on the light, took one look at my face, then said, "Jesus Christ, Jessica. What happened?"

And I told him.

CHAPTER 18

Nina

We got Lou to pretend he was sick so that he could call out from work on Black Friday to take care of the baby. Jessica put me in the front of the rental car with her to navigate, and Ma sat in the back with Irene. The two of them with their purses on their laps and their chins raised, offering feedback. "If I was you, I would not take Forest Avenue right now. We're about to hit rush hour," Irene said. And Jessica mumbling so that only I could hear it, "Well, you're not me. Are you?"

Already on the road we had to stop three times so that Ma could run into the gas station to pee and Irene could stretch her legs and buy a pack of cinnamon sugar-free gum. "Chacho, that bathroom. Sometimes women are just as disgusting as men."

The car we rented was large enough to comfortably hold all four of us and our luggage and, hypothetically speaking, Ruthy. If we could convince her to come back to us—though sitting there, the idea became more impossible by the second. What if when we arrived in Boston, Ruthy turned around and said: "Get the fuck away from me"? I cringed and repeated the scene over in my head so many times that this disaster seemed inevitable. I remembered when I was eight and Ruthy had looked at me indifferently when I asked to come with her to a party at a friend's house. Worse, I started to worry about how Ma would react once we saw her in real life. Would my mother start crying uncontrollably? Smack one of the cameramen in the head with her purse? Try to drag Ruthy into the car as if she were still in eighth grade?

I had always been afraid of my mother.

I had always been afraid of my mother making a scene.

Not only the way her emotions would swing from zero to ten at any given moment, but also and especially the way she overperformed being a mom. For so many years, it had felt like she was trying to overcompensate, for having kids so young or for growing up poor or for being Puerto Rican. She would repeat the same jokes from the American TV moms we watched that week on TGIF, the stories they told about their PTA meetings or shopping trips to department stores. She'd cite the Bible unnecessarily and in the next breath roll down her car window and scream at somebody trying to cut her in line, "Motherfucker, I dare you." God, all the times she'd embarrassed me in front of teachers. In sixth grade, in that dark green classroom at IS 61, when I'd failed English for the second time in a row, she told Mrs. D'Angelo, "I always tell Nina, 'If I hear a problem about you in school, I'll believe the teacher, not you.'" She made eye contact with me as she said it, then turned back to Mrs. D'Angelo and laughed.

I hated English, hated how the questions could be so ambiguous and unclear; you can look at what somebody wrote a hundred different types of ways. And there on the test, the first question, *What is the main idea of this passage?* But in my head, there were so many main ideas, and all of them burst forward like a star when I had to sit down for an exam.

Now, in the car, I turned to my mother and said calmly, "Ma, when we get there, just leave it to us, okay?"

Which annoyed Jessica.

"All right, Nina, relax," Jess said. "Don't come in this car barking out all these demands, like you paid for it."

The whole way up I-95, Jessica wouldn't give up the radio. She was an early-eighties baby, but like also super corny, so she loved to listen to a multitude of Light FM shit that drove me crazy: Vanessa Williams. Lionel Richie. And the entire drive to Boston we argued about whose right it was to change the station.

"It's a rental," I said.

"Yeah, but I'm the one who's fucking driving," Jessica argued, which earned us forty-five minutes of Marc Anthony, at my mother's request.

"To keep the peace," Ma said, passing us the CD.

Still, me and Jessica went on jabbing each other in between the chorus of "Hasta ayer." About if it was even a good idea to drive to Boston. About me not wanting to go because now I didn't even have a job. And do you know how hard it is to get a job, Jess? About it being harder for Jessica and what did I know about being a mom? (We stopped there for a moment to sing the end of the song with Marc Anthony, Irene, and my mother, *¡Eh, yo te quería tanto, mujer!*) Again, about me not wanting to go to Boston in the first place, that it was stupid, a stupid idea. About me not caring about Ruthy as much as Jessica did: "You're always so fucking selfish. That's your sister, your own flesh and blood, and you could not care less."

"Ya, enough, the two of you!" my mother shouted from the back, then pushed her head between our seats. "I AM THE ONE that cares for Ruthy the most. All right?"

This made Irene chuckle.

About Jessica always bossing people around just because she was the oldest. Ever since we were kids, everything had to be her way. About me not caring about anybody but myself. Exhibit A: the expensive room and board Ma had to take out a loan for when I could have just gone to a goddamn CUNY. "But nooo...make Ma pay eight thousand dollars to go to some stupid Richie Rich school." About Jessica thinking she was better than other people, just because she was the *oldest*. Ever since we were kids, the way everything had to be her way, even when we played whatever make-believe game—she always was the tyrant, forcing other people's Barbies to play the roles she wanted them to. About me thinking I was better than people just because I went to college: "Pues, look at that, Miss Big Shot folding panties now. Oh, wait, but that's right: you were fired. Ha!" She banged the steering wheel. "Can't even fucking sell lingerie." About Jessica being jealous. Jealous that she never finished college, couldn't even make it past that first semester, the College of Staten Island at that.

"Oh, and how, Nina? How was I supposed to continue going to college when I was the one helping Dad take care of—" And here she stopped short of saying *Mom*, because she remembered that Ma was in the car.

About me acting like a stuck-up little white girl who couldn't even speak good Spanish, not even the basic shit. And all that education good for what, Jess said nastily. "God, we go to a Mexican restaurant, and you order in English. So freaking embarrassing."

About Jessica being a stereotype, knocked up, not even married, barely got her GED. "At least I'm a real person," I said, even though I did not mean it. She had hurt me with that comment about acting like a white girl, and I needed to find something that would hurt her equally. In truth, there was nobody I admired more than my sister.

"Oh my god, Nina. You are so fucking corny. Do you ever realize how corny you are?" Jess banged the steering wheel. "A real person? What the fuck makes you realer than me? What makes you realer than me, Nina?"

"I got a life," I said. "I got *options*, bitch," I added for good measure.

"Call me a bitch one more time," Jessica said. "See what happens."

"Bitch."

"One more time, Nina, I dare you."

Now, the words *I dare you* were not to be taken lightly in my house. There were consequences if you took the dare, you see, but there were also consequences if you did not. As the youngest of the family, I'd earned the nickname *Punkin* when I was seven years old for *punking* out of jumping off the top bunk bed onto the floor. That nickname lasted a decade. Literally. I had to go to college to erase it.

So, I made my choice. And I'm not ashamed to say it. "Bitch," I muttered underneath my breath and looked out the window.

The heater pushed the plastic smell of new rental car at my face, and I braced myself for what might come.

"How 'bout you walk back I-95 by yourself? Then we'll see who's jealous of who, now that your ass don't got a car. Let's see how long it takes you to walk home, Nina."

"Go ahead," I told her.

"Okay."

"Go ahead." I even snapped my fingers next to her chin.

Jess shifted her face away. "Okay. I got you," she said.

My mother's and Irene's protests buzzed in the back, but all me and Jess could see or hear was each other.

"Why aren't you stopping, though?"

"Bitch, I am stopping. I'm stopping right the fuck here."

Jessica pulled over to the right shoulder of the highway, reached across my lap, and popped open the door. "Go ahead, Big Thing, Miss I Got Options. Walk the fuck home."

Which put me in a predicament, because I hadn't expected Jessica to actually pull over, and now, as the outside cold chilled the car, I didn't know what to do. I sat there for thirty seconds without a visible comeback in sight, which could only mean that Jessica would win the argument.

"*Vete*. Go."

"I am going. God." I unclicked the seat belt and let it zip violently back into the roof. "You're really something, you know?"

"Jessica, stop it! Now," my mother said, then started hitting us both in the arm with a rolled-up *Oprah* magazine. "What is wrong with the two of you? Jesus Christ."

"That's right," Jessica said to me while leaning away from Ma's swipes. "Now you know that I am *something*."

"Animal!" Irene shouted in the Spanish way, really stepping on that long *i*.

"*Really* something," I said, "leaving your sister by the road." I stepped out of the car.

And as Jessica pulled away, she turned up her Light FM station on the radio so that I could hear Patrick Swayze sing, *She's like the wind*.

Irene and my mother looked at me from the back window.

Do not move, my mother mouthed with a finger pointed in the air. *Stay right there.*

Irene was turned around, too, her raccoon eyes staring at me, and her little pinched mouth.

I stood there for a while, stunned by the cold, and waited.

For the car we'd rented to exit the highway, loop back around, and pull up along the shoulder of the road.

We found The Balloon Factory, a very long eight hours later, next to the Catfight Condo. It was already nine o'clock. Plastered on the telephone poles were flyers that read: BLACK FRIDAY SPECIAL: GROWN AND SEXY WOMEN FREE BEFORE TEN. A line of girls wrapped around the block, shivering in their short sequined dresses, waiting to enter the building. Every now and then the sidewalk vibrated with the sound of the bass blaring through the speakers inside the club.

I stood up out of the car to stretch. My legs were cramped from resting on top of Irene's suitcase. And I felt nauseous. There was so much perfume between all those girls waiting on line, it was like you could taste it inside your mouth, even in the cold.

"Okay, so what now?" I asked Jessica, as if she was in charge.

I was trying to make up for our fight in the car.

"Before we hit up the club, let's see if we can catch them coming out of their apartment building," Jessica said.

She was still wearing the bottoms of her green scrubs from work, and she looked wide and short and stout. There was something scraggly about her long curls clinging to her polyester shirt. The top of her tramp stamp peeked out from the waist of her pants as she bent over to tie her Keds. She was asking some of the people entering the building if they'd seen or heard of Ruthy/Ruby Ramirez, showing them a picture of our hypothetical Ruthy that she'd printed off the internet. Meanwhile, I snuck into the lobby and argued with the doorman—who looked like a Latino Orlando Bloom with black hair, elfin cheekbones, and a thin, perfectly manicured goatee—to let me go upstairs, for just one minute, please.

He clasped his fingers on the marble front desk. "Nobody has notified me that they were expecting company."

"You don't understand," I told him.

Then I hesitated.

The doorman couldn't be that much older than me, but I felt strangely intimidated by his good looks. Probably this kid was getting paid two times more than I was—shit, maybe three. Who knows? In New York, the folks who worked buildings like this in Manhattan got hundred-dollar bills for Christmas tips. An old girlfriend once told me that the management companies hiring for the buildings just wanted to make sure that you were the right type of minority, erased of any cultural tics that would cause discomfort to residents; and oh, the right candidate should be grateful, yes, so *always* grateful for the job... Look how beauty and subservience had so much more currency in this world than a bachelor's degree in biology.

I wanted to ask the doorman how he'd managed to find such a great fucking job.

"She's my sister," I said. "I'm here to surprise her."

"Uh. Okay." He didn't even look up from his computer.

"I'm serious, man. We're related."

But he waved me away and started talking to the woman behind me in some type of weird transatlantic accent. "Oh, Ms. Wagner, how smashing you look tonight." He nodded and pulled his lips into a neat smile, as if I had disappeared before him.

"Oh, yes, so smashing, Ms. Wagner," I said, imitating him.

Then once she was on the elevator and the doors slid shut, the doorman turned to me and said in a completely normal-ass accent, "You need to get the fuck out my building before I call the cops."

"Oh dear," I said with that same transatlantic flow. "What poor manners." Then I retreated outside, where it had started to snow.

Jessica was leaning against the car and shivering in her scrubs. Already she had helped herself to one of my cigarettes, but I didn't even feel like arguing about it.

"Dude in there is a self-hating Latino," I told her. "No way we're getting in."

Jess snorted and made some type of comment like *Look at the pot calling the kettle black*, but I pretended not to hear her.

"Let's just sit in the car. Sooner or later, she's going to have to either leave or enter the building. Then you all can go up to her," I said.

As we walked back to the car, my mother rolled down the window: "¿Qué fue? What happened? Did you talk to him?" She pointed at the doorman, who was clearly glaring at us through the glass door from his well-lit lobby.

I got back into the car. "Yeah, I talked to him. It's not going to work, Ma. He's being an asshole."

I leaned back into the seat and closed my eyes.

"Let me go over there. I'll explain it to him," my mother said.

She slid her purse onto her shoulder and zipped up her coat.

"It's not going to work, Ma. I'm telling you. And he's being mad disrespectful, too."

"Yeah, but sometimes, Nina, you don't know how to be nice and talk to people. You girls act like I never taught you manners," my mother said.

Still, she unzipped her coat and took her hand off the door handle.

She squinted into the dark.

For half an hour, we sat like that, watching the line shrink as one by one the girls disappeared into the club. Sometimes the wind whipped debris around the light of the streetlamp, or a plastic cup came rolling down the block to hit one of the girls in her heels. In the cold, they drew closer to each other, but none of them left the line.

What was worth that much time in the cold?

I couldn't remember the last time I stood on a line like that. I couldn't imagine waiting that long for some type of ambiguous fun.

"Enough of this," my mother said.

She unbuckled her seat belt. Wrapped her scarf around her head and stepped out of the car. Irene, who had been powdering her face, took a tiny bottle of lotion from her purse and rubbed it into her hands before wordlessly joining her outside.

"Can't go to the club looking ashy, huh, Irene?" I said.

Jessica looked up from her cell phone and rolled down the window. "Whoa, whoa, where are you guys going? Ma?"

My mother ignored her. Her attention was focused now on the long line of girls chattering in the snow. Only Irene turned around to wink and give us a little sarcastic wave.

"Fucking Irene, man," Jess said as she rolled up the window.

We got out of the car and followed them into the cold, but had the good sense to hang back. The wind made it hurt to breathe.

Somehow, they had already engaged with a group of young women standing in the back of the line. Irene was showing a picture of Ruthy to the girls, and they gasped, covering their mouths in surprise. Instantly, I understood the strategy. My ma knew what she and Irene looked like to those young, shivering women—one of their own mothers who could potentially be searching for them in the future. All of a sudden, now the girls were shocked out of the joy of being young and pretty and alive by the reminder that they, too, could at any moment go missing. They drunkenly hugged Irene and my mother. Carefully, they held their cigarettes as far away as possible from Ma's and Irene's faces as they pulled them into their arms with a sympathetic cry.

Listening to Ruthy's story, one of the girls even started to weep, her hand clutching her mouth in surprise. Old Irene joined her with the tears, as if she were auditioning for *María la del barrio*. And with her head held up high, my mother parted that line of girls as if she were Moses and their young bodies were the sea.

"Thank you. Oh, thank you so much. Mira que linda, look at that one," my mother said dramatically, clutching the breast of her peacoat, as another one of the girls let her move to the front.

"Be careful, though," Irene could not help but add, eyeing the length and stretchy fabric of one of the young women's skirts.

Me and Jessica watched them, stunned, as one by one these beautiful drunk girls let my mother and Irene skip in front of them until they reached the bouncer.

"Holy shit, I think they're actually going to get in," Jess said.

We went back to the car and let Ma and Irene work their brujería as we shivered, watching them with the window open.

The bouncer was a big dude, couldn't have been more than thirty-eight years old, and some type of Latino, with an extravagant mustache that looked like it belonged in the eighties. He flirted with Ma and Irene, asking for identification to check their age. And my mother flirted right back. Even though it was impossible to tell for sure from the car, I thought I could see her wink.

"Look at Ma, smiling like a little sixteen-year-old," Jess said.

"I mean, you got to admit it. She's still got it."

Ma's hair was still pitch black, and she had a way of curving one side of her mouth up slyly when she was amused with you. Growing up, I'd seen dudes unnecessarily hold doors for her. The rude ones whistled, then commented on the size of her ass and what they would like to do with it. It was gross, me and my sisters always thought. But now that I was older, I could see my mother more clearly for what she was: a beautiful woman.

After carefully looking at their IDs, the bouncer played a little game of being surprised by their ages. He looked down and then up and then down again.

"No way is this *you* in this picture." He chuckled. "Is this a fake? You're playing games."

Beside me, I could feel the heat Jessica's eyes generated as she rolled them. "All right, dude. Now you're doing too much. Just let them in," she said, shaking her head.

The three of them shared a laugh before he opened the door and sent Ma and Irene into the club, giving their shoulders a gentle pat.

Through the brief opening of the door, we could hear the crowd go wild as the DJ moved into another song. The windows were blacked out, so you couldn't see anything that was happening inside. But you could feel the music shaking the walls. It even felt like the sidewalk was moving.

This was our opportunity. Quickly, we scrambled out of the car and jogged up to the bouncer before he could welcome the next group of girls into the club.

"We're with them," we said, pointing to the closed door that Ma and Irene had disappeared behind.

A couple of girls in the line started to complain. One very

annoyingly dragged out the word "Heellloooo." Another shouted, "The line is back there."

"Bitch, shut up," Jessica said.

The bouncer was annoyed. He threw his head back as if he was literally disgusted.

"You just let in Dolores Ramirez. And the old woman, her name is Irene."

The bouncer sighed. "Hold up." Then he opened the door and shouted inside the building. "Ladies! They with you?"

It was Irene who poked her little head out from behind a green velvet curtain separating the outer door from the inside of the club. Looking like the Wizard of Oz; all you saw was her face.

"These two young ladies are yours?" the bouncer asked again.

Irene frowned. "Them?" she asked, as if she were confused. She raised that infamous eyebrow of hers to inspect our faces and shook her head. "No, sweetheart, sorry," she said to the bouncer. "I have never seen them in my life." Then she winked at us and disappeared again behind the curtain.

We stood over there for a second, frozen on that snowy sidewalk, dumbfounded about how Irene had just played us.

"She's lying," Jess said. "I know her!" Jess pushed past the bouncer and poked her head past the curtain. "You're a liar, Irene."

"I can't believe Ma let you come," I shouted over Jess's shoulder, right before the bouncer pulled us away by our elbows and directed us to the back of the line.

"All right, ladies. Nice try."

CHAPTER 19

Dolores

Already, the smell in that place, Dear Lord, I knew none of this was going to be good. All around us reeked of rotting cilantro—the walls and the slippery floor. The crowded bar. And the smell just hung in front of you like 102-degree weather. Poor Irene has asthma, so she had to spray the air in front of us with a free sample of Elizabeth Arden perfume to protect her lungs. "Ay, fo," she said, trying to wave the smell away with the palms of her hands.

I said to her, "At least, now that those two are gone, maybe we'll actually get something done."

"Blah, blah, blah. That's all they do, the two of them. It gives me a headache," Irene said.

By ourselves, already we had learned that Ruthy and her little friends always came to this club. This is what one of the girls had shared with us outside when we showed them the picture of Ruthy that we'd printed off the internet. They were fans, most of the girls, or wannabe *Catfight* cast members. They dreamed about being on TV and picking up nicknames that sounded like ice cream flavors. For what? I did not understand.

"Does that show pay you a lot of money?" I'd asked.

No, they said. These girls, they just wanted to be known.

The dance floor was packed and dark, and there was nothing happening on the stage.

"Ay, pero, maybe we missed it." Irene checked her watch.

Already it was 10:05 p.m.

And there was no sign there would be any type of performance, just a crowd of people bobbing up and down, not paying attention to who they were stomping on. Everywhere, nobody had any sense of personal space, except the bartenders, who danced around each other as a line of girls stuck their hands out over the bar, begging for a drink. ¡Qué lástima! How in a few years they'd realize they'd wasted their beauty on *this*. Standing on a line for thirty minutes, slow-roasting their insides with cheap menthol cigarettes. Drinking and jumping up and down in heels that would give them hammer toes in twenty years.

I took every chance to inspect each girl's face more closely, but in the dark they all looked the same. Any of them could have been Ruthy, and I prayed that any of them were. I had hope now, and I didn't care if she ran away from us on purpose, if she hated me, if she did not want to talk to me ever again, as long as she was alive. I would forgive her, Dear Lord, and I would ask for her forgiveness, too. In my pocket, I felt for a small gift I'd brought her, a Madonna medallion that she had always loved growing up, that I'd never let her touch because it had been my mother's. How stupid I was, thinking one thing more valuable than the other. You could have anything, Ruthy. Just come back.

Somehow, we got pushed up against the bar. And Irene kept raising her hand at the bartender as if she were trying to get the teacher's attention. "Excuse me! Hello."

The bartender grabbed a rag to dry his hands. "What can I get for you, ma'am?"

"Nothing," Irene said. "I don't drink. And neither should you."

Irene had sworn off liquor ever since her husband died of cirrhosis of the liver in 1992. Couldn't even stand to smell the stuff. If I opened up a wine cooler while we watched old episodes of *Cristina*, olvídate.

"Listen," she said to the bartender. "Do you know when these young ladies will be doing their dance performance?"

The bartender raised both his plucked eyebrows. "The dance performance?" The young man laughed.

And I love Irene, but she cannot stand to be laughed at. Chacho. She told that poor boy. "You know exactly what I am talking about. There's a performance scheduled TONIGHT at ten p.m." Then raised her pointer finger to pound on the bar but had second thoughts about it when she saw someone's blue drink spilling over the edge. So she grabbed a napkin and wiped up the spill instead.

"Here." I slid the bartender one of the promotional flyers the girls outside gave me.

He looked us up and down and laughed. "I wouldn't have pegged you two as part of the target demographic."

Livid, Irene turned to me and said out of the corner of her mouth, but loud enough for him to hear, "Is he talking to *me*?" Slowly, she got louder with each syllable. "Because his mouth is moving in my direction, but it does not sound like he is talking to me."

"Cálmate, mija," I said, trying to pull her away.

"Because if he WAS talking to ME, I would warn him to be very careful in how he addressed me. Tú sabes," she kept on.

"Come on. Déjalo eso. Let's go. I need to find a bathroom," I told her.

The bartender couldn't stop laughing. "Aw, I'm sorry, ladies. Come on, come back. I got a drink for you. I'll make you a couple of Old Fashioneds."

Irene turned around. "Me cago en tu madre," she said. "You hear me, young man . . . I shit on your mother."

Which only made the bartender's grin wider.

I pulled Irene away from his laughter. In the bathroom, there was a pool of piss from the hundreds of girls who apparently missed the toilet completely while they were crouching over the seat. And I had to have Irene stand on her tiptoes to hold the door with a piece of paper towel so I could pee.

The walls were decorated with dozens of hearts, hearts that looked like faces with arrows in them, hearts broken in half. And all the same old shit we used to write on the walls in the seventies. Above the toilet paper, scratched into peeling paint: *Kelly and Deandra Best Friends For Life 2006.*

And: *I hate fucking feeling this way.*

And: *Maria O'Sullivan's vagina stinks.*

On the door, the club had taped a piece of paper that said: *If you're in trouble and need someone to call the cops, order a Connecticut Punch. No questions asked.*

"I'm going to need a long shower after this," Irene kept saying over the door.

Beside us we heard the faintest sound of someone farting as they pissed.

"I don't know, maybe the show was canceled," I told Irene while we were washing our hands.

But then one of the girls in the bathroom, after hearing us speak in Spanish, turned around and said, "No te preocupes. This club is always like this." She flipped her long black curly hair. "They'll be like a half hour late, but you didn't miss anything."

She waved a tube of purple lipstick as she spoke, and I couldn't help feeling proud, even though she was not my daughter; such a beautiful girl, with good manners.

I sent a prayer up to God that she would get home safe.

CHAPTER 20

Jessica

I texted Lou.

> we've been standing on this fucked up line foreverrrrr. I feel like
> my cellulite is going to freeze off.

Inside my chest, my heart was pounding, though. And I could feel my fingers tremble from the thought of seeing Ruthy again. Every time the line moved, my stomach dropped.

Once we finally got to the front, we clutched our IDs with our numb fingers and lifted them up to the bouncer. In the cold you could smell the brown leather of his jacket.

"Well, here we are back again," I said.

He inspected the IDs as if he didn't recognize us. Snow fell on his cap and melted on the leather jacket as he bent over to squint at our cards with his fogged-up glasses. "All right, two of you ladies, that's going to be twenty dollars, ten for each of you."

Nina jerked her head back. "Twenty dollars! I thought this shit was free." She pointed to the marquee. "What happened to Grown and Sexy Ladies No Cover?"

The guy smirked and I thought to myself, Nina was really leaving herself open with that one. With her discount glasses, and me in my scrubs and week two of unwashed hair. I was expecting dude to turn around and say, "Exactly. Grown and *sexy*. That's *not you*, lady."

But instead he opened his arms and shrugged good-naturedly, lifting each chubby hand. "That was before ten p.m. We're almost at ten thirty."

"But you didn't charge those two girls in front of us, did you?" Nina asked.

"There's a grace period," he said.

He gestured for Nina to step aside and gazed behind us at the next clique of girls waiting to come in.

Nina snapped her head back into his field of vision. "So, we're not in your grace period, huh?"

And if I didn't move her stupid ass back in two seconds, it was going to get ugly. Ever since Nina went to college, she had the terrible habit of thinking everybody owed her something, like the universe had scammed her out of a larger life. Twenty-two years old and still acting like you're the baby of the family. I kept telling her, Nobody owes you shit, Nina. It is what it is.

The bouncer had his mouth open like he was about to go in on her.

"Sorry, my sister is just a little tired," I said, pushing her aside.

For a second, I considered telling him the whole story, but I was afraid he'd just think we were unstable instead of regular-ass pitiable. "We drove all the way from New York, and we've been waiting in the line for a while. You gotta understand. We're just tired."

He ticked his head to the side, confused, like why would anybody drive all the way from New York to come to *this* club?

"We came with my mother and her friend, who you let in. But we were here before ten o'clock, remember?"

Of course he did.

"That's right. *Before* ten o'clock," Nina repeated, like she was my hype man. "Ten o'clock." She pointed to an invisible watch on her wrist.

The man tugged his mustache and then shrugged. "Sorry, ladies. I don't make the rules. I just work here." He pointed to two girls laughing behind us. "If I let you in for free, I gotta let them in for free." He lifted his hand and pointed farther away at the endless line of women shivering down the block. "And then the ones behind them, too."

"Fine," I said.

I started digging in my purse for cash, through the tangled strips of receipts and empty gum wrappers, a pacifier coated in lint. But all I could find was a piece of chicle that had come unwrapped and was speckled with pieces of a broken cigarette. "Nina, you got twenty dollars?" I asked.

God forbid!

She made a big show shaking her head as if she had reason to be offended. "Why would I have twenty dollars? That's like three hours of work."

"Jesus Christ," I said, then stopped.

It was too cold to argue. And I felt a thread of muscle at the back of my neck seizing every time I trembled in my scrubs.

"I'm the one who just lost her job to go on this little excursion. You forgot that, Jess?"

Better to just reason with the bouncer. I asked him, "So, now we got to find an ATM, come back, and wait another twenty minutes on line?"

The bouncer huffed and adjusted his cap. "All right, just go in," he said, clearly exasperated by the thought of having to deal with our asses again.

"Thank you, thank you, thank you so much!" I could have kissed him.

He pressed the stamp hard on our hands, two black X's, and gently pulled the door open for us. A blast of music emanated from the darkness buzzing inside. Nina moved into the building and then pushed through the dusty green curtain hanging behind the door.

CHAPTER 21

Nina

The club was inside the basement of the building. And we could barely see the steps in the dark stairwell. A pair of girls behind us almost fell when one of their stilettos missed a step. Downstairs the whole space was packed tight with bodies rubbing up against each other. Pink and yellow fluorescent lights sliding against the crowd of faces. There were some dudes there, but mostly the club was full of young women—girls with their hands extended in the air, spinning while their girlfriends circled around them and cheered: "Okay, I see you!" Girls with their eyes closed and their mouths open as if they wanted to swallow the light. There were girls who couldn't dance for their life but were too drunk to care, switching their hips from side to side to a hidden rhythm bumping inside their heads. Then there were the girls who laughed at those girls who couldn't dance, while waiting for their boyfriends to call them. And there were girls so talented that every one of their gestures seemed to be composed of a litany of smaller movements, imperceptible from the next, that would be impossible ever to mimic or understand.

When I moved, I felt so painfully aware of every dragging second it took me to imitate a smile.

"I don't see them," Jess said.

We kept on scanning the club until I saw Irene hugging her big black bag in front of her, as if someone was going to snatch it away, while the DJ, hidden behind his turntables, put on Lil Wayne.

"Look. There's Ma and Irene," I said.

They were pushed up against a wall next to a stage with three go-go dancers, about fifty sweaty people ahead of us. One of the dancing women looked like she was going to accidentally slap Ma in the head with her butt.

The lights now jittered across the crowd, projecting vibrating green squares of light on the stage. Irene had scrunched up her shoulders, hugging her purse even tighter, as if she were trying to disappear into herself. "Looking like one of those See No Evil, Hear No Evil monkeys," Jessica said.

Just then, a half-naked purple-wigged woman in white high-heeled boots started gyrating next to Irene. She was wearing the type of pink lacy boy-cut panties we sold at Mariposa's. Two pairs for $29.99.

"You know," I said, "I changed my mind. I'm glad Irene came."

Meanwhile, next to us a girl who had been dancing to Flo Rida's "Low" had the unfortunate luck of collapsing on the floor because her heel had skidded on somebody's spilled drink. Or throw-up?

Who knows. At this point it was hard to tell; the lights gliding across the room had erased the boundary between the wall and the floor. And now the girl's friends were lifting her up by her elbows while she slid her hands over her wet dress. "I'm not drunk. I promise." Her friends just laughed and shook their heads. "I'm not drunk," she insisted.

"I don't know why Irene is pouting over there. She and Ma should feel at home," Jess said. "This is just like a bad day at church. All the women falling down on the floor going cuckoo for Christ."

I looked at the stage and shouted back into her ear. "Oh man, we gotta get over there. That go-go dancer's about to drag Irene up onstage."

As we pushed through the crowd, a weird techno song came on, and the lights began to pulse against the ceiling, then swirl around the room, highlighting the drunk faces in the crowd before leaving them again in darkness. For a while, there was no way to move forward. Everybody was standing shoulder to shoulder. And I was stuck breathing in the burnt strands of somebody's blowout.

To our right there was a line of women waiting for the bathroom, and every time the door opened, a whiff of bleach and piss floated toward us as the bass vibrated in my chest. We were two nondancing girls walking like zombies through a crowd that seemed to throb to the beat as if it were one many-handed body.

At one point we lost sight of my mother and Irene, but we kept going in the same direction, pulled and deafened by the noise of the speakers, hoping we'd see their faces again. Jessica squeezed my hand. And at first, I didn't think anything of it. I kept on moving until she tugged the sleeve of my hoodie more sharply.

Over our head the DJ shouted, "Are you ready?"

The crowd, mostly women, answered with frantic screaming. One girl shouted so loud she started to cough.

Jessica pointed in front of us to the stage. "Oh my god. It's Ruthy."

The go-go dancers had left, and in their places stood the *Catfight* cast posing on the stage, their backs to the audience, their arms frozen at ninety-degree angles like mannequins'. The only way we knew they were the reality TV stars was because each of them wore a shirt with the show's logo on the back.

"No, I don't think you're ready!" the DJ said. "'Cause I don't see y'all really paying attention."

Suddenly he stopped the music, and it was silent in the club except for some of the women in the audience who started whistling and cheering in the back. Then we heard Nelly Furtado's voice over the speakers: "Am I throwing you off?" And Timbaland answering. "Nope."

Now everybody turned their faces to the stage and started cheering.

Furtado giggled through the speaker: "Didn't think so." Then the *Catfight* cast turned around together and began swinging their hips at the same time, in the same direction, in some type of choreographed dance.

"Oh god, this is painful," I shouted in Jessica's ear. "Please make it stop."

Jessica grabbed my hand and pulled me forward as we tried to get closer to the stage. We had to push hard through the crowd and sometimes a girl would turn to us, ready to jump: "Bitch, watch where you going." Other times they'd push us back for accidentally shoving too hard as we moved up to the front of the club.

Neither of us paid attention to that, though.

There was no time to fight.

We had to get to the stage before our mother did. Or else who knows what she would do once she got her hands on Ruthy.

For some reason, now confetti burst from the ceiling and landed on the crowd like snow. A chunk fell on Jessica's head and got stuck in her hair and in her eyelids. Her nose. Metal colored specks of it clung to her dark eyebrows. All that glitter! It made it look like her face was melting in the dark.

"Stop laughing at me," Jess said.

"I'm not laughing."

"Yes, you are."

Then she dragged her fingers through her bangs and shook the confetti out of her hair, so that some of it got in my mouth. The glitter was like dust, and I started to cough as the song changed to "This Is Why I'm Hot." I'd forgotten to bring my pump, and the fog machines were fucking with my asthma. As we got closer, the speakers made my heart feel like it was going to pop out of my chest.

Irene saw us in the crowd and waved her hand frantically at us, as if for help.

Jess shook her head. "See now how the old bat recognizes us."

I tried to scream over the song to Irene, "Where's Mom?"

But Irene kept on throwing her hands in the air and shouting back, "What?"

We were close to the front of the stage now, and we could see the faces of the *Catfight* cast more clearly. Ruthy/Ruby was in the middle grinning, her hair freshly dyed *Little Mermaid* red, the piercing in her lip glinting as she mouthed the words to the song. The beauty mark of her childhood stretched beneath her left eye.

And finally, we found our mother to the left of the stage, frozen, her gaze locked on Ruthy.

In the background, a crew of cameramen lingered behind the *Catfight* cast. The fog made their feet disappear, so they looked like they were floating. Smiling, the girls onstage ripped off their glow-in-the-dark shirts to reveal rhinestone-studded bras. A thin film of glitter sparkled all over their bare skin. And they looked like a strange combination of slut and fairy. Somehow, someone had given them boas, and they were flossing them against their necks as they bent over and shook their breasts for the crowd. Then in one utterly confusing moment, they straightened their backs, lifting their chins in the air and kicking their legs up high as if they were cancan girls flexing over the Mims lyrics.

We had expected to find our mother's face twisted in distress, her respectability politics exploding in her head. But instead, she squinted as if she were trying hard to concentrate on an invisible math problem, as if she were making some type of complicated calculation. Her face was completely still, except for her mouth, which opened ever so slightly with what looked like hope.

Then it happened. One of the girls dancing onstage, Gem, turned towards Ruthy, lifted her hand in the air, and smacked the back of her head. Hard. You could tell that when Ruthy's mouth slammed shut, she must have cracked a tooth or bitten her tongue. The whole crowd started whooping around us, whistling and laughing.

"Get her ass," some bitch screamed out from behind me.

Cradling her jaw, Ruthy/Ruby swung around to fight the girl who'd hit her. But then McKayla crept up behind Ruthy and pushed her toward the edge of the stage, into the crowd. Ruthy stumbled forward, her arms raised and flailing, as if in worship. She fell. But there was my mother at the bottom of the stage, ready to catch her body. She landed in my mother's arms, and Ma gently brushed the hair out of Ruthy's face before pushing her back up on her feet.

"It's me, baby," she said, "it's Mami," as she got Ruthy/Ruby back onstage.

But now the whole cast had turned on Ruthy, and they were jumping her. This one slapping her face, the other one pulling her long red curly hair. So that Ruthy now had fallen backwards and started to scream, "*Stop. Please. Help.*"

That was it for my moms and Irene.

They hopped up on that stage and started swinging. Pure craziness. My mother was unleashing some of her Jesús Cristo Karate on the *Catfight* girls like they were her stepchildren. And Irene was up there hitting bitches in the head with her big black purse. It looked like she'd even snuck in a rabbit punch.

It was all *boom, pow, bang, crash*—like in the comic books.

"Oh my god!" Jess rushed towards the fight, and I tried to push past the crowd, who were laughing at the commotion on the stage, taking pictures and selfies beside these women killing each other.

Meanwhile, my mother started punching the sorority girl in the back of her head. The go-go dancers for no explicable reason joined the fight, too. And one of them with long straight blue hair had come up behind my mother to attack her, except now Jess was up there in her scrubs, tackling the dancer.

The mic had picked up her voice. "That's my fucking mother." Jess had pulled the go-go dancer's wig off. "You going to touch my mother, bitch?"

The frail dancer shook her head, terrified. Old girl was maybe 105 pounds, and Jess was clocking 165, at least.

"Because it looked like you was about to touch my mother," Jess said.

Then Jess pushed the dancer off the stage so that she crashed down into one of the speakers.

I could hear security already pounding down the stairs. When they sprinted across the dance floor, they started screaming at the stage, "Break it up, ladies! All right, that's enough!"

Upstairs, the bouncer was probably shaking his head, regretting ever letting us in. I could picture him lifting his cap in surprise to smooth back his thinning hair when security told him about the two older women throwing punches, and then later that night joking in bed with his wife, "I knew there was something up with those two. None of that made sense to me, those women wanting to go into that club."

There it was, my whole family fighting onstage, all of our mess displayed in public for everybody else to witness. Jess pivoting to catch somebody in the back of her head. My mother fiercely delivering blows to whoever might dare touch her daughters.

I took my glasses off.

I put them in my purse.

I hopped up onstage to join them.

Eventually the police came, too, their walkies beeping from their waists. When I looked up from the fight, I saw that cops and security had formed a circle around us and were quickly closing in, grabbing this one's elbow, that one's leg. Jessica and my mother were still at the center of the brawl, absorbed with whatever blow they were landing or receiving.

When this lady cop came up to me, immediately I put my hands up and said, "We're leaving, okay. Sorry. Look, we're leaving right now."

But one of the cops had already restrained my mother. Another had Irene. And the last one, the biggest of the guys, cornered Ruthy, who had accidentally clocked him right in the jaw. He picked her up as she kicked her skinny bruised legs into the air. "Let me down. You let me the fuck go, you creep."

Her long red hair lashed around her head as she struggled, and when she whipped her head back up, we all gasped. It was not the bloody nose or the knot rising on the top of her forehead, not even the girlish tears that shocked us. It wasn't the scratch somebody had carved above her upper lip, or the way in her fury she started to comically mix her curse words: "You *fucking mother*, you *bitch of a bitch*."

No.

Me, my mother, my sister, and Irene all stood there, frozen, stuck in place, because there was no longer a beauty mark on Ruby's face.

No beauty mark at all.

Nothing. Just pale brown skin below her left eye.

It was a fake. The mark, she must have penciled it in every day in front of the mirror before she got in front of the camera. It must have wiped off during the brawl or gotten smudged away with her sweat. Limping towards Mom, Irene started smoothing her hair down and straightening her blouse, embarrassed. The look on Jessica's face was unreadable. She tilted her head to the side, just staring at Ruby and blinking, as if she had woken up from a dream. And the great weight of our mistaken hope turned inside my stomach.

When my mother saw up close the woman who could no longer be her daughter, she stopped struggling. She shook her head, covered her mouth, and said, "No, no, no, no, no, no, no, no."

Then went limp in the cop's arms and slid to the floor.

In the morning, after a night of lockup, on the car ride home, I found the Light FM station for Jessica and turned up the volume. She was sitting there driving, staring intently into the long stretch of road in front of her as the radio host spoke about a Wal-Mart Black Friday worker who'd been trampled and killed by a mob of idiotic shoppers in Long Island. When Jess changed the radio station, I kept quiet and let her play whatever song she wanted.

Every now and then I checked the mirror to look for signs of emotion on my mother's blank face. Sitting beside my mom, Irene could not stop weeping.

Back home, the next week, me and Jess laughed at clips of a crazed Jessica being pulled away from the fake Ruthy on TV.

Pointing at her televised butt, Jess said, "Shit, man, I'm fat."

They'd blurred all of our faces, but the cameramen had made sure to zoom in on Jess's scrubs so that you could see the outline of her dark blue underwear. Its pink polka dots and beneath that azure layer of polyester, the faintest suggestion of cellulite.

Sometimes we imitated the scene.

I would pretend to be Jessica, and Jessica would pretend to be Fake Ruthy. Then I'd run dramatically through the hallway to Jess, from the bathroom to her bedroom, and throw my arms around her waist. Other times, we just sat there quietly on the couch as the commercials replayed my mother shouting at Ruby, "It's me, baby, it's Mami," over and over again. "I'm coming." The cameraman sometimes would focus on my mother's horrified face when she realized that this Ruby we'd chased hundreds of miles from New York was not our Ruthy but some other poor woman, exploited on TV like so many other brown and Black girls and women, but not ours. Not an imposter, but a sister of ours in her own right.

I picked up some wine coolers, because I knew Jessica liked that Froot Loops–flavored shit they sold in six-packs at the deli. Jess liked all of her liquor to taste like aluminum pouches of Capri Sun.

Ma had somehow magically managed to put the baby to sleep

early: "'Tate quieta, mija," she'd say if Julie started to fuss. My mother sang to her in Spanish the same song Grandma sang to her more than forty years ago. And then nothing. Quiet. Mom emerged from Julie's nursery triumphant.

When Jessica expressed her awe, Ma simply lifted one eyebrow and waved her hand at us. "Amateur."

Lou was working a late shift, so we had the house all to ourselves. There was going to be a fight between Ruby and the rest of the girls living in the apartment, because the cast suspected she'd been lying and stealing money from their purses while they slept as revenge for that fight on Black Friday. And blond McKayla and the punk girl named Gem were plotting a coup to take over the house. They were going to jump Ruby when she got home, because they wanted to get her kicked out. If she lost, she'd have to pack up all her bags and leave the set immediately. "Watch me," whispered the sorority chick in the confessional booth, smoking and lifting her pretty knee to scratch it, "deport that bitch." All of this we'd seen in a preview that aired nonstop that week.

I got nervous for Ruby. Seeing her at the club that night, I could not help but feel bad for her, remembering her audition tape and the small, dark apartment to which she would have to return.

"Put the volume up," Jessica said.

The episode started with what we'd seen in the preview, the girls scheming in the confessional booth together while passing a bottle of Alizé between them. Though they had pretended to make up with Ruby, they were still not over the fight. They were going to make her pay, one way or another.

Fifteen minutes later McKayla and Gem were giggling in a nearby closet, pretending they weren't home.

"So vicious, these girls," my mother said.

Now the cameras showed Ruby exiting the elevator, opening the door, walking down the long white marble corridor, and tossing some shopping bags on the pink couch, announcing out loud, "I'm home, bitches."

Nothing. Ruby looked around confused at the empty, quiet condo. "Hello?"

There was suspenseful music playing now that only we viewers could hear. Innocently, Ruby walked around the first floor, looking for her roommates, then laughed. "I know these bitches did not go out partying without me. Like, I know that they did not." And for a moment I thought I could detect genuine hurt on her face. Could Ruby be sincerely lonely, or was this all part of the act?

Then, finally, as she made her way back to the corridor, the girls jumped out from the dark in the corner where they were hiding and grabbed her. All three of them fell and slid across the white marble floor. And you could hear the metal of Ruby's purse bang against the wall. A close-up of her chapped orange lips twisted in pain: *Motherfucking bitch.*

We watched her scramble to push herself up from the floor, the sound of her bracelets banging against the marble. "Get up," my mother said. "Get up, you got this."

And we watched as Ruby fought, the way the muscles in her back moved underneath the strap of her sequined tank top, as she twisted one of the girls' arms behind her back. And we rooted for Ruby, not caring whether or not our voices woke up the baby.

"¡Wepa!" Jessica shouted.

We rooted for her when she tore Gem's face apart, when she dragged her across the floor by her new extensions. And then sometimes we rooted for Gem, as she pushed Ruby up against the wall.

"Get her!" we said.

Because we were angry, angry that Ruthy'd been gone, angry for what might have or might not have happened to her, or to our mother, or to our father, or to *us*—if in reality Ruthy had decided to stay or if she had not been taken.

And we wanted to see Ruby get hit.

McKayla jumped in now and blasted Ruby's back with her fists. "I'll beat your Mexican ass like a piñata."

"Pendeja, I'm Puerto Rican," Ruby said, kicking her in the knees.

And then we laughed.

We cheered for Ruby, our Ruthy lookalike. Our Ruthy imposter. How many girls in the world were there who looked like Ruthy, talked like Ruthy? Laughed like her? How many of us were missing?

After a few moments the cameramen broke up the fight, and Ruby fell backwards, legs open so that her crotch was blurred on TV.

"You're so [*bleeeeep*] gone," Ruby shouted from the floor, taking down a vase when she grabbed the leg of an end table to stand up. The vase toppled, and all of the fake flowers fell on her head.

McKayla looked down from the top of the stairs now, singing, "I'm sorry. Speak English."

Then the camera cut to an image of Ruby being escorted by the producers to her room, where she packed her bags. Without looking, she frantically filled her suitcase with makeup and bras. The lingerie spilled out the edges of her luggage and got caught in the zipper. Some ripped to shreds. Then Ruby looked around the bedroom, which she shared with McKayla, who'd used masking tape to delineate where Ruby's space ended and hers began.

Background music played while a look of mischief grew on Ruby's face. A dark chord, the note so ominous it was comical. They were cartoons, all of them, the track seemed to suggest, these women. *Look how stupid and funny they are. Their silly rage and superficial desires.* Ruby tiptoed over the border of masking tape to McKayla's night table. She opened a drawer and pocketed a string of her pearls. Then in one corner, Ruby found a garbage can and emptied its contents on McKayla's bed as one of the cameramen laughed in the background. Now the camera focused on somebody's used tampon rolling toward the pillow, its string stained with blood.

"Dirty bitch," Ruby shouted through the door. "All day I'm surrounded by dirty women."

Here came the producers, moving in quickly again, trying to restrain her, while she asked mock-innocently, "What? What did I do now?"

They lifted her away from the bed. Told her to stop screaming. One of the men's arms hugged her stomach as her feet dangled three inches above the floor, the tips of his fingers somehow ending up underneath the band of Ruby's skirt.

"You calm down now, honey," he said.

Ruby managed somehow to shrug for the camera, smiling as if she didn't even care, even though a red bump was slowly forming above one of her smudged eyebrows where the punk girl had hit her with a cell phone.

"I don't give a [*bleeeeep*]. You think I care? I'll never care. Do you understand?" Ruby shouted.

"Lord," Jess said. The light emanating from the TV screen made her face look skeletal.

I couldn't stop laughing. It was as if someone were setting a handful of balloons free inside of my chest.

"That's enough," the producer said, as if she were a child.

Another one picked up her bags. Underneath his thick, hairy arm, a blow-dryer dangled from her golden purse.

Ruby dragged a half-zipped suitcase down the stairs and started yelling behind her shoulder upstairs at the two girls, "I'll get your ass outside TV, bitch. There'll be no producers then. Watch, you're gone."

Now there was a new shot. From the window, McKayla threw Ruby's leftover makeup onto the concrete, where the camera focused on it shattering; a broken tube of lipstick rolled down the sidewalk.

"No, you're the one that's gone!" screamed McKayla.

And then the show faded to its theme song, a bright dance hall hit that used to be big at the beginning of the millennium. A commercial followed the music, trying to sell us some other new type of bullshit, to fix our faces, to get us home faster, to make us skinny. Another pill! Another chemical to reduce the size of our pores, to wipe the kitchen counter clean, to make us happy (with the least amount of side effects to our livers).

"Good*bye*, Ruby," Jessica said sarcastically, lifting her wine cooler in the air.

"Goodbye," I said, trying to read the traffic of emotions intersecting on Jessica's very pretty face.

My mother stood up from the couch. "All right, girls. That's enough," she said. "Pobrecita. It's sad, what these shows do to these women."

I stood up from the recliner to turn off the TV.

In the silence now, we could hear that Julie had woken up. And we twisted our heads to decipher her noise. The baby's voice arched above us and then hiccupped.

"It sounds like she's laughing," I said.

"No." Jessica lifted herself up from the couch and limped toward the stairs. "She's crying."

Then all three of us, we went up and opened the door to the baby's room to whisper, "It's okay. Don't be scared."

You are not alone, baby girl.

You are loved.

CHAPTER 22

Ruthy

The light falls across the school as the sun rearranges itself in the sky.

It is very, very, very cold.

Look, there is Ruthy Ramirez dragging her book bag full of Regents study guides against the sidewalk to the concrete yard the school uses for recess.

Coach is going to have the team run down the hill on Castleton towards Goodhue and use the track at St. Peter's. Tenaja is there with Yesenia and Angela, trying to teach them the Tootsee Roll, how to turn their knees in, then pivot their feet out in one smooth, quick movement.

Ruthy walks past them, sits on the concrete in front of Coach, and pretends to be focusing on stretching. She is wearing her shorts and a red hoodie, but now she wishes that she had worn tights, because the cool air makes her body shrink, seize, and tremble. She can feel the fake diamond in her stomach snag skin every time she bends over and stretches her arms to lock her fingers around each foot. Slowly, an ant crawls up her knee, stopping to inspect a stray hair that escaped the blade of Ruthy's pink razor that morning.

Already her lungs are acting stupid. When the girls start to walk down that narrow strip of Castleton—one side a field of trees, the other side cars—she can hear Angela whispering behind her and laughing. Ruthy mouths the words to "Siyahamba," trying to remember the music in her head to drown it out.

At St. Peter's she begins her laps around the circular track. The inhaler jiggles in her shorts like it's trying to remind her that, at any point, breath here is optional. And who's to say it even belonged to you to begin with? Yesenia is behind her, trying to catch up. Ruthy can feel her shadow.

But forget that. She is going to run through it.

Any type of pain is just noise. Inconsequential. All those girls are just sitting there, jealous in the background.

In through the nose.

Out through the mouth.

Ruthy is a stronger runner than Yesenia. She knows it. If she can just control the breathing and concentrate on what is next. First, there is a wall of weeds stuck on a chain-link fence. *Just reach that fence.* Then there is the red wall of the Catholic all-boys school. *Just reach those bricks.* Then a yellow van parked on the side of the street, in which somebody has hoarded stacks of boxes and paper. *Run past that car.*

When Ruthy repeats the loop, she cannot hear anybody behind her, but she sees Coach at the center of the circular track watching her run.

"That's right, Ramirez," she keeps repeating as Ruthy pumps her arms and finishes the mile.

Afterwards, bright red and breathless, Ruthy looks back at the other girls struggling far behind her and finds that Angela Cruz has bent over to throw up in the grass.

Coach dismisses them, and as Ruthy wipes the sweat from her face, she looks over to Yesenia to detect any signs that she has received the letter, the letter Ruthy wrote and put in her locker after eighth period, before changing for track, asking if they could please talk.

Ruthy does not want to be seen caring. At least not by the other girls. But perhaps it is too late for that and too obvious that she cares. There is no way to hide it.

So be brave, Ruthy, she tells herself. Just wait until she looks back up at you. Do not care that the other girls are watching.

It feels almost impossible. To lift her hand. But Ruthy does and she waves it at Yesenia, hoping that she will wave back, that she will smile, that she will walk over to Ruthy and apologize. But Yesenia doesn't.

And so instead of following the girls back to IS 61 to take the S48, Ruthy stays behind at St. Peter's boys' high school and walks the opposite direction over to Henderson Avenue to take the S44.

And this is where we reach the end of Ruthy Ramirez's story. It is not a happy one; I hate to say it, because I like happy endings. Most people wouldn't think that about me, but most people are dummies. And I reserve the right to hope for a joyful end to my story, too.

Listen, though.

Jess. Nina. Ma.

Are you listening?

Can you hear me?

This part of the story is for you.

Here's something wonderful about what Ruthy is thinking as she walks down Clinton Avenue alone, that is, before the random man pulls up, before he offers to drive her home, and she looks at his greasy face, the way his skin looks so thin and plastic, before she says no, and he says, "Come on, you don't want to wait in this." Pointing at the cold damp sky, and she says, "Leave me alone, you old, corny-ass motherfucker," her thirteen-year-old mouth twitching with the words she just learned the week before from you, Jess.

His corny ass, you had laughed in the kitchen on the phone, probably talking about some poor boy who loved you, who waited in math with his heart pounding hopefully in his teenage chest for you to walk inside the room, Jessica.

Before the strange man opens the door, before Ruthy stands there startled by his shape, before he drags her into the back seat of the car, and she screams, but there is no one there to hear her. Before he knocks her out, locks the doors, and drives away. Long before a crew of construction workers building the new mall by the Staten Island Ferry finally find Ruthy's body with her school ID hanging off the lanyard, almost twenty years after she disappeared, before you cry on the phone with the coroner, Ma, this is what Ruthy is thinking as she waits for the S44:

About how this time, when Coach had them sprint, the ground seemed to have softened beneath her sneakers. She could smell the grass, the sweat on her skin, and the air darkening. Free, she'd figured it out. The rhythm, how to resist the demand for breath, even her own body's nagging. Ruthy had measured it this time. In through the nose. Out through the mouth. And she could feel her coach smiling at her as she sprinted past all the other girls, who were just too slow.

"That's right, Ramirez," Coach said.

And Ruthy was eager for another stretch of road. The world around her seemed to melt away, to disappear.

And for a brief moment, for just one small moment, nobody was able to touch her.

ACKNOWLEDGMENTS

An acknowledgment page always reveals the people behind the scenes who listened, read, and critiqued a book into existence, and probably more importantly the people who loved and saved the author from themselves.

This novel took me almost a decade to write.

It began as a short story in 2013, when I was an MFA student at Vanderbilt University: a strange story about a long-lost sister, a raunchy reality TV show, and life working retail during the 2008 recession. With the persistent encouragement of my thesis advisor Lorraine López, the tale bloomed and started to take shape. I am grateful for her feedback then and now and for always believing in my work, even when the first drafts of this story felt slippery and out of control.

After I graduated from Vanderbilt, I came back home to New York City to adjunct and work at the Gerard Carter Community Center and the Staten Island arts council. The whole time, I kept revising and submitting the short story to different literary magazines but could never find it a home. Eventually, I tapped out of adjuncting and decided to go back to school for a PhD at the University of Nebraska-Lincoln, where the story landed in workshop again with Jonis Agee who explained to me that there was a very simple reason why my short story was not getting picked up. "This," she said, "is a novel. Now, write the next 80 pages for workshop."

I was horrified.

I did not know how to write a novel.

But luckily, some of the other students in my class did. For that, I am thankful to my fiction cohort at the University of Nebraska-Lincoln who read some of the first drafts, especially David Henson who would push me to finish it, even when I felt I had written myself into a corner and didn't see a way out.

I have also been fortunate enough to have a strong community of writers outside the classroom who cheered on the work, while also providing me with incisive feedback. Thank you to Xavier Navarro Aquino, for pushing me to think critically about the impact of colonialism on our literature and the power of our stories. To Olufunke Ogundimu, who told me to slow down the ending. We've gone through so much in Nebraska together; now, we celebrate! Thank you to Ángel Garcia, Saddiq Dzukogi, Jill Schepmann, Linda Garcia Merchant, Tenaja Jordan, Lee Conell, Christy Hyman, Cara Dees, Joshua Moore, Joshua Everett, and Janet Thielke, whose writerly wisdom and friendship guided me through my own self-doubt and uncertainty.

Thank you to Nichelle Jolly, my dear friend since 1998, Staten Island Technical High School, for explaining to me the ins and outs of nursing. I love you and the family so much.

Thank you to my fiction cohort at Vanderbilt University, who read early drafts of the story that would eventually become this novel.

Thank you to all my professors at the University of Nebraska-Lincoln and Vanderbilt University, who have helped me grow as a writer, and to my dissertation committee, including professors Joy Castro and Luis Othoniel Rosa for their thoughtful readings.

Thank you to the brilliant Dr. Kwame Dawes, who taught me how to listen. Every day I feel so fortunate for your mentorship and for the ways you have shaped me through example, not only as a writer but as a person. Thank you to Professor Lorna Dawes for your kindness and wisdom, for literally opening your doors to me, as I learned how to become a mother.

Thank you to Timothy Schaffert, who, when I was struggling with the structure, told me to write it straight, and for meeting with me all those years ago for drinks when finishing the novel felt impossible.

To Susan Kenney, who was my first professor of creative writing and has continued to teach me almost twenty years later. And for my fiction professors at Vanderbilt University, Nancy Reisman and Tony Earley.

Thank you to Belinda Hinojas, for your expertise and grace. I write fiction, but colonialism, racism, and femicide have been forces that have shaped my reality and the way I am seen or not seen in this world my whole life. Depicting these forces in fiction at times was painful, and I was lucky enough to find Belinda who taught me that I could not do the work of being a writer without first taking care of myself.

Thank you to my New York family: Cindy Choung, Boris Rasin, Caitlin McGuire, Kadeen Rafael, Katherine Delfina Perez, Stephen Gargiulo, Douglas Macon, Francine Rivera, Ozzy Ramirez, Zen Glasser, Noemi and Ruthy Feliz, Debra Fredrick, and the Maradiaga and Ouaaz families for checking on me, for reminding me to come home.

Thank you to the Midwives at CHI Health Birth Center and the doctors and nurses at St. Elizabeth Hospital for their excellent care, as I finished writing this book and defended my dissertation from the hospital.

Thank you to my kick ass agent Jane von Mehren, who read and critiqued many, many drafts of this novel; who patiently waited, until I finally figured out its shape; and whose enthusiasm for this story never waivered. You made my dreams for this book come true.

Thank you to the talented Maggie Cooper, whose sharp and careful eye further brought the novel into focus, and for your generous spirit and energy.

Thank you to the talented team at Grand Central: Stacey Reid, Andy Dodds, Theresa DeLucci, Autumn Oliver, Lauren Bello, and to superhero copy editor Laura Cherkas for catching all the little things that escaped me. Thank you especially to my wonderful editor Seema Mahanian, for not letting me or my characters get away with a joke during hard moments, and for pushing the characters to admit on the page when they feel. Thank you for taking this book on. You work hard for your authors, and it shows.

Thank you, Damion Meyer, for taking care of us, for making the dinner while I finished writing a chapter, for listening to me reread the same sentence aloud over and over again for a half hour, for helping me nail down the plot, for walking the dog, and driving the baby around the block until he stopped crying, for locking the doors and turning off the lights downstairs at night. I love you.

Thank you to my mother and father, who brought me to libraries and gifted me a passion for reading and storytelling that has forever since opened up the world for me. You were my first teachers.

And to my sisters for kicking my ass and keeping me honest. Thank you for making me laugh. This book is for you.

ABOUT THE AUTHOR

Claire Jiménez is a Puerto Rican writer who grew up in Brooklyn and Staten Island. She is the author of the short story collection *Staten Island Stories*, which received the 2019 Hornblower Award for a first book from the New York Society Library and was named a finalist for the International Latino Book Awards, a New York Public Library Favorite Book about New York, and Best Latino Book of 2019 by NBC News. She received her MFA from Vanderbilt University and her PhD from the University of Nebraska-Lincoln. In 2020 she cofounded the Puerto Rican Literature Project, a digital archive. Currently, she is an Assistant Professor of English and African American Studies at the University of South Carolina. Her fiction, essays, and reviews have appeared in *Remezcla, Afro Hispanic Review, PANK, The Rumpus,* and *Eater,* among other publications. *What Happened to Ruthy Ramirez* is her debut novel.